LAMP IN THE NIGHT WIND

Colum of Derry

LAMP IN THE NIGHT WIND

an account
of the coming of St. Columba
to Scotland
in 563 A.D.

by

EONA K. MACNICOL

WILLIAM MACLELLAN

First Impression 1965

Printed in Scotland
at the Scottish National Press
by
William MacLellan & Company Ltd.,
240 Hope Street,
Glasgow,
C.2.
Bound by J. & W. McQueen Ltd.

CONTENTS

This is my name — I tell a secret! —
Cul ri Eirean. *My Back is Turned upon Eire.*

The
Island

MAN was possessed by this sea. Its salt essence went through and through his being, penetrating every fibre. One felt no more than a sea excrescence, a blob of sea-wrack lifting and collapsing upon the tides. When one was abandoned to the feeling one was happy, if freedom from hope is happiness. But now and again one was engulfed in horror, nausea rose from the stomach to the throat.

Young Diarmaid, the Abbot's attendant and bell-keeper, pressed his mouth hard down on his arm.

They had been so long upon the open sea! Even though the sailor monks declared it was no great distance between Eire and Dalriada, and said, " Soon it will be over. Soon, soon! " it was an eternity. Even when Diarmaid shut his aching eyes he saw the horrible sleek mountains of water rise and fall. His stomach turned as the light ship, their seagoing curragh, jolted upon a suddenly rising wave and a lash of salt spray fell across his burning face. With the sickness surging up again in him there surged up the shocking realisation that between his quick flesh and the abominable deep there was only the thickness of a hide stretched over wooden spars.

But even as the thought rolled sickly in his mind and he suffered the extremity of actual sickness, he would become all helpless and spent again.

He lay thus, inert, all strength gone out of him. Only his eyes could move with movement not the ship's. He watched Rus and Fechnus the sailors. One would think they were a part of the curragh itself, so easily did they lend their bodies to its jumping and swirling round, leaning out and stretching up to handle the ropes of the sails. Snatches of sea songs came from their lips, though the winds swallowed the sound. Or they would shout a command to Lugne, a boy Diarmaid's own age, but how much better at sails and oars, and as for swimming—! Among all the young men of Ailech he was champion.

Their faces flushed with activity, they were the only men who were happy on board. Though not all were as afflicted as Diarmaid, there were others languid and pale: Grillan the farmer, and Carnan the miller his helper, and Scandal the builder who also knew about herbs and about bone setting and would serve as a doctor to the new community—they were silent, and yawned often, and endured the time weary for dry land and for grass, trees and the work of the good earth. When one sat here, not called upon at the moment to row or help with the sails, one had too much time to think, too much time to remember they were going away from Eire, like exiles, not to return.

Ernan the bishop, the Abbot's mother's brother, who had come from his own great community in Laighen to Derry to cast in his lot with them on this journey, Ernan sat staring out over the curragh's rim at the heaving sea. His face, ready as the Abbot's own to crease in laughter, was sober with fatigue now. And yet surely not for him the sharpness of that leaving Derry —hours that seemed not hours but ages ago—when the people crowded down to the shore to watch them go, kings and simple folk all mingled in a common grief together; not for him the anguish for that lengthening wake as the crowds grew small upon the beaches and the land itself went back from them, far hills rising that had been hid before? Worse than seasickness and sea horror was the knowledge they had left Eire forever. For Diarmaid it was not so much thought but simply a haunting vision of Gartan, his birthplace and the Lord Abbot's own, wild swans floating on the slow river, the little houses with a stout turf smoke rising from their morning fires.

Ernan sat hugging in his arms the few books, in leather book-shrines, they had brought from the Derry library, sheltering them from the spray so that no water should enter in and spoil the precious words. Tochannu and Eochaid the priests had similar care, and they guarded also the cross and the abbot's staff, and the cup and spoon and platter of the Mysteries.

He himself, Diarmaid the door-keeper, was in charge of the abbot's bell, the symbol of the Lord Abbot's authority. But of what use is a bell or a bell-keeper to a abbot who sits still as a man of stone? Most destroying of all things, beyond sickness, horror or exile, was the sight of the Abbot Colum. He

10

crouched, where earlier he had stood, in the stern looking backwards always. He had eaten no food nor slept nor spoken more than one word to anyone; but stayed still, unwilling to stir, unable to turn his back yet on Eire. The swinging seas outlined his still shoulders and head, strange frame for so familiar a profile! Diarmaid knew and loved almost to adoration each line and contour, broad brow heightened by the tonsure from ear to ear, bright brown hair, the jut of the chin and cheekbone, the deep sockets for the grey eyes.

Beside him in the stern knelt Baithene, his cousin and abbot heir, ready to offer food or measured sips of their fresh water, readiest to help those most at any moment in need, and now by the Abbot, watching him in a silence full of praying.

Ah, but the Lord Abbot was kneeling too? Surely, for their errand was most holy. To carry the light of God to a new land! It was the sinful weakness of Diarmaid himself that had suggested to him the idea that the Abbot Colum was deep in a gulf of despair. And not only the heart's death of exile, but an agony of contrition for the battle fought and won by his Ailech kindred and the death of men on his account. So they said before they left, in Derry. But how could he in reason take such guilt upon himself, kindest and most compassionate of any under the sun? And yet Diarmaid felt, if it had not been for Baithene who was holding his spirit up over its abyss of pain—.

He tried to pray himself, but found he could not. Instead he idly watched the other men. The farmer Grillan took hold of a sail rope and hoisted himself awkwardly up to Fechnus. "Where are we? When shall we see land?"

"Why, I can see it," Fechnus answered, "Or I could before this mist came round. We've never been very far from land. We are sailing north east, not far from the coast of the island of Diura. It was the high mountain tops of it that I saw to the east. Rounded mountains, very lovely they are, blue on a sunny day. I saw them last when I went to the royal palace of Dalriada. Dunadd that is. It stands inland a mile or so."

"Are we near enough yet to get sight of their longships? It would be a cheery sight."

"Time was when you would have seen the longships of Dalriada all around here. When I was here last, Gauran was king, and his ships went nosing up and down like watchdogs. Now there's a bit of a change, so they say. Things have not gone well with them. I've seen no ships certainly."

"When shall we be at Dunadd?"

"We are not going there at all. Were you sick or asleep or what that you don't know? The Lord Abbot said we were to sail north. That is, as far as the currents—"

"Not going to Dunadd?"

"No. It seems he is making for the community of some cleric, I forget his name. He'll ask advice about where we should set up our community. Only after that will he see the king. Connal it is now, Gauran's cousin."

"Don't look so glum!" Ernan rallied them. "Dalriada is a Christian country. Wherever we land we shall have no difficulty in making our way to some abbot or priest."

"To tell you the truth," Carnan said, "I am glad myself if we are making for a community. I was afraid it might be to some wild lonely place we might be going to make a penitentiary. It's this desolate sea, and the leaving home that turned my mind that way."

Grillan nodded his head. "I was afraid of that too. But now so long as we get to land at all I will be pleased."

The sea was getting up again. Diarmaid's sickness like a wakening beast stirred within him. He filled up with that disgusting knowledge that they were on the sea, that swung and swirled and eddied round and round. Sickness and horror—were they two evils or one? Two beasts or one? From confusion of mind he passed into the oblivion of sleep.

From fevered, stale, crude sleep he had been wakened to see their approach to land. Tall rocks, grass-topped. Oh could it be? There shall be no more sea. Between them and this wonder there was only some half mile of sunlit sea, dancing, bird-crested.

They pulled in, and were silenced by a kind of awe as the curragh struggled in the shallow water and sagged a little on her side as she ran on sand. They clambered out. Diarmaid saw Fechnus steady her, and Rus help Eochaid out with his armful of books. They beached the curragh in a yard or two of sand among the rocks.

They lay together in a beatific swoon. Beneath them they felt the earth rise and fall and laughed at the blessed absurdity of it. The still stable earth, waiting at the end of every voyage to comfort those who have tossed upon the sea. They took up the fine sand in their hands and trickled it between adoring fingers. They raised leisurely eyes to the cliffs and watched the grasses moving in a gentle wind. The sun warmed their backs, they stretched cramped muscles in the heat of it. They spoke softly together, lying where they had thrown themselves down, exhausted, given up to peace. "When I hear that lark sing," one of them said, "I cannot believe we are not still in Eire."

Baithene said nothing, as he played with the sand; said nothing, but made his thought clear. This soil was Alban Dalriada. They had passed as if through death to a new life in a new land. His hand moved among the sand and short seaside flowers as if caressing and blessing.

"But, the Lord Abbot," Diarmaid asked uneasily, "Where is he?"

Baithene looked up and smiled, "Sure he's off with the sailors exploring to see if we are near a community."

"What if we've gone too far—beyond Dalriada into the country of the Cruithnians?"

"Fechnus was sure this is within the confines of Dalriada. He says he once ate supper in a house on this island."

"It's an island?"

"It is. And there was a settlement of clerics upon it. It may be they will ask us to stay and join them."

"At least we may stay until King Connal grants us a site for our own cashel."

Soon animation came on the wearied men. Some had got up and were doing what they could to make a meal. Grillan and Carnan were picking up driftwood from the shore. Scandal and Lugne were climbing the rocks, finding a dulse one could eat. But Diarmaid did best, for he found shellfish in a rock pool and laid a pile of them on the sea grass. Eochaid had a flint, and nursed up a tiny fire with it. The earth, blessing on it, was soft as swansdown in this delectable place.

"Here are Rus and Fechnus."

They went to meet the sailors. "Did you see where the settlement is? Did you find the cleric?"

Rus and Fechnus sat down on the grass. "We found the cleric. He is a disciple of the Abbot Oran."

"Oran of Latteragh, who died some years ago?"

"The same, sir. He has only a small cell here. He says Oran's great cashel lies north of here, on an island where the kings of Dalriada are buried. He has not been to it for years, for he is an old man and unfit for travel, and also he says it is not quiet in Dalriada now; he stays where he is, tending his few people."

13

"Are we to settle here with him?"

As if for answer the Abbot came swiftly among them, scattering them like a dog among hens. "Put out the fire!" he cried. And when they looked at him as if in disbelief, "Put it out! Put it out!" he cried again, stamping on the little fire with unsandalled foot. The handful of shellfish spilt out over the flat stone they had found to bake them on. "Back to the curragh. Come on. We mustn't stay here."

"But where can we go, Lord Abbot?"

"We must sail farther north."

They could not restrain themselves. "No! Let us stay here, father. It is Dalriada, not so far from King Connal's dun. Let's stay at least for a little while."

"Not an hour!" he cried, "Come away, will you? I put you under obedience to come away with me."

And he strode off down the rocks to the sandy place, and bound by such a command they had to follow. He wrenched the curragh from its bed and pushed it unaided to the edge of the sea. The sailors then by force of habit took it over from him. They pushed off, reluctantly, and set sail and were out again upon the sea.

When they were jolting again upon the waves he turned from his moody watching of the water and looked at them half laughing, half in earnest.

"Forgive me, forgive me. If we had to go it was best to go soon. I climbed a little hill above the shore and I saw Eire. I saw it far off in the south across all that sea. We could not settle with such a temptation. At least I know I could not."

14

STORM was brewing. You could smell it in the air. A train of birds went over above them with desolate crying, seeking the shelter of the land. A spurt of spray rose and drenched the curragh. The sea was rougher indeed. And there were currents here and there into which the curragh went spinning before they could stop her, shaken as a rat is shaken by a dog. Someone said they should loosen their habits lest in an accident they should have to swim, if swim one could in such a sea as this. Fechnus and Rus were hardly able to reach up to shorten sail.

As for Diarmaid, his sickness had overpowered him again, and he asked for nothing better than to slip down into the dark water and drown. He drew his cowl over his face and lay exhausted. His body lolled this way and that with the lurching ship. His head bumped on a wooden spar and he groaned. He was half aware that his head was raised and propped against a knee.

He awoke to a confused crying. The sun was down, though the May sky was still flushed with green. He raised his head to peer: there were dark shapes about, what he could not tell. A toss of the curragh brought his chin down with a horrible impact on the ship's oaken rim, his teeth went into his tongue, the shock waking him completely from his drowsiness. The Abbot was getting to his feet from where he had sat: so that was who had held him?

They were among rocks. All but himself were standing in the curragh, Fechnus and Rus were hauling down their sail. It was all they could do to hold it, with Lugne helping; and Carnan gasped as he held on to the shaking helm. They were among rocks, whose dark shapes were all around them; and in the gloom they saw the lines of white where foam broke over hidden reefs.

15

They swung from side to side; two of the men were rowing now, but were afraid to pull hard lest they should run her aground. There was a jar and a thump as the ship's bottom went over water too shallow; they waited tense, but she was free again. Carnan gave a sob of despair, "I can't get through. We seem to be enclosed."

"Let her drift then," said Rus.

But Fechnus cried, "There are rocks on our lee side, and a strong current." The waters boiling upon the reefs made a noise like loud singing.

One or two tried to speak but their throats could not get round it. Even the sailor monks were looking glum.

'Here, let me take a turn of it,'" said Colum to Carnan, putting him gently aside. The helm was leaping like a live thing, and the Abbot had to lean his whole weight on it to steady it. The rowers pulled gingerly where the waters were darkest. And so they came through the rocks into the clear sea.

But in their manipulating the rocks they had lost their bearings. Land forms rose dark above them on every hand. Only by the faint green coloration still left in the night sky could they tell where west might be. And they fell again into a swirling tiderace.

"Pull now if you can still pull at all," said the Abbot to the rowers," "We'll take her aground here. I can see a bay."

As they approached they heard the sound of waves breaking on a pebbled shore, the hissing suck of water and the tumbling of stones one against another. The dark wall of land before their prow took dim shape as they came nearer. It was a double bay. They made for the nearer inlet. There was a grating of the spars upon the pebbles, for dizzy moments they were clashing among the clashing stones. Lugne and Fechnus clambered over and went waist deep into the sea, staggering on uncertain feet. Rus joined them, and Carnan, until they had pushed the curragh above the level of the tide. They went scrambling up the beach over piles of stones only half visible in the thin starlight of the May night.

"There would have been an easier way maybe," Rus said to Fechnus. "Maybe we did not row on long enough. But we're lucky to be out of the storm. I've never known such strange currents."

"And those rocks round us on every side—what seas are these? We've never been this way before."

16

The rest heard in a lull of the wind.

"Where are we at all? Do you not know?"

"Pray God we have not sailed too far north beyond Dalriada."

"If this is Cruithnian territory — "

"No, no. It's not likely," the sailors reassured them. But the thought lingered. "There's something moving over there."

They forgot weariness in terror. Indeed the rock faces on either hand were menacing, like huge men, like horsemen standing still watching them.

"Father," even one of the priests whispered to the Abbot, "I wish we had not landed."

"Better the curragh," Grillan frankly said, "Than a strange place like this."

Someone stumbled on the yielding stones and fell, pulling his tired companion down with him; and they cried out as if ambushed.

"Don't be frightened," Colum said, "There's no one there." And he called. But for only answer they heard the sound of the sea and the sucking of the tide upon the pebbled shore.

"Let's make a fire," Ernan said. "As soon as we are above the level of the beach we'll make a fire."

They went in couples to gather driftwood, groping for it half-heartedly. Fechnus kindled it with the third spark. The Abbot cupped the little flame in his hands and blessed it as it struggled up, though it revealed in its glow the haggardness of their faces and made more dark the dark rock shapes. "I'd rather it were dark," Lugne said secretly to Diarmaid.

"Tighten your girdles for tonight," said the Abbot, "We'll hope to eat tomorrow. And keep close together for warmth and company. I'll keep watch and see that nothing worse than ourselves comes by this way."

So watched by half-shut eyes he sat by their camp fire. They saw him handle the books, take out one, his own Gospels from its leather carrying satchel and hold it carefully before the fire. With Ernan and Baithene and Eochaid he knelt on the sand, lips moving as if saying an Office. It dawned on some as they stirred in their sleep that this was the eve of Pentecost, and if they were awake long enough they wondered whether the thought blessed or appalled them that they would keep the familiar festival in this eerie unknown place.

T HEY said their prayer at earliest dawn with throats parched after the voyage. The sea water was no good at all to drink, for all it glistened in a blink of sunshine with seductive beauty, and made the diverse coloured pebbles on the beach flash in the ebbing tide.

Gulls wheeled crying on the rocks around. It dawned on the monks, the birds they heard were not tormented with thirst like theirs. There must be wholesome water somewhere near. The thought made them overcome the lassitude of fatigue, and go inland up the grassy little valley at the head of the double bay, and climb the rocky knolls that overhung its sides.

It was a sort of moorland that they entered; an expanse of rock-strewn land covered with heather and small wind-warped trees. They climbed one knoll after another, trying to get height enough to spy out the surrounding land. Carnan it was who shouted suddenly, "It's an island." An island it was: to east and west of them they saw sea. To the west it stretched immense with islands far in the north like thin blue threads. To the east across a narrow strait they saw high hills, "The mainland of Dalriada, very likely," Rus said. "Though it might be one of the many large islands. I wish I knew where we are."

But water? A covey of wild ducks went overhead. "We'll go to the west where these sleek lads have come from," Grillan said. And in a few minutes back he came to the rest his hands filled with bog moss, red and green. "A loch, my boys! And so many wildfowl drinking of it, unless you hurry they will leave none for you."

It was great luxury to kneel at the lochside and drink. The little loch lay silent and solitary as if called into existence for them. Round them they could see only loch and moor, and far below, the shore.

"Come, let's push on to the north; there's a gully going down yonder." Loaded with their things—rugs, the empty water skins, a knife or two and a spade, the holy vessels and the Abbot's staff and bell, and the books, the books!—loaded they made their way down the gully. And as they went they saw the lovely plain below them to the west. Green like a hosting place of the immortal ones, it sprang into sight, edged by a dazzling white shore. They were no longer stiff with the curragh. Lugne dropped the spade and the two rugs he was carrying. It was a miracle how white the sand was, how wide and flat and green the grassy plain.

"Good for grain, I wonder?" Grillan said. "And for grazing."

The clamour of their talking roused some creature. "A sheep. There must be people on the island if there are sheep set to graze here."

Towards the northern limit of the plain the land became wooded and wild again. But to eastward the grassland rose gently, enticing their curious feet. They found a bit of land which seemed once to have been ploughed; there were furrows in the earth, and among the grasses what seemed to be a kind of barley sparsely grew. "Surely there must be people here," they said; and were glad, for it would be pleasant to see a house and smoke going up from its roof, and hear a word spoken, and eat hot food, and have a roof over one's head at night.

There were a number of sheep now feeding among the rocks that stood above the grassland. "These are ewes," Scandal said. "We could milk them if we could catch them! If their owners are subjects to King Connal they will not grudge it to his kinsman and his men."

"We will first see the other side of the island," Colum said.

So they went on, following a slender sheep run. Though they had hoped for it, yet coming suddenly on it they were startled when they found a small round house of wattle and clay standing in the shelter of some crags. Its clay walls glinted silvery with the mixture of white sand. Its roof of heather was whole as if it were an inhabited house. But it was empty. Though the Abbot went up to the open doorway and called, they found no one inside. Some little distance away there was another little house, and again another with a rowan tree in leaf and flower-bud by it. But no human being was anywhere around, nor were there cooking pots outside though there were the blackened circles where fires had been.

19

"Yet there is a faint smell of turf smoke," Lugne said, "Isn't there?"

On that they were divided. If the sweet summer air held the tang of smoke it was faint indeed.

"Well, well, let's go on," Colum said. For they seemed reluctant to move, or to stop puzzling over the little houses. "Have they been deserted? And if so, why? Could it be some disaster—Christ save us!—sea robbers, or pirates seeking slaves?"

"Or the army of the Cruithnians—"

"Surely in this island place, not the yellow plague?"

"O come on!" Colum cried, "Have we escaped the perils of the sea to fall into such perils?" He led the company along the path that now turned north eastward. And as they mounted a height they saw the sea on the east, a narrow strait between the island and the adjoining land. And then suddenly they saw another plain. Sloping gently to the strait, grassy and green, it spread northwards a long way, sheltered by the northern moorland which rose to a hill. But no farm, no house, no coil of smoke going up into the bright air, no human voice anywhere to be heard.

"They must be rich in land then in Dalriada, since they do not farm here," Grillan said. "For that looks good land to me though I shall have to see it closer."

They went down to the shore which was rough with rocks, though here and there the rocks, relenting, gave place to the white sand. No footprint, no sign of curragh; but across the strait they saw houses down by the shore. Fechnus caught three flat fish with a sharpened stick on the floor of a little bay, flounders, and they cooked them over a fire of dry seaweed.

Their grace took longer than their meal! Soon they were walking up from the shore; they found a sort of causeway across the swampland above the beach, a track rough paved here and there that led up from the beach to the grassy plain. There were circles on the ground which were clearly the foundations of houses, and they came upon a heap of willow wattle and wooden beams, rotting on the ground.

It was strange the whole place should be so desolate. "It would do us fine," Grillan said. "If we find no one living north of here, on the other side of the moorland, if the island is for the taking—I could till this land, and the land on the west side."

20

Baithene who had gone south a little called the others. He had found, not inhabited houses as they hoped — but burial places.

There were a few small cairns. One the smallest, had recently been made, for no moss yet bound its stones. Nearby stood an upright stone pillar.

" They were not Christians who were buried here," Ernan remarked, " Unless it is the custom in Dalriada to use the old burial." He examined the standing stone, running his fingers down the corner edges for inscriptions. He cried out at the name he found, and felt over the stone again to be sure. " Domangart! Is that not a name known in Dalriada? Was it not the name of one of their kings?"

Colum came quickly and felt the stone beside him. "It is a name of Dalriada. But there could be other Domangarts." He found the place where on the corner edge the incision was sharpest, and he gasped in turn, for the name he found was Gauran. They called Tochannu and Baithene. There was no mistaking it; five names were inscribed and the names were Loarn, Fergus, Domangart, Comgal, Gauran.

" These are the names of the kings of Dalriada!" Baithene cried in astonishment, " Our kindred."

"They make little ado about memorials then!" Ernan said, with a wag of his head. " Only the name, and the last not even well lettered."

" Can this really be the burial place of the Dalriadan kings? This island, so strangely deserted, the graves unwatched and untended—? "

" Cairns set up for Christian kings?"

Only Colum was silent, standing with his hands pressed against the upright stone.

IV

"**THEN** this must be the island where Oran's community is?" They were so deeply absorbed by the question that they did not hear the splashing of curraghs approaching nor the footfalls of men on the grass. Indeed the men seemed to have little mind to be heard; a half score or so of fishermen with tunics gathered up above the knee wet with the sea. They asked a little timorously, "What do you want with these graves?"

Their speech was the speech of Eire though with an odd accent.

"Greetings to you!" Colum said, his people echoing him. But when they moved nearer the fishermen retreated and made a sign for them to keep their distance. They spoke among themselves: "They are dressed like monks. They do not seem to be armed. Yes, but why are they here, close to the burial place?"

"You are surely not afraid of us," Ernan said, "This is all we are. You are in your own country with friends near at hand. Besides we are Christian clerics. Are you not Christian too? You are men of Dalriada?"

They spoke again among themselves, some in the speech of Eire in the Dalriadan tones, but others using a language not quite the same which was strange to the monks. Then they asked, "How did you come to the island?"

"We beached our curragh last night in a bay south of here."

"That's true. I saw it and wondered. That's why I sent to the Young Men."

"Shipwrecked?"

The monks smiled wryly at the recollection of the voyage. "Not exactly."

22

More men had come in curraghs and now they ran up. These were all young men, some were boys, in the coloured clothing of nobles, but tattered and weatherworn; one or two were armed, a sword or a hunting knife or a stick. "Are these the strangers? Where do they come from? Are they clerics from the Brythons in the Far South? Or from Reged maybe—from Teach Martain? Or only from Strathclyde?"

The monks answered, "From Eire. From Ailech."

"From Ailech!" A stir went through the young men. "Yes of course, they look like men of Eire and their speech has the right ring. Then where are the fighting men? When are they coming?"

"We have nothing to do with fighting men. We are as you see us."

They looked vexed at this. And some of the fishermen noticing the change of mood asked uneasily, "What have you done to be sent over the sea?"

"Keep quiet!" one of the young men bade the speakers. "They are holy priests. Don't you recognise the tonsure and the dress?"

At this a ripple of fear seemed to go through the fishers, some going straight back to the little bay where their curraghs were beached, others remaining at a safe distance. The young men stayed close, and the one who had last spoken, a tall comely lad with dark burning eyes, explained, "We thought for the moment that the kings of Ailech might be sending men. Connal, our king, is in sore need of them." Colum shook his head. "Then why have you come to this island?"

"Are you not used to seeing monks from Eire landing here?"

For only answer the young man stared. Then he called to the fishermen and they brought food, barley cakes smelling strongly of fish, and a honey cake. "You have a big hunger!" they said kindly as the monks ate.

Colum asked, "Those cairns and the burial stone—"

"What do you wish to know about those? They are our concern."

Colum tried again, "Do you live here? We found houses, but none lived in."

"The fishers live across the Sound, over yonder. They used to live here. Not now. Some of us still keep our sheep here."

23

"Your land across there," Fechnus asked, "Is it the great
island of Mula?"

"Yes, it is Mula."

"Then we are well within the confines of Dalriada?"

They paused at this. One of the fishers called out a remark
in the strange language and the rest chuckled. The young man
looked at them angrily, even made a slight movement to his left
side as if to draw a sword. Then he answered sullenly, "It is
Dalriada."

"King Connal's land?"

"It should be King Connal's."

Another young man explained, "It was his until recently."
Someone among the fishermen laughed and said, "He would
like to think it was his. But he must hold what he would keep."

"How far are we from the King's dun?"

"That depends on where he is now making his dun." There
was another burst of laughter.

They argued with one another, some in anger, some in fun.
A fisherman said to the monks: "We are simple folk except for
the young men here. They were knights of Gauran's, trained in
the palace. But for us—it is all one to us who holds the land.
We sow and reap and fish and sleep as we always did."

"These graves," Colum asked the young men, "They are
marked with names. Are they indeed the graves of the kings of
Dalriada?"

"These are their graves. We guard them."

"But the cairns—these are not Christian burial places?"

"Yes they are Christian! They were Christian kings. That
is why we brought them here for burial. Even though it was by
the skin of their teeth that his sons brought Gauran to the island,
yet they brought him, and they gave him Christian burial saying
the prayers their mother taught them when they laid him down.
They had only time to sprinkle earth on his body. Afterwards
when their pursuers were gone away we came back and heaped
the stones over him. And still we guard him, for we were his
men and drank his mead."

"In Eire the graves of Christians—"

"Do not despise them!" the young man cried hotly, "The
times are bad, we cannot mark the graves with greater honour
or they will be robbed. But the royal seed of Dalriada lie here."

"The only quiet kings in Dalriada!" Laughter broke out;
an older fisherman explained to the monks, "It is not lucky to be

noble in Dalriada now. We simple folk have less to fear from
the Cruithnians. We are in any case of both bloods here, many
of us. And why not? Isn't all blood the same? "

Colum drew aside the young man, " Why did you say they
were brought here, the earlier kings? Has it been a Christian
place? "

" It is indeed. It is the site of a great community."

" Belonging to whom? "

" To the Abbot Oran. A very holy man."

" Oran of Latteragh? "

" I do not know him by that name. But I know he was born
in Eire. He came over to teach the people of Dalriada. My mother
heard him. It was through his teaching she came to follow Christ.
She called me after him." He said shyly, with pleasure in his
eyes. " My name is Oran also. He was the chief Abbot of
Dalriada, and had his greatest cashel here though he went round
everywhere. That was in Gauran's time when the people were
safe. Now Gauran is dead. And Oran is dead; he died of the
yellow plague in the year when it took so many."

" Deisuil! Deisuil! " they all cried hurriedly.

" Where is his community then? To the north of the island
where we have not been? "

" No, no! His site is here. That is his harbour, and causeway.
There's where he had his farm, yonder over there. You must have
seen the foundations of his cells and his church. And the rampart, look, see where it ran round. And here where we stand is
the ground he hallowed for the kings, though they had been
buried here before—"

" But it is in ruins! "

" Everything in Dalriada is in ruins."

" Has no priest continued his community? None of his
men? "

" Yes, yes, there are priests here." a fisher said. It started an
argument.

" No. They are not proper priests." " Yes, but they are."
" No, they are not. They have broken down Oran's church and
his cells."

" They are priests of a different kind."

" The priests who live here now are very holy. They know
deep science, it is dangerous to speak of it. They can make or
withhold rain. They can make the sick well and the well sick,
as they wish. They can change shape—deisuil! "

25

"That hill yonder," they pointed, "up on the top of that hill they practise their potent rites. It is not safe for the unlearned to stay on the island any more. We come only to bring them gifts of fish and eggs and grain, to keep them from cursing us. And they allow us to keep our sheep here, in return for a share of the wool."

The man who spoke broke off and gasped, the rest stood still in horror. Then without further word they turned and ran helter skelter to hide among the rocks, simple and noble alike.

V

SWIFTLY from the crags at the edge of the moorland two men were coming towards them. They were dressed in self-coloured woollen robes, somewhat like the monks' own, their hair tonsured too. But round their necks hung amulets of sparkling stone. They came so fast there seemed menace about their approach. Colum stepped forward with Diarmaid and Baithene following. They did not pause before speaking. " Brothers, we greet you! " said the shorter of the two. " We are bishops like yourself, and we have settled here to teach the people. This island is ours. There is no need for you to come. Seek another island and be bishop there."

" I am not a bishop," Colum answered, " I am a priest."

" Bishop or priest," said the taller, frowning, " You are of the new way, you are Christian clerics. And so are we. So go without delay and find another island."

" That is fair," said the shorter man, smiling.

" You are odd Christian clerics," Colum said. " Though you are dressed like monks, you carry charms round your necks. And the tonsure you have is like—"

They spoke to each other in the language Colum did not know, such as some of the fishers had used. Then they turned to Colum again, and spoke in his language, politely.

" My brother here," said the shorter man, " My brother here is a great Christian bishop; if you doubt that we will show you." The taller then raised his arm, his hand held with fingers spread as in the Christian benediction.

" But we can show you more! " said the other eagerly, noting the effect this had on the monks.

As if acting a bardic legend they both went back a few paces so as to be better seen. " Look now. We can do what you do. We have been taught."

27

They moved their hands, as if over objects spread on a table, then lifted up some imaginary thing, chanting in a not too bad imitation of the Holy Office. The monks watched them spellbound. "Kneel," the shorter man bade them in a whisper, and made as if to offer the spoon to Baithene's lips.

Colum gave a cry of anger, and they stopped their acting. "You ought to have knelt, brother. Besides, you do wrong to cry out, and be disorderly when the secret symbols are being shown. The unlearned, who as you know are not far off, may hear and discover your mysteries. We are most careful to keep such secret from those who know no science."

"You are druids!" Colum cried.

"We are Christian clerics, brother, like you. Only we also know the old religion. We know both ways. In this we are superior to you in learning and in power."

The taller said, " Beware of our power. Although we know your secret rites, you do not know ours. This island belongs to us. We have our holy temple on top of that hill where there are the ancient stones. We mean to teach our disciples there again as of old. Unless you know our mysteries, do not stay. We have the Eye that can see far off. Did we not see your coming yesterday? We saw you struggling among the Torran rocks. And we have seen all you have done since you landed. We know where your curragh is. Our Eye follows you everywhere you go. If you want to keep yourself and your men safe from harm, take your curragh and go away immediately."

"It is you who will go away! You are druids, not Christian clerics at all. I claim this island in the name of the Abbot Oran whose cashel lies desolate, waiting to be rebuilt."

"Why, brother," the shorter druid said, so calm in his reproachfulness that Colum could not for the moment find anything to say, "What have you against us? Are not all religions the same? There may be small differences on the surface. The deep beliefs are the same. We are of Oran's faith."

"How dare you say such a thing! You have let his church fall into ruin if you have not pulled it down. You have let his fields lie untilled. You have driven his people away."

"How do you know what we have done? You are newly arrived from distant Eire. And you have no Eye of knowledge with which to see."

"And why should you say our form of religion is not Oran's? It may not be the Christian faith of Eire, but it is his."

"Nonsense! Did he build temples among the ancient stones on the tops of hills? Did he and his disciples wear magic charms?"

"It is at any rate the religion of Dalriada."

"That is not true. The men of Dalriada are Christian and are led by a Christian king."

"They call themselves followers of the new way. But in times of trouble men remember the old gods."

"About that we shall see," Colum said. "I am the kinsman of King Connal of Dalriada. I am claiming this island. You will go away, and you will cease to practise your rites where Christian monks have lived and where Christian kings lie buried. The King will defend my cause."

They spoke together, then turned to Colum. Even the good-natured druid looked angered. "Why all this talk of Oran!" he said, "and Christian clerics. It is an island anciently holy. It was not always Oran's."

The taller added, "There are more kings than Connal of Dalriada. Do not think because he is farther away our own king is less powerful. And in the east there is the High King."

But they held a secret consultation with each other, and at the end of it faced Colum again. "For the present we will go. But not for long. We will return in power. You may well wish you had taken our advice and gone when the time was good. You will never live safe here or unmolested. We can put such curses on you—"

Colum stepped forward in great rage threatening them, and they retreated from him towards the shore. The fishers hurriedly pushed off and rowed in all directions scattering before them like seabirds.

The echo of their words remained in the air like an evil odour; remained in the mind, for in the gathering summer dusk the monks became possessed by fear. A shape would seem to come from behind a rock, a bush would rise and menace them. So they slept and waked and said prayers the night through among the ruins of Oran's community.

VI

BUT they were well pleased with the site of Oran's cashel. The land lay in the shelter of the high moorland, safe from the great sea gales of the western side. And it ran to the eastern Sound so gently as to be almost level. They longed to have the buildings up on it. A little north of the site a stream ran out of a small loch, with rushes growing all ready to be picked for lights, and with clay on its shores fit for making walls.

The first task, the one they all turned to, was to remake the cashel wall. For this, if unable to protect them, made manifest their claim to Oran's ground. They found ancient walls connecting the battlements of crags all along the edge of the moorland. On the grassland they could detect the lines of the eastern cashel. It was of an odd shape, more square than round. " Some peculiar custom among the clerics of Dalriada?" someone asked. " Well, we shall find much that is new to us in this land. There are still people living, it may be, to whom this shape is dear. So let us keep it in all humility." So they kept mostly to the lines of the cashel they found, though they rounded off the corners.

Carnan and Lugne were singing a ditty in time to their measured dig and throw; Rus perched on top of a pile of earth joined in as he beat it smooth.

Sheltered the site might be; it was also overlooked by the druid hill to the west of it. The people who came to watch their labour murmured about the Eye. Some shook their heads, others laughed. " Why are you building the old boundary wall?" they asked. " You do not really mean to stay and settle here after the Wise Masters have told you to go away? You will not dare?"

And, " Of what use is a wall? If you disobey them, will a wall like this save you? They know science, they will cast spells "

"We are building a wall of prayers against that," Baithene answered them, "an unseen wall as we build this wall you see."

They were rebuilding two of Oran's cells. Clearing off the rooted vetch and clover with sharp stones they dug down into the sandy soil, and set in the rounded walls, weaving thin willow branches together and daubing them with clay that dried in the summer air. For thatching they used heather from the moor. With these cells up they could shelter from rain their books and chalice and pattens until the church was built. For the church they were clearing the former site from heaps of earth and mouldering wooden beams.

The days were warm and dry and long for building, and they were eager to put up more cells. Ernan was planning where to place the abbot cell; a knoll stood at the head of the gentle slope giving a view not only of the grassland but of the fishers' houses across the sound. The work went on well; it was all they could do some days to break off for morning and evening prayers.

More and more of the neighbouring people came to watch them, men brought their womenfolk and families to see. "Is there some marvel?" the monks asked.

"It is a marvel you have lived so long. Perhaps the Wise Masters plan to come upon you, however, at the longest day. For that is the day of the power of the Bright One—Deisuil!" And they muttered a prayer to Lugh.

"If you should survive," one of the watchers said to Grillan, "I could show you where the soil of the island is best for oats and barley. Round about here it is best for pasturing cows and sheep."

"My sons and I," said one of the fishers, "will bring you some oil for your lamps if you wish. There is an island of seals near here."

"They are thin with hunger," a woman said. "You must send them grain. And cows. They must be tired of fish and cockles and dulse."

"What is the use if they are going to die soon?"

But the longest day came and went; the yellow iris was fading on the swamp and on the rocks the white campions and sea pinks appeared. And they were still alive; and more, they were very busy. The mill stream was cleared, the water running sparkling to the Sound. The mill and the kiln had been repaired. Lugne,

climbing along the shore had found a flat rock which could be
lifted and chiselled into a foundation stone for the church.

"Who said they were going to die?" the Young Men were
saying. "They are not going to die! Not until they have rebuilt
the community. We are here to see to that." And led by the boy
with the dark eyes, Oran, they drilled and practised warfare,
making such a great noise about it the birds rose protesting from
the shore and the older monks took their lips between their teeth.

The Abbot himself turned from the work one day and went
up alone towards the druid hill, for here lay the danger he fore-
saw for his men.

His mind filled with the thought of other settlements he had
seen: Ciaran's, ages ago! when they were little more than
students; Cannich's in the peace of Aghabo; Brendan's at Clon-
fert; Comgal's — O and his own, his own! He did not see any
longer the rough rocks and heather of the slope he was ascending,
the desolate hill and round it the desolate seas. He was going up
again the familiar track to Derry, children running laughing out
to him. The speech of Eire was in his ears again, the true accent!
He remembered how Donal the Ailech king had given him his
pleasant site of Derry, near to the palace, so that he could watch
over both people and kings.

Who was there to watch over them now? How were they
faring? What calamities might have befallen them, sickness,
accident, and he not there to help? He was fretted with cares like
an absent mother, picturing now one, now another.

From the height he had reached he could see far out over
the sea southwards. As if overpowered by a magic spell he was
unable to move, unable to stop gazing, gazing, dreaming that he
could discern a tiny faint speck of land that might be the Eire
shore. Though what was the good of seeing it? He must not go
back to Eire. He must turn his back on her in spirit as in deed.
The curragh that had brought him here had no command for a
return journey. He might as well bury it below the shingle of
that bay where still it was lying beached.

He had thought he was alone. But with a sudden movement
from behind a tussock of heather a young man came into view.
It was the young Dalriadan who had said he was called after the
Abbot Oran, and who certainly outdid his fellows in noisy zeal
for their building of Oran's community . He stood hesitant a
moment—as was to Colum's mind—then leapt across the bog to
his side.

32

"You should not come alone up here!" he said breathlessly.
"It's too close to the Masters' temple. We cannot protect you
against such perils. A man cannot keep away the Eye with the
edge of a sword!"

He squatted down to talk, not seeing the averted face. "I've
heard your men saying you have met Wise Masters before, in Eire.
They say you built a church in the middle of a circle of ancient
stones. That may be all very well in Eire where the land is
largely of the new religion. Here it is the old ways that have the
power."

When Colum went striding off he followed at his heels. "I
think I know why you came up the hill. You are looking for
beams to build the new church with, isn't that it? I once saw a
church building, I watched them at it when I was a child. They
did not use clay and wattles, they made it of good oak wood.
When I was a child Dalriada had many churches, on every hillside and every promontory. Churches or cells at least. That was
before Gauran died.

"I have been much about the palace of Dunadd. Though
my father was Brython, my mother was of Dalriada and she
suckled Aedan, the younger of Gauran's sons. He and I are
fosterbrothers; though I like the elder, Eogan, better. I and those
other Young Men, we were part of Gauran's bodyguard, or we
should have been if we had been older before he died. He was
killed in battle, a sword cut through the face and head. His
brains ran out of him, and he stood waving his arms and gibbering like a beast until death came. And he so noble! I would
have died to save him, and I would not have been the only one.
Since I cannot defend him I am defending his grave."

"If you will come up this glen," Oran then said, "I will
show you a store of wood seasoned and ready to use." And in a
cave among the rocks overhung by trees so that its mouth was
hidden, he showed Colum a pile of planed timber. "It is yours.
For it was Oran's. And if it is not enough I will get the boys to
carry more over from the mainland. Only you and your monks
must pray us safe from the Masters' cursing."

When the Abbot thanked him, he shook his head. Putting
his hand out to touch the Abbot's hand as if taking an oath, he
cried, "And we will help you. Your power will be strong, won't
it, once the church is built? That's where the holy symbols are."

"The church vessels!" Colum corrected him laughing,
"Scarcely the same thing."

C   33

"And the prayers."

"One may pray anywhere. God's church is in the heart of a man before it is anywhere. But the church is the centre where people come to worship."

And as with the young Dalriadan for company the Abbot made his way down by rock and heather to the grassy plain, to the half ruinous half rising community, and heard the lowing of cows and a man's cheerful shout and the slapping sound of the builders' work, he could almost see in the empty air his finished cashel and people coming into it from all sides.

VII

THE trenches for the church foundations had been dug in the ground down to the dark earth below the surface of sand. The stones, shaped now, had been dragged to the site. The wood had been brought down to the edge of the moor, ready. Next morning they would hold solemn Mass and dedicate the founding.

There was some little commotion at the end of evening prayer. Eochaid and Tochannu were reproving some of the Dalriadan boys. But they seemed to have reached agreement, for Colum saw his two monks draw the young men around them to sit on the ground. Eochaid had their precious Gospels out of its shrine and was holding it gingerly to the light of the rush lamp. When the labour of the day was over, they hoped to instruct them in the faith, for they had strange ideas of it; and strange practices, saluting the rising sun, prostrating themselves before the new moon, forever turning their thumbs sunwise with a murmured word against ill luck. There had been grave outrage among the monks over a proposal by one of the Dalriadans that they should carve on the altar stone the sun and crescent moon!

The Abbot left them. For he himself knew he must find some place to be alone. The seashore drew him. He made his way northward over the starlit machair, past the sand dunes with their rough bents, to the rocks of a little bay. The sea came whispering in, cold and clear·

Baithene stood at the northern rampart watching him dimming in the half-light as he went farther and farther away. Diarmaid made a move to follow him with his cloak, but he was called back by Ernan. Grillan and Carnan and Scandal went across the stream to see the cows in their shelter, heaping bracken to keep them warm as if they could thus ease for the Abbot the cold of the sea water and the pain of cramped limbs and the length of the long long night from evening prayer till dawn.

So, though surrounded by the thoughts of his men, the Abbot went alone to his cross vigil, and knelt on the sea drenched stones of the little bay, and spread his arms out on the ledges of rock, to conquer sleep and give his soul to pray for the new church at its founding.

Yet the cold of the sea water, the hardness of the rocks on which he knelt, could not distract his mind from its haunting pain, let alone stay it on God. Night was around him, night was in his soul. Almost he might have been plunged in the druids' hell, lost in eternal cold, eternal woe. In his darkness of spirit he could believe they had power to harm him, those who had confronted him with their claims to the island.

These were fancies. The spectres of his own conscience were reality. Why had he come? To what end? Could he hope by deepest prayer to gain light and blessing? For what was he — a man of violence to found a church, a man unable to conquer sin in himself to fight the world's sin! What was he—a deceiver as much as the druid priests had been, more, more! For they could be detected. But twelve men believed in him as abbot and guardian of their souls.

Sin was not past, it would never be. He sometimes could not endure men round him, for his heart was in Eire across the sea. The accents of the men of Dalriada still irked him, what then of the Cruithnian men he might meet? His body had obeyed his Lord, but his heart would not. Would not, for all the suffering of the night here.

But he thought of his men, one by one: Ernan, Baithene, Fechnus, Grillan, Diarmaid—what was it had brought them here? Loyalty to an abbot? Not that alone. Loyalty to the will of God. What else had set them singing as they builded their cashel in a strange land? The cheerful talk and laughter that had sometimes so sorely vexed him comforted him now as nothing else would. They were at peace in their minds, his men, though he was not. They were kept by God. God was their friend and would even here call up for them many more.

Perhaps he lost consciousness; perhaps touching the bottom of despair he rose up again from it; perhaps the Holy Spirit returned to him.

At any rate by the time the birds were crying on the sands on the north of the island and the day made its first greyness over the sea, his mind cleared. Words of the Mass came into it, familiar, well loved, powerful to keep light in. They had not come to this land to die unfruitful, his good men. They were in God's hands: and he, even he.

As the dawn came in, its light revealed a strange land indeed. As if he had never seen it till now he saw it with astonishment and a kind of sweet perturbation. Clearing itself of shadow, the shore across the sound put on the beauty of green and rose, the grass mantling the granite rocks. The sea danced in brightness. It was like a vision. A new land, a new work; and the work not his or his men's but God's. The surge of his spirits mocked the anguish of his cold stiff limbs· He stumbled as he got up.

As he clambered with difficulty over the rocks towards the sand dunes, he saw someone standing amongst them, still, as if watching himself. The rising sun's light made him clear; it was the young man, that dark-eyed Oran.

"What brings you out so early, my son?" Colum asked him.

Staring at him with anxious face the young man replied, " I have been here watching you since first I knew you were on the shore. For hours I have been watching—deisuil!—Why do you come here alone at night?"

Colum smiled, putting his hand on his arm, " So you shared my vigil!"

They walked together. Oran slowing his steps for the Abbot was still stiff with cold. He was a fine young man, for all the hardships he must have endured, stalwart and lithe as any of the boys of Ailech, with his head held high, and broad shoulders on him, and long striding legs.

"Father," young Oran asked as they went, " Has no word come back yet from Connal?"

"No word. But I do not know that my message ever reached him."

"He is said to be back in Dunadd now, though we have to keep it secret. And wherever he is, the message we sent should have reached him. There ought to have been an answer before now. He is a Christian king, for all they say against him, and would be sure to grant you the Island at your first asking for it.

"I think it is rather that Connal needs help from you! The land is in such a plight. The old queen was gently reared, she comes from the Far South, Breconia: it is hard for her to live like a beast on the hillsides. And Connal's wife, the young queen, there was nothing in her rearing either to make her able to bear the hunger and the cold. It is hard for us all. Connal has

37

been made a vassal to this heathen king Brude. Some day he will make an end of us altogether. I think we are going out like a lamp in the wind, and something better than ourselves is going out too."

They stood a moment or two looking up the long gentle slope, hearing men's voices. "Do you really believe you will build a church here again?" the young man asked with rapid breath. "Will an abbot's bell ring and voices chant the way it was under the old abbot? I have heard my mother say, if only Oran's church stood we should be safe and happy. She said that stronger than Gauran's sword was the Abbot Oran's bell!"

"Most certainly we will build a church here again. I hope it will be up before the worst of the winter. And by then I shall have sent to other communities — to Lismor where my friend Moluag is.

"And you yourself will be at the prayer we are now to make when we dedicate the site and lay the foundations in the ground."

"You must say strong prayers then," Oran said, shivering. "That is when they will try to confound you and your building."

"They?"

"The Wise Masters. No, do not shake your head. You must believe me. I know this land. It may be you were safe from the Hidden Ones in your land of Eire, but here, danger lies in the very soil. When you set your foundation stone in, at that time there will be the greatest danger."

"Come then," Colum bade him, "Come and help us."

"I will come," the young man said, gazing with a look curiously solemn and earnest at the site, "I will help all I can."

And he drew from his belt his short sword, and put its hilt to his mouth.

VIII

STANDING between the trenches as they held Mass to dedicate the foundation of their church Colum pictured it complete. Small indeed it might be and low, but able to bear the island gales; and plain as yet, whereas in Eire his churches had had the jewels of kings for their adorning; but adorned by the very obedience of its being there, and by its holy function, for here as in any church the sacred vessels of the sacrament would be stored and the books of the Scriptures full of the word of life.

By the time it was complete Moluag of Lismor might have come to see them, and others from churches in Dalriada and Alba. A library would grow. And he pictured in his mind the buildings that would go up around, the cells not only of his present community but the clustering cells of the men who should come to join their rule. He saw the ruined causeway of the Abbot Oran supporting once again the feet of many men coming to the Island to learn and confess and pray.

Ernan the bishop, with Eochaid, was now speaking the words of the Mass, high and remote and yet familiar and dear. Around their little company, almost to be seen, came the presences of many other men, those he had left in charge of his communities up and down Eire, Cannich and Comgal and Brendan his friends, priests he had heard of in Gaul, in the lands of the East, in Rome. The oblation of the Sacrifice made before twelve men was made before all the Christian family.

Twelve men? More. For as the joyful words of the thanksgiving rang out over the quiet Island, up from the shore had come fishermen and their neighbours from across the Sound, in by the gate space of the rough made rampart, over the clovered grass and the places where Oran's houses had stood. They halted a safe distance from the absorbed monks, absorbed too, listening

39

to the Latin words which were strange though the meaning had been explained to many of them in the past days, and yet made old childhood memories echo in the mind. The great arch of sky enveloped one and the other company, enveloped the whole site and the Island itself as if in one vast church of God. Colum's love went out to them and in the space of intercession he prayed for them and all those who were unknown as yet to him in the unknown land.

They listened and watched till the last hymn was sung; and when the monks went to their several tasks they watched them still.

Colum went with Rus and Fechnus to where on the edge of the heather the pile of wooden beams and pillars lay. It was a day to build, dry and clear, and the Abbot was very eager to begin. The young men raised a beam and carrying it upon their shoulders went in step down on to the grassy plain, to the site. The Abbot called to them to send another man to help him carry another beam. The sun was making the Island beautiful. The sea around was deepest blue yet came in green and palest green upon the white white sand. There was a patch of gold on the swamp below the grassland where the wild iris still bloomed, and on the rocks the sea pinks challenged it with their colour. It made him think of a manuscript ornamented in gold and colours. But what would be written as the text? What joys and what cares, what marvels, would unfold themselves here?

He could see the slabs of stone being dragged into position, Grillan and Carnan and Lugne straining at them. Colum hoped they might get help from the young Dalriadan men, Oran's companions. He had seen Oran stand watching the ritual of the Mass, still rapt with shining face. He had looked different from other days. For he was dressed in a white tunic and on his hair was some sort of chaplet of leaves, like someone celebrating a festival. He had helped so much, indeed it would be fitting if he took part in this first stage of building, as in Eire where princes would be glad to be invited to raise the first pillar upon the foundation stone.

With some thought of calling the Dalriadan young men to help he looked down at the site and the workers. Baithene was coming up towards him with Rus and Fechnus. Some singing was in the air. The Abbot turned towards the sound of it and saw the young Dalriadan men some distance away coming towards the site. They were walking slowly, singing, as if at some rite: a figure in white which might be Oran was leading them.

And then a cry cut through the air, through all other sounds in it, through the Abbot's brain. He dropped the beam he was hoisting up and looked down, saw a commotion in the very centre of the church site. Then he saw a number of young men in flight, running in all directions, some to the shore, some to the track to the western side of the Island. Shouts followed them, cries from the monks.

What could this be? Had there been some quarrel that had become a fight? Had Eochaid perhaps, enraged at some irregularity of belief or practice, rounded too sharply on his pupils and been struck by them—or struck? Surely not. More like that some light word among the boys themselves had sparked off a fight. One of them was running his way, blindly with head down; the Abbot caught him and asked what was the matter. It was not guilt that showed in his white face, nor anger, but a sort of sick horror.

An accident? A tumbling stone, a man pinned beneath. The Abbot let the young man go, and ran with long strides down to see.

His monks were clustered round one of the foundation trenches. He called out to them as he got near. But it was as if they did not hear him. When he was close they became aware of him, but for only answer drew in together as if hiding something, and they would not meet his gaze.

"God, God, God!" Ernan prayed between his teeth, "Let him not see it," as if by a miracle sight might leave the keen eyes.

It was no mangled flesh pinned under a heavy stone they were hiding. The body lay whole and shapely on top of it. Who was it? Who? Colum's heart was thudding the question.

It was not one of his monks. The long legs trailed from a white tunic, a chaplet of green-brown oak leaves lay fallen off the dark head. Young Oran. With a cry the Abbot dropped to his knees beside him. Scandal the doctor got up then and with a little gesture of abandon stood away to let him make his own examination. Colum felt for the pulse on his forehead and throat, and put his cheek to the mouth. He took up one hand which dropped limp from his grasp when he let it go.

The white tunic was stained with blood, blood trickled across the stone he lay upon. The tunic was stuck to his left ribs — a knife wound. The knife lay beside the trench on the shorn grass.

"This was no accident then?" Colum asked slowly with a stiff mouth. "Which of them did this? Which?"

"Who was it? Tell me!" he commanded roughly.

41

Ernan took him by an arm, "Come away, Columan. You can't bring him back. You can't alter anything. Don't ask."

"Who saw it happen? What did they quarrel over? On such a day! Who struck him? Who?"

"No quarrel. No one to blame. Except his friends in so far that they allowed it. We found them walking in procession singing a strange heathenish song. We came to admonish them. But it happened so suddenly, before we knew. Most of us were thinking of the building. We saw the knife flash in his hand, and they cried out to drown his death scream. His body tumbled down as it lies now."

"He did this himself? What had we done to vex him? Who has said words to make him despair?"

"Colum," Ernan put his hand on the Abbot's arm. "You do not understand."

"What? Why has he done it, why? Do none of you know what was in his mind? And the rest of the boys, why have they run away?"

"They are wise to run!" Ernan grimly said. And then gently, "Come, Colum, you cannot hope to change old ways in so short a time. This is the old evil practice of a man giving his life to the ground to make a building secure. I have met it once or twice in my youth in Eire. He did this to make the church thrive!"

And as the Abbot said not a word: "If this is the state of the Christian faith in Dalriada!" Tochannu the senior said, and Eochaid answered him, "Poor child! If he had only lived we might have taught him. But he has died the death of a pagan, God pity all men."

Grillan said trembling, "Can we build the church here after this? The ground is polluted."

Fechnus and Rus clamoured, "No, no! We must not build here. We must not even stay. We'll get the curragh ready and we'll go. Anywhere."

Eochaid demurred, looking over at Ernan, "But the site is chosen and blessed. We must build on it now. Let us quickly take the body of this stranger, his friends can lift him up, and row out and bury it at sea at ebb tide. God's currents may carry it away from us."

Then Colum called loud out, "The church will assuredly be built here! And if I dared I would lay his body under the foundation stone. But since that would lead them further astray

—we will lay Oran's body in the ground. He shall lie with the kings, with Gauran whom he honoured, in the soil hallowed by the Abbot Oran whose name he was glad to bear."

He said as they lifted the body, "Touch him reverently. Whatever his error, it was noble. He gave his life for us, and he so young too. There is more of Christ our Saviour in his error than in all our righteousness."

And on the third day when they had buried the young man he said to Baithene, "He will never see now what he longed to see, the church complete. He was the first man of Dalriada to join our brotherhood and the first to die. His sacrifice shall not be in vain." And that very night he called the seniors together and said, "I see that I must leave you to get on with the building. God keep you."

"Leave us now, Colum?"

"I must go across to the mainland without delay. I must go to Dunadd; or if the king is not there I must search the whole of Dalriada till I find him. I must find what his state and the state of the land is. Whatever their plight, we have come to bring help."

"You will not go alone?"

"I will go with God. But not with any of you—none can be spared from this building. The fishers can ferry me over to the mainland when the day is light."

Dunadd

IX

NO sooner had Colum landed on the mainland shore than the fisherman who brought him from the Island leapt into his curragh again and rowed off with alacrity as if he preferred the sea.

It was a pleasant land, this Dalriada, with little hills and glens nestling between them. In some of these, sheltered from frost, the rowan trees were still partly green, and hung scarlet berries in the wind. Bracken made gold brown tracks down the beds of streams. There were grassy slopes that could have fed cattle. But no sheep or cows grazed them. And land that must at one time have been under the plough was now rough with weeds. Colum walked the best part of a day without seeing any human being. And when after a night in the wild he did come upon houses they were empty, roofless indeed and falling down. One, the largest, had its beams blackened with fire.

It was an event to smell peat smoke again and know he must be near humankind. But when he reached the little cluster of houses he found all the doors barred. From one a voice challenged him, asking what was his errand, and after he had said he was a priest, the goodman put a gaunt face through a hole in the mud wall. The eyes of his family peered from lesser holes here and there. When Colum asked him if he could help him to find King Connal he stared glumly at him. It was only when women's voices urged from inside, " He is a priest, see he is carrying his book!" that any answer was given. " If you want Connal you must ask at the dun."

A fortress was visible to the south set on a high ridge. Colum asked if that were Dunadd.

" No, no. It's the dun of Fergus our chief. He is there now. He is always there, guarding the pass to Loch Awe. He cannot leave it ever, not even to join the King and the rest of them at—"

A woman's voice cried, " Quiet!"

The man said loudly, in a fright, " What have I said? I have told him nothing. Go to our chief Fergus's dun; if he thinks fit he will tell you where to find Connal. We dare not. We are simple people, and have been forbidden to speak."

Colum made his way to the dun, and there they received him and gave him a place to sleep—though little peace, for they rained questions on him. Was he indeed a priest? And from Eire! Not one of Oran's men? Was he passing through Dalriada going to Strathclyde? Most of the clerics, folk said, had gone south from there. Was it to Teach Martain he was going? Where were his retinue? Who was his patron prince?

There was no milk for supper, though they had children who could have made use of it, and no bread, instead a handful of hazelnuts dried and roasted. Sadly they showed him below the hill their field of corn, burnt before harvesting by a band of raiders from Cruithnian country who swept through one night from Loch Awe. They had got only a swathe or two round the edges of the field, but were thankful enough to have that same, and above all, mouths still left to them, hungry though they might be.

But when in the morning he asked directly where he might find Connal, the chief shut his lips. "Who told you he was in Dunadd again? What do you want with him?"

Then he relented. "Well, I will show you the way to Dunadd. We were a Christian country, and I must show so much civility to God's priest. Take this track south, keeping by the side of these raised fields. Good earth it is there, ploughed for hundreds of years. I wish to God we had the crops of them! Then you will come to an open valley where the ancient stones are. It is wise to say prayers there in the passing. There is maybe little good to be had from it; still, there is no harm in keeping on the good side of the old gods. Who knows? Maybe it was for neglecting them we are so harried by the Cruithnians now. If you go on southwards still you will come to the Great Bog. You must keep to the track and avoid the softest places. I am sorry I cannot show you. You will see the palace then, God save it! and will have to find means of crossing the River for the bridge is down.

But I did not say you would find Connal there!"

So at last he came within sight of the royal palace, Dunadd of ancient story, taken by the kindred from the Cruithnians. It rose abruptly from the moor and marshland, a citadel towering over the width of land. The Long River glinting like a coiled snake made a rampart of water round it.

X

THE lords of the Great Isles, Isla, Diura and Arran, and the Lord of the Headland, were bawling at one another for they were of different kindreds and apt to disagree. When Connal tried to shout into the din they turned upon him, one menacing him, with fists since he was weaponless. A cousin of the King's from the eastern territory cried out at the outrage, but the rest laughed at him, saying, " Where is the King? We have no king, we have a petty chieftain."

And Connal rose and left the council that was more like a brawl among the slaves. And none cared enough to rise in honour to him. He went alone, slowly, up the winding stairs to the little tower room where he knew he would find his wife. And there she was indeed. She sat by a little smoking brazier crouching forward to get its meagre heat. She was suckling their latest baby. Connal went and stood against the wall, looking out of the narrow window in which was framed a vista of his land. If he put his head out he could see not only high Cruachan but the Arran mountains, and the round hills of Diura, the boundaries of his dominion. But the mountains mocked him as the men below had mocked him. Everything he saw mocked him. Below the window on its shelf of rock was the ancient crowning stone. He remembered with what trembling delight he had placed his foot in the Step, so awful with the carved symbols round it. And now the memory of that day was sharpest pain. He was called to be king when there was only ruin to succeed to.

He turned in his secret anger to his wife. When first he had seen her suckle a child he had felt deep peace and fulfilment. That was when Connad was born. But there were several now, he scarcely knew whether this was the fourth or fifth; and it was a bondmaid who had named him, so that they called him Nechtan as if he were a Cruithnian! And yet for a moment peace came to him again, for his wife was not regarding him, nor was the sucking child regarding him, nor did the bitterness of his own thought regard him. This, he said to himself, is to be a man instead of a fighter. If they had asked him to be a good man, a wise councillor even: but they must make a fighting man and a leader of him, and he could not lead.

"Do you know what they wanted me to do?" he said in a voice too loud for the little room, "They wanted me to get ready to lead a skirmish into Cruithnian territory. Winter and all. They said if we could retake and keep the other end of Loch Awe it would guard us from attacks."

"But will you, Connal?" She spoke absently, immersed in her own misery.

"Will I Connal!" he burst out in irritation, "Are you not listening? They wanted me to lead an attack on the Cruithnians. I'd like to see those fellows suffer what happened to me. O they fought, no doubt, and were wounded before they ran away. But which of them had to—" The memory of his shaming was too dreadful, his tongue froze in his mouth, he could not speak. He might tell her, for she was gentle to him, his woman. But she was Gauran's niece and royal in blood. He found himself shouting again, "I've a good mind to let them have their way. By all means let them go and attack Loch Awe or anywhere. They can scarcely make our state worse than it is now. And it might put them where they would have to hold their tongues! You should have heard them at their so-called Council, shouting and interrupting one another with no thought of precedence; expecting me to sit and listen to plans not one of us dares fulfil. By all means, let them attack if they can find a leader.

"It's your fault!" he was shouting at her again. "Without you I'd never have come back to Dunadd at all. I wish we were back in those caves—or in that shieling on the mountain—I had some peace from talk at anyrate."

The child gave a wail, she put it sighing to the other breast. And she said patiently, "Did you not want to come back?"

"Only for your sake. Do you think I want to see you endure a winter like last?"

He turned down his mouth when he thought of it. She had given birth to her child in the open air. They could hear the howling of the wolves in search of the blood when they halted for her delivery. And the cold, the cold! It had tormented their ill-fed bodies. The children were pitiful to see. And it made them all old: it had withered and aged her, and he had been sad in heart for her, and listened to her as she harped on the comforts of the palace. "Connal, I want to go home."

50

"Well, you're in the palace now," he said to her, "Your old Bog Castle! You're back in the palace, or what's left of it. We would be as well in the caves as in this draughty place." He laughed with a kind of amusement at the look she gave him as if she were terrified he would try to make her flee again.

He said, "Another thing. You may feel safe because you spent your childhood here, but I warn you we may be attacked any moment—whether my brave warriors attack the Cruithnians or not."

"I only want a little comfort," she said beginning to weep. "Do you wonder? I have another child to bear in the spring."

He pressed his lips in with his teeth, and walked a pace or two, and then sat down beside her, running a finger on the back of her hand, and at last he spoke quietly as he should to a woman.

"I had two messages today."

"From whom?" she asked, accepting his offer of apology.

"One was from Aedan." She glanced at him questioning. "Your cousin Aedan is still hoping to gather some men. He writes in good spirits. I don't know what Aedan would have done to pass the time if he had been born in a time of peace."

"Where is he, Connal?"

"He was at Alclydd when he wrote the letter. It has taken some time to get here. Rederech could do nothing for him, of course. What did he expect? The man is harassed by foes at home, not to speak of having to do his share in keeping those Saxons at bay. But our Aedan nothing daunted means to go east and bully or coax a soldier or two here and there among the Brythons and rearm Dalriada. He may make you some day a real queen, gold and chariots and feather beds and all!"

She shook her head, "Who was the other message from?"

He twitched his shoulder again, as if the pain he felt was in it.

"From that priest who says he is a kinsman of ours from Eire. The one I had a letter about from Donal of Ailech. Do you remember, I told you at the time? Donal bade me protect him, with curses like to freeze your soul in hell if I did not. I was to give him all help and honour. I got the letter somehow while we were on the hillside. It amused me. Remember the name—Colum mac Felimid mac Fergus, a prince of the North Niall. Well, then I heard from one of Isla's men that some monks from Eire had landed, somewhere on an island he did not know

51

just where. And now, today, I get a letter from the man himself, saying he will shortly pay me a visit in the Palace, he is on his way. Now what do you think he can want with me?"

"Tribute, you thought, for his king."

Connal got up with an oath, "Then I'm damned if he gets in here. I'm damned if I give him a welcome for all his kinship. I honour and help him! They never sent one man over to help us in our troubles. Tribute indeed! The only tribute I can give and it's one I would like to give them, is—"

It gave him a spiteful pleasure to think of Donal's envoy coming to Dunadd and finding an attack on. His royal Ailech blood would look the same as any on the ground.

"Didn't you say," his wife was asking, "He was a priest, this Colum mac Somebody? It isn't usual to send priests collecting tribute. Are you sure that in King Donal's letter—"

"It isn't usual to be so clever as the Ailech kings. They think we cannot refuse a holy man admission. Then once he's in, he's a prince and bringing the demand of his king. But I shall be as clever as themselves, for I will not see him."

Connad their eldest child slid like a cat to his mother's side. Connal shuddered with distaste at the sight of him. He was left-handed to begin with, and now he coughed, keeping them awake at night as they lay huddled on their mattresses. He stood over the boy asking impatiently, "What are you up to?"

"Look what I've found, father!" And the child was sharing out to them some cakes and apples which he had been carrying in the breast of his tunic.

"Where did you come by these? They're scarce enough these days."

"It was easy," Connad said, "You can find them every night now on the flat stone beside the great door."

"It's Savaintide," said his mother to Connal, and her eyes filled with tears. "So many have lost kindred.—You should not touch what is laid out at the door. It is robbing the dead."

And Connal pushed the gobbling child away. "You'll stay in the hall at night, that's another thing, and not go wandering out, do you hear? The great door is kept shut at night, shut and guarded. I will give stricter orders to the guards. They should never have let you go."

He was thankful he had not let his son know the fullest extent of his anger. It was no fault of his if he reminded his father always of the Crowning Stone.

XI

EOGAN was the only man who had pitied Connal, as he made his clumsy way out of the hall. Connal was after all his cousin, his father's brother's son: it was not good to see him so sorely shamed. He had been in his childhood rather fond of Connal, and admired his skill in hunting when he was a little lad and Connal half grown. He could still remember one cold night, one winter of the four Connal spent at the palace learning warfare, when he was wakened by Connal coming to his bed to tell him of the great stag they had brought down; he remembered the chill of the raindrop that fell from his cousin's mantle on to his own warm neck as he sat up from his pile of fur rugs. Good-natured, kindly, easy-going Connal — a pity he should have to suffer being laughed at, and by men no better than himself, as the way of life is!

No more,—ah not so much, he thought later that night as he sat up in his bed, not so much as he himself was suffering. He was Gauran's own son. Gauran had loved him, the very difference in their natures seeming to unite them. In his devout humility he had often wondered how it could be that the magnificent warrior king could love a boy better with words than with a sword. But so it had been, this miracle and splendour. Gauran had always shown him a half humorous gentleness, and in later years asked his counsel and even taken it. One would have thought he would have ignored him for Aedan. For Aedan, though younger, had from his very cradle seemed to show his warrior powers.

Now Aedan was gone from them, the one active person from a crowd of useless men. Connal had had a letter from him, Aedan was in their uncle's kingdom of Strathclydd. He was using all his cunning and a patience unlike his years in his efforts to persuade Rederech that he could spare fighters for Dalriada's need when he had not enough for his own! If Rederech to the end denied him, in spite of the influence of the queen, their father Gauran's sister, he would go round the chiefs and wheedle men from them before they were aware it was for himself he asked them. He would also go east to the Men of the North as their mother called the people of South of the Bannag, and use his uncle's name to get men to his own cause. Aedan was sly. And he was doing this partly indeed for his country, but partly because, simply, he was hungry for fighting men. As other boys are hungry for meat or apples, so Aedan had always been hungry for fighting men.

But as for Eogan himself, he could see nothing to gather men for. Since he had witnessed his father's death in battle he had ceased to be fully alive. He and all the men of the bodyguard who had seen Gauran fall and not saved him, they were like ghosts flitting through their violated hall. It would be more decent for them to die and be done with it, at least they would not be tormented by thought of their own inadequacy. They were so wild in their manners now they would draw knives on each other disputing a share in the roast meat, but they would not draw a sword to win back their nationhood. They were dead and buried more truly than Gauran in his grave on the Island.

Aedan and he had carried their father's body to it, though Brude's men were on the look-out for them. They had been met on the shore by one or two monks, quiet and grey, the last of Oran's men. They had helped them to lift their father out of the boat, and led them to the burial place of Dalriada's kings. There was no splendour to mark it. One of the monks said he would carve the name upon the memorial stone. He and Aedan then sprinkled earth as the monks said their prayer. They had scarcely done so when their companions screamed to them from the other boat—a longship of the Cruithnians was rowing swiftly towards them. They had thrown on the body a few stones lying to hand on the beach, then run for their lives; leaving Gauran a second time, leaving him alone, the new dead with the old.

Lluan their mother had wanted to know what prayers had been said over the body. She cried out and covered her face when she heard about the cairn of stones. She said Gauran should have had earth burial, he was Christian. As if it mattered!

But sometimes now that he had little to do he himself worried a little over the burial. It would be dreadful if they made him suffer in some death kingdom for their omission. He sometimes wondered if those monks had been monks at all: he had heard it said in spring they were druids and not priests who were at the Island now.

He could think of his father in no dim death kingdom, though. He had been so much alive, his broad shoulders moving among his men, his loud voice commanding, his keen eyes flashing. If he did return, he would come striding in, gallant as ever, and call them up bravely and fill them with courage again. But he smiled at the dream. He knew there was no returning. He had cast the stones on his father, and better to leave him so. For Gauran if he came would find only what would grieve him, his hall broken, his men heartless, and his elder son sitting idle with his back against the wall.

He was roused by a movement near his mother's bed. He was alert instantly. For if he could do nothing else he could protect her in her helplessness. Since Gauran's death her thoughts were all confused, she wandered in her sleep at night and talked wildly at times by day. But all was still. He lay down and went to sleep.

XII

LLUAN the widow of Gauran glanced through her long lashes at the sleepers in the crowded hall. The ache for Gauran was gnawing at her breast, and she pressed the hand that held her mantle over the place to still it. She could feel her rings hard as she clenched her hand, but no longer remembered the pleasure she felt sometimes that through all the spoiling, she had them still. Softly she rose, and stood, trembling with fear, lest anyone should wake and see her.

They must all be asleep now. In any case the fires were dying down. She whispered to her little bondmaid, and the girl woke yawning and got to her feet. "I have it!" Lluan breathed in her ear. "Help me carry it."

They made their way softly among the prostrate forms. Now and again a spurt of flame would reveal the scene in the hall. Lluan drew her mouth down. They lay in one another's arms, and who was to say if they were married or not? There was no chance of marriage ceremonies; still! She jerked the maid by an elbow, ashamed that she should see such sights. "In my hall!" she said angrily. But she forgot her anger in fear like the girl's. that they would be discovered, that if anyone awoke he would see them in the firelight. She watched the King's couches sharply. The boy Connad coughed now and again and twisted in his sleep. But they got safe to the door.

The slave girl was afraid as they began the descent of the stairway. "It is forbidden, Noble Lady. The King has expressly forbidden anyone to go out at the door by night. I am afraid to disobey."

"Afraid?" Lluan asked. Turning her head a moment she looked at the girl with far-off eyes.

"There are sentries—I am afraid of men at night."

"Of my men? They will open the door at a word from me, my little one. I am the queen."

56

"You are safe enough," the girl said, rude in her terror, "They will not harm you. You are noble, and you are crazed. But I am young, and of the other people. Connal will punish me."

"Connal!" Lluan said, and her face coarsened with anger so much that the girl whimpered and the lamp swayed in her hand. "This is Gauran's hall."

She went on down the steep stairs, and the girl stifled her crying and followed. The wind blew cold and whined in the passage as if the great door were open, but when they turned the last corner they found it was shut and two sentries lolling up against it, yawning and grumbling with each other.

They stood up straight, however, when they saw people approaching, and called to them with an oath to stay where they were. Lluan held up her lamp, the small light flickering in her fine-featured distraught face. One of the men muttered, "It is the old queen!"

"Open the door!" said Lluan.

"Noble Lady, the King's orders—we may not."

"Open the door, will you! The King will have your heads for refusing to obey me. Open the door, or I will bring the matter to my Lord Gauran."

"Hush, hush!" cried the girl, clapping her hand over her mistress's mouth. "Gauran is dead."

"Open the door!"

"Noble Lady, we dare not. The King has given strict orders—we would risk too much—Go you," one said helplessly to the other, "and tell the King, and ask what we are to do."

"Connal is lucky that some of his men obey him," Lluan said, with the corners of her mouth down. "Have I no rank now? No kinsmen to protect me? I have Gauran, and sons."

Connal appeared, his mantle pulled tight round him for the draughts of the passageway, his face fuddled with sleep, but his manner kind.

"Fostermother—"

Mollified she put her hand on his arm, "Connal you too—you are like a son to me. You will help me? I must go out. Tell them to open the door for me."

"Listen, Noble Lady. You must understand. It is not safe. Inside at least we have some protection; outside, who can say? A band of raiders, one single raider even—it is of your own safety I am thinking."

"I am not afraid to die," she said contemptuously, "And I am too old to fear rape. For that matter it can happen inside the hall."

"Why do you want to go out?"

She paused at the direct question. Then she dropped her voice to speak gently, reasonably. "I know Gauran died. Do not think I am mad." She could not say more, but pulled the girl forward, pushing back her mantle to show what she was carrying, a dish of meat and bread, a skin of wine.

"Our mouthfuls are counted!" Connal cried, "Why do you take this outside? Where did you find the wine?"

"I will not waste it, boy. It is for him. He will come and take it."

"Ah!" he said, understanding, "Savaintide." And he was shocked. Though he had not heard a priest say Mass for many a day, though prayers he had been taught were fading from his mind, still he remembered enough of the teaching he had received as a child: especially the teaching he had received in the palace here. "Are we Christian people or of the old religion? You yourself it was who taught me when I was trained."

She drew her breath in, and hung her head.

He followed up his advantage, "You learn such ways from the bondwomen." Then more gently, "Come now, come up with me again. It is safe in the hall, and warm. The nights are cold now, you are shivering. Come back to the warmth of the fires."

She burst out into a torrent of wild words. "Warm, safe! It is all you think of. There was safety and warmth in Dunadd when Gauran was King. Now the winds whistle through the walls. Mend the walls. Why will you not? I know. Because you do not mean to defend it. You will take to your herdsman's hut again, and Dunadd will be abandoned. It will pass to the Cruithnians who had it before."

"Lead your mistress back into the hall," Connal said sternly to the gaping girl, "And see she does not wander at night again."

"I am ashamed I fostered you!" Lluan sobbed as she turned away. "Your ways are not a king's ways. It is right our enemies degraded you to a chief's status, you could not be more. But our people—my husband Gauran's people—my own sons—"

Eogan was standing now beside them. She hid her face in his breast. "Eogan! Eoganan! You know what season this is. How can you lie warm, darling, and your father out in the cold? See, I have made a meal for him, the kind he likes. Do you remember

how we used to eat supper together sometimes in the little room?
—Now I must go out and set it for him. But Connal will not
let me go out by the door. The door is locked—Don't you say
it is not our custom! I know it is not our custom. I know it is
not right. But I must do what I can. I am so grieved he died,
Eogan. Even if he cannot come, he may see and he will know
we have not forgotten him." She began to weep, the two men
gazing unhappily at her. "Open the door, and come out with
me, then, Eogan. I have no one but you. We'll put the food on
the flat stone beside the gate."

Eogan looked over to Connal above her head, and Connal
shrugged. "O go out with her then. Look out for yourselves.
And mind the great door is locked and barred behind you.—It is
such a waste."

XIII

THE ache for Gauran gnawed at Lluan's breast again, and she rose from her couch laying back the fur rug and pulling her mantle round her still slender form. The little slavegirl was asleep and she did not wake her, but made her slow laborious way alone through the hall, stepping this way and that distastefully among the sleeping men and women. She went holding her small lamp down the worn and broken stairs. The sentries by the doorway were, as she hoped, asleep. She put a hand to the door but she knew it was too heavy for her to open unaided. Sighing she went to the slit window and looked into the starlit night.

. . . She was making her way back quickly, quickly, heedless of the muttered protests, the angry oaths, of the sleepers she trod on on the floor. Her lamp spilt hot oil on her dress. She came and crouched over him—"Eogan! Eogan!" She was afraid he would cry out in waking, but he woke silently, getting to his knees and pulling his hunting knife in one movement from his belt which he was wearing.

"Hush! It's I—mother," she whispered to him.

He said urgently, "Which way are they coming? The door —For God's sake, do not tell me we left the door—"

She made a wordless sound in her throat as if stilling a child.

"Aedan then, is it? Has news come? Is Aedan killed?"

It was she then who cried out, "O God forbid!" and she signed herself. Then she took him by the hand, "Eogan!" she said laughing low, "Wake up, dear! Listen to me. The food is gone!"

"The food—?" Sleep was coming back over him; he sighed and was for lying down again.

"The food we put out for him, for your father—the food is gone!"

"Well, how else should it be?" he asked peevishly. "There are enough hungry men around."

60

She shook his arm impatiently, " Why will you not believe me? Gauran has come and eaten our food, do you not understand?"

He said with equal impatience, " Gauran my father is dead. The sword cut through his face, through his skull, and he— he —till he fell dead on the spot. I saw it, I was standing there."

But she drowned him out, speaking in a voice like singing, " Now that he has eaten he will renew himself, he will put on new flesh. He cannot go away. Come with me, Eogan, we will go out to meet him. Who should be there to welcome him but his wife and his son? Put your cloak on, so, it will be cold. Poor boy, you are cold already, your arm is goose-fleshed. O let us take him in! Who knows how long he has been waiting for us?"

Eogan got up reluctantly, pulling his clothes on with an ill grace. But from force of habit he obeyed his mother. She was going on and on in her crazed way. "—When the hero dies, the hero lives again. In my girlhood when the heathen Saxons came to harry our eastern borders it was Ardyr who fought for us. He was our saviour. And in the very year that Ardyr was killed. Gauran married me and took me to this northern kingdom; and it was strange to me, but I felt safe again. He was like Ardyr. Perhaps he was Ardyr? At anyrate he was the Deliverer. And now that my lord Gauran is dead he comes in new guise. You will see. You need not stare so sadly at me. You do not realise these things, you are only a child. But I have lived longer and known other lands; I have seen it come to pass.

" Look out of the window, Eogan," she bade him. " You are tall. Tell me if you see him."

Eogan put his eye to the slit window, grimacing as the cold struck it.

" Is the stone not bare? Is it not as I told you, the food is gone?"

She asked again. " Eogan? Why don't you speak?"

—" There is a man out there."

" Gauran."

" No!" he said angrily. " Not my father. How could that be? But some man is kneeling—"

" Let us go out to him."

" No, mother, no! It may be a trick of the Cruithnians. Whoever he is he can wait till morning."

" Give me a lamp, Eogan! The one on the wall, for the oil is done in mine. And come you and get this door open. Never

mind those men, they are fast asleep and will not heed us. God
will help us.—When the hero dies, the hero lives again."

He knew he must do as she said if he were ever to get back
to his sleep. The beam of their lamp in the open doorway shone
through the dark, and the man at the flat stone rose to his feet.

"A priest?" Eogan whispered. "God of Light, can it be a
priest? Tonsured from ear to ear, and a book slung at his side.
When did we see a priest come travelling this way before?—Ah,
now I see! It must be the kinsman from Eire that Connal told
me about; he had a message from him. But he was hoping to
avoid seeing him—and now we shall have to let him in!"

The man came towards them as they stood bemused in the
doorway. He came slowly, because the path was far from smooth,
and he appeared very tired. Eogan stood where he was, staring.

"I am Colum, a priest from Eire."

"Kinsman of Donal of Ailech?"

The stranger replied quickly, "Kinsman of King Connal.
But you are right, I am from Ailech."

"Sir, we have heard you were coming. My mother—"

The stranger bowed, and then blessed her. She bent her
head to him, making a deep obeisance, and said in a clear formal
tone, "I am Lluan, daughter of Brychan, wife of Gauran. We
are most happy, holy father, to welcome you. You are a priest!"
She laughed lightly, like a girl. "I have two nephews who are
priests. One of them is Cadog, you must have heard of him, even
in Eire? Son of my eldest sister Guladys. The other too is famous,
my sister Meleri's son. O do not think because—" her eyes filled
with tears, her face flushed with shame as she implored him.
"You must have seen it, I am afraid—the Savain offering? I am
to blame. The times are bad, one tries all ways. But I am
Christian, born in a Christian land. My father was a prince in
Breconia, a land of churches, with priests and even many layfolk
speaking in the Latin tongue. Both my father's and my mother's
families have been Christian for generations, since before the
Roman legions went away! It is a land of gentle manners and
fine living; it is not as it is here.

"Come in, father, O come in! You are welcomed in Gauran's
name by his queen."

Colum said softly to Eogan as he turned from bolting the
door, "You must be Gauran's son?"

"He is our elder son Eogan," Lluan answered for him. "He
is like his father—in looks."

The priest said softly still to Eogan, "I have come from your father's grave."

All shyness left him. "From the Island? And the grave—?"

"The grave is unharmed. No one has disturbed it. Not that you need care, for his soul is gone to God. Still, their bodies also lie in peace, and they will lie so, for we have settled there."

Lluan, scarcely heeding them, was saying, "Come in now, father, O come in! Why was I not told of our kinsman's coming?"

Grandly she led the way up the battered steps, shining the lamp courteously at their guest's feet—and indeed he had need of it. Eogan dreaded the moment when the door would open and they would enter the hall.

They got their guest over the unclean and crowded floor. Eogan made him take his bed and rug. He could not sleep himself, in any case, and was glad to walk up and down. His heart was thudding. Almost he shared his mother's crazed exaltation. If they had not admitted Gauran himself by the door, they had admitted someone whose influence was like Gauran's. If the graves were safe—who knows? Hope rose like pain in his mind. If Gauran was at peace, his people might rise again into prosperity. He walked restlessly around until the fires were relit by the servants, and the grey of morning stood in the window slits.

XIV

OGAN averted his eyes as he came to the King's couch. He had not yet learned to tolerate their lack of privacy. In the wilds this sort of crowding together did not seem to matter very much, but here in the hall of his father's dun! The queen was his first cousin, gently brought up; and he was ashamed to see her with all her children about her, stared at and jostled even as she rose and tidied herself. She was suckling the baby for all to see; she, a princess by birth and with a right to be called queen by her marriage to Connal, had not so much as the decency of a woman's grianan.

She was gathering the children to take them to find food, though Connal was still in bed, snoring through all the stir of rising. Eogan went to the pile of frowsty fur rugs, and shook Connal awake.

"Connal, listen to me!"

"What, is there something wrong?" Connal got up on one elbow, sufficiently awake.

"No, but in the middle of the night—"

"I heard nothing. Has Aedan come? You don't mean Aedan has brought fighting men here from Rederech?"

"No, no. It's our kinsman from Eire. The cousin of Donal of Ailech, the one he wrote to you about. He's inside the dun, here in the hall."

"No!"

"But he is. He is waiting to meet you."

"God damn it!" Connal leapt up, biting his lips with the pain of his wounded shoulder which he had moved carelessly. "How did that happen? Who let them in? Someone must have opened the great door in spite of my express command."

"The queen my mother and I, we let him in. It was when she was making her offering of food—you remember. We saw him waiting out in the cold, and we opened the door for him."

"Your mother is crazed with her Savain offerings, and you are as crazed as herself. Could you not have bolted the door again, confound you, and come away back to your beds?"

"He is our kindred."

"O but I know!" Connal said grinning in a fury, pulling on his outer robe with clumsy haste, "I ought to remember. It was all set out in Donal's letter, all the wonderful genealogy like a bard's Naming. Why for the gods' sake did you let them in? What am I going to say to him? You great fool, with your man's stature and your boy's brain!—And his retinue? How have you accommodated them, I wonder? And how are we to find food to fill them all?"

"He has no retinue. If I had known, I would have ridden with a spare horse to meet him and escorted him here."

Connal cried, groping impatiently for his shoes, "Why, man, have you no spirit? You are more tolerant even than myself. I've seen your father beside himself with rage when these tribute messengers came. He would have brained them against the lintel of the door, if it were not for their immunity. By God, the only tribute they got out of him was a meal and a bed for the night and their skins left whole on them!"

"Connal, he's a priest."

"I know he is a priest. The letter said that too. A priest and an abbot. He is famous. You have heard of him, haven't you? He has founded communities all over Eire. How hard it is to remember what Eire is like! All the churches and the schools and the books and the fields well tended—I wish I had my brooch still, Eogan! It is a pity they took my brooch and armlets away. O they are clever, aren't they, those Ailech kings, very clever! It is not enough to send a man of the kindred, they must send a holy man into the bargain. If we refuse we offend them and have his curse on top of everything. What are you dreaming of, confound you, with that smile on your face?"

"When I saw him come out of the dark, tall—and his voice —Connal, he made me think of— I don't know how to describe him. Only when he spoke to me he reminded me of my father Gauran."

Connal gave a wheezing laugh, "Of Gauran!"

"He seemed to look into my thoughts, understand what I was thinking. Connal, the graves are safe! This priest has been on the Island. Nothing is harmed."

"You and your mother! If you are not quite crazed, you are like bards so full your heads are of dreams and wonders. How could a priest look like Gauran?—I suppose, Eogan, he hasn't come to bring us aid? Didn't they say he prayed on the side of the North Niall when they made insurrection against the High King and defeated him with great slaughter and spoiling? Some men have all the luck! If he would do as much for us, who knows, we might even push back the Cruithnians? But no! What are we to him?"

"My mother is calling to us." Lluan indeed was calling them, vexed sorely at the delay. Connal following Eogan kept his hand on the collar of his mantle covering up the place where his King's brooch had been. Now the thought struck him as never before how forlorn the hall seemed. Gaunt dogs nosed in the foul rushes, whining to be fed. Men and women were pulling their clothes about them, grumbling and yawning, children were coughing.

It was his own child. There was his wife, and Connad standing beside her. Domangart was being swung up in the arms of the stranger, with little Nechtan clamouring to be swung up in turn. The small sound of Domangart laughing was like a bright flower in a peatbog. Connal stared at the stranger who was laughing too. He stared at him, watched him, as Connad was coughing, take the boy to him and look intently at him. His wife was talking earnestly to the stranger, "It was the winter! The cold was too much for him. We had a hut on the hillside but the water came into it. And when the snow came we could not get out for food. I had these children, and this baby."

"Now you are back in Dunadd. And you can get Connad a thicker mantle, and shoes. And proper food.—You must get cows from those parts of the land which have escaped the raiding."

"What's the use?" she was saying, "What's the use?"

"How he fares now will affect his health and strength in manhood."

"His manhood—?"

"Certainly. He is already almost a man."

Connal thrust forward between the stranger and his eldest son. "This," Lluan said in a clear disdainful tone, "Is our King Connal who has succeeded Gauran."

The stranger priest's eyes rested now full on himself. He bowed and made a sign of blessing, and then he smiled. "I thank you for your hospitality, Gentle King."

66

Then Connal found his voice. "Cousin, you come to a disordered dun. We will keep you safe as long as you are here, but it is not easy. I cannot answer for it. And in regard to the matter of the tribute—"

The priest looked at him in surprise. And he went on, "You see we are in no position to send it, even supposing the claim were just. We have been many years in Alban Dalriada, we cannot go on paying tribute to Ailech for ever. They must remit it. At least these years."

"Tribute!" The priest threw up his head and laughed. And then the children started to laugh too. "I come on a different errand."

XV

LLUAN and the young queen had decreed a feast, and
Connal had to see to the hunting in good earnest. He sent
a score of young men out, and they brought back hares and
badgers and a wild boar to add to the deer brought down
by good chance the previous day. Salmon and carp they could
find at any time in the River. The ladies meanwhile made search
for any plate or ware which might have survived the spoiling of
Dunadd by the Cruithnians. And Lluan's maid found some.
unbroken too, and her mistress praised her, omitting to ask
questions as to how she had found it so soon. Before the night
was old they were sitting down in style.

Connal sat at the head of the trestle tables, and looked
cautiously along either side at the faces of his guests, cousins and
chiefs of the Headland and the Isles. He hoped devoutly there
would be no brawling or defiance of himself; and was relieved to
see them eating with good humour and drinking contentedly even
though the mead was scarce and there was no wine. They were
all glancing from time to time at the tall grey-eyed stranger priest
from Eire, observing how he ate, for in four generations they
might have forgotten the niceties of the code of manners of Eire.

Connal himself felt strange once more to be host at an
ordered table.

All were constrained a little except for the queen Lluan who
was very much at her ease. He watched with admiration her
elegance and dignity. She had found a blue silk gown, treasure
of her bride gear of long ago, and a gold ornament or two. But
her queenly attitude was her best adornment. She talked
pleasantly. He remembered as a boy he had loved listening to
her strange stories, the stories that held her own children around
her like bright-eyed mice,—stories of the great ruined houses in her
homeland with the trees sprouting from the many coloured floors,
of the wide straight smooth highways, of warrior bands riding out
on them clad in sparkling armour. She was trying now to impress

the stranger priest. Her thin fingers on which the rings slipped up and down handled the Roman ware with love and ostentation.

"This Roman ware was part of my dowry when I came here as a bride. How fearful I was of coming here! For mine is a cultured land, of fine buildings and richness and gentle ways. We have churches and hermits' cells, many priests and abbots all conversing in the learned tongue. Even the nobles speak it as well as their own tongue."

Connal was glad to let her talk, so that he himself could sit in silence. For he needed peace. The day had tired him more than a fight. The stranger had shown great interest in the palace, and he Connal had to show him round. They had gone through the hall, followed by a tail of gaping folk, from nobles and young fighting men to slavegirls. The stranger had taken up Gauran's great sword, which Aedan had saved in battle taking it from his father as he fell, and the huge shield of their ancestor Loarn Mor which Eogan had carried about with him through all their wanderings and flights. The stranger was different from other men, he had an odd way with him, a sort of relish like a bard's as he is telling his story; one forgot the present. He asked about the history of Dunadd, and even himself knew a story of young lovers escaping who slept three nights here. Then he asked questions as to the weight of the weapons. One could not tell whether he were in jest or earnest. Connal had taken steps with the shield, forgetting his bad shoulder, and the priest had seen him wince, and inquired as to the reason and had examined the wound, so hastily doctored and so slow to heal. The priest had made Connal tell him how many men were in similar case in the palace, and offered to see them all. It seemed he was something of a doctor, and that was a luxury.

A bard would also have been a luxury, to make this a true feasting. But Alain had fallen in battle by Gauran's side, and of the other bards of Dalriada Drost had gone back to his own people who were Cruithnian, and Ferradach had gone with him, ashamed. It was as well the old queen could talk and entertain the guests.—" My marriage was the arranging of our cousin in Strathclydd, the former king. I have a number of sisters. But none of those at that time unmarried would go, and it had to be myself, the youngest. I was afraid at first of him, my warrior whose speech was not mine, who fought with loud shouting and without armour. But I soon came to love him and trust in him.

And indeed I had less to fear than my eldest sister Guladys, who was reft from our very doorway from the midst of her sisters in broad daylight by her ruffianly king. Gwennlew was his name, one of our own rougher princes. You may have heard of him, even across the sea? A terrible man, full of ungodly wrath and of passion. And yet my sister tamed him, and their son is holy, and Gwennlew himself was baptised in the faith before he died.

"Ah, but I remember, child though I was at the time, the terror of her taking. My sisters were all sitting together in the sunny doorway at their embroidery, talking and innocently laughing as girls do. I sat leaning against her knee, for I was the small one. He came upon us like a thunderclap, before any of the men of the household could interpose. He leapt from his huge black horse and with one arm caught her, and then it was the sound of the hoofbeats lessening away. We found a great hoofmark on the purple silk she had been embroidering, right among the patterns of flowers."

She lacked only the harp! Connal thought . . . They had gone out of the hall, and Connal had managed to get rid of the company. Together, just the two of them together, they surveyed the ruined courtyards, the women's grianans especially on the sunny side of the hill. "We are going to have those rebuilt before anything else," he heard himself saying, and the stranger nodded approval.

The stranger was gazing at the view, the Long River and the wide Bog that kept Dunadd so safe from sudden attack, and at the fertile fields on the lower slopes of the surrounding hills, and the far flicker of the sea beyond the Crinen Loch. Connal might have let it stop there, for the priest was talking about Ailech and the view from the palace. But he found himself leading him straight to the crowning place. He showed him the ancient stone, with the Royal Step in which he had placed his foot when he took vows as King. As King!—words froze in his mouth.—But the stranger was not looking at him, and so he was able to speak, to blurt out with stiff lips, "You are not used to talking with defeated kings. Your Ailech kings win their wars. But I cannot help it. I did as bravely as I could. They are a great and powerful nation, our enemies, you know nothing like them. For years we lived in peace, extending our borders by a raid here and a foray there, encroaching on the territory of the Cruithnians. But luck like that doesn't last."

The priest had answered, " There are bad times and good. And both are in the hands of God. It will not always be a time of shame in Dalriada. Do not think I do not understand defeat. Our cousins of Ailech may win their wars. But I have lost battles in my own soul."

What he meant Connal did not understand. But his mind warmed itself at the hope for Dalriada, as a man warms himself at a fire in winter time.

Now at the supper table, they were asking the stranger questions, his wife looking gay as she had done before the war. They were asking questions about Eire, how the queens were dressed, had they many gold ornaments to choose from, what breadth of girdle did they like, had they nothing of Roman origin about them, nothing? Lluan watched, silent now, smiling in kindly pity, for to her Eire was nothing, the lands of the South were all.

Connal sat silent and smiling too. He had no questions to ask the stranger priest. He had asked him questions already and had his answers, and he desired only now to sit in peace revolving them in his head. He had asked, "Are you going then by land to Teach Martain? Your way lies through Strathclydd. I will send an escort with you to King Rederech, and he will give you an escort on."

The priest had answered, " But I am not going to Teach Martain. I mean to stay in Dalriada."

" How long will you stay? Donal expected you to return to Eire—"

" I am never going back to Eire. I am staying with you."

71

XVI

WHEN the meal was done, and the women gone to see to their children's bedding, the men sat on talking, almost as if in council.

"If you are minded to stay," Connal said to the abbot, "Come and build your community near the palace. Once in the Royal Valley there was a cell of the abbot Ninian the founder of Teach Martain. He built beside the ancient stones. And in recent years Oran had a church here. I will do all I can to protect you."

"But we have already begun to build on the Island. We had to build even before asking you, Gentle King, because our claim was challenged. We are building a new church and community on the site of Oran's cashel."

They stared at him when he said the word new.

"It is near enough to Dunadd," Colum went on, "for me to come and go freely, and for you to come to me. Yet it is remote enough for us to get on with our prayers!

"It is a good little island," he still went on, as the king did not answer him yea or nay. "There is land for pasture, and land for tilling; enough to support a community. Will you grant me the Island, Gentle King?"

He stopped, for Connal's face was convulsed with shame. Two of the chiefs leant over to him, "Let him have it. Why do you not grant it? Why are you saying nothing?" And Eogan with more understanding said in his ear, "They will respect clerics. It is as safe there for them as it is here."

Connal said, at last, "You may have this Island indeed, as far as it lies with me. Glad would I be to think of you founding your cashel there. It is holy ground. And it is not far from us. And if you wanted more ploughland I could give it you—But—"

He cried then, loudly and bitterly, "It is no longer my land. No land is mine any longer. All is King Brude's. You are wrong, father, to call me by the title Gentle King. I was degraded in

72

status. I am no more now than a chieftain, a fourth grade prince.
Brude is my overlord. I had to go to him, and submit to being
stripped of my sword and my ornaments and my royal mantle,
and he put on me in face of all his people a drab robe no better
than a farmer's. And dressed so I had to kneel down on the
ground to him, and take an oath of submission for myself and
my followers."

"Deisuil! Deisuil! Deisuil!" they all cried in a dismal
chorus, coughing and hawking in their throats to drown out the
unlucky words.

"Chieftain you may be," Colum said when they were silent,
"to Brude. But to me, to your kinsmen, to all these loyal men
—you are king as before, king and lord."

There was a sudden fall of silence after his words, broken
only by the murmur of sleepy children or whining dogs, for at
the table no one had words to say.

"Well," Connal said softly after a while, "I can grant you
the Island, but it is an empty gift as long as it is not ratified by
Brude."

A shiver went round the men, some looked over their
shoulders.

"Well now," said the abbot, "This Brude. Tell me about
him."

"What is there to tell? We do not find it easy to speak about
him."

"He is High King of the Cruithnian peoples. Tell me about
them."

"We did not think it would so provoke them. We thought
they were occupied with the invasions of the Saxons, so we went
in raiding through the passes as men do, carrying the people
back here as bondmen and bondwomen, and placing our young
men in the chieftainships there. Perhaps it was when we got
into the rich valley which is like Eire,—that they could not spare!
Perhaps they feared we would cut their land in two, and join
with the Saxons. At any rate they came with fury upon us."

"They appeared one day suddenly out of the mists, to the
north and to the south at the same time. They caught the flower
of our army between their two forces and cracked us like a nut."

"They gave no quarter. It was kill, kill. Never a prisoner.
But when they came here, right through our Royal Valley to the
Bog itself and up the slope of this hill—then they took our king
and the kindred captive. And them they spared, to shame them."

73

"There are so many of them. It is a wide country. The High King called men from all the seven provinces. So many and so powerful—"

The men were talking all together, scarcely coherent in their awakened terror. And for good measure one or two women had come to their sides. Lluan with wide distraught eyes was crying out, "Who can withstand them? They withstood Rome! I thought I should see peace in my time, after my troubled girlhood. I thought I would live safe in Gauran's care. But they killed Gauran! Until we are hid in our graves there is no peace."

"They are devils in battle. They strip off their clothes and no one can catch hold of them in a fight."

"They prick their skins in patterns and confuse the eyes — they make themselves invisible — they appear out of the mists and up from the bracken or the heather."

"It is because they are protected by the old gods who are cunning. We have sinned in failing to worship the old gods."

"Come now, tell me truly," Colum said half sternly in a lull. "Tell me what I am to understand of Brude and his people."

"It is true, father, that they are powerful," Eogan said then, "Brude mac Maelchon was King of the Northern Provinces of Alba, being himself by birth ruler of the province of Murav. His dun is in Murav, where the River Nesa runs into the sea. His power grew till he shared the High King's state with King Gallan of the Southern Provinces. They ruled for one year, and they unified and strengthened under them the whole of Alba. It is true that they do not fear the Saxons, as in past days their ancestors did not fear Rome. Then after a year, how I do not know, Gallan died. And Brude became Paramount Lord of the whole land, North and South. He rules from the Bannag hills in the South to the farthest Northern Isles. And even the people in the West who are of the old stock acknowledge him."

"And he is of the old faith?"

Connal answered, "He is indeed! In the Southern Provinces there are Christian priests and communities and churches, it is true. And in the North the faith was once known. But there it has been put down. They say it is dangerous so much as to say a prayer such as we say, or to talk with respect of the new way. And they say even the thoughts of the mind are visible to the druids." He turned his thumbs sunwise. "For in King Brude's own home province lives the Archdruid—"

"You call him Brude mac Maelchon. Whose son is he?"

74

"He is king through his mother, who is the sister of the former king. It is the custom among the Cruithnians."

"His father?"

"It does not matter for the succession. They say his father was some visiting king, from the Brythons of the Far South."

Lluan with a cry interrupted him, "He has terrible blood in him! I know! Maelgwyn was king near my father's country, an obdurate pagan, a man of blood, ready always to avenge never to forgive. For Gwennlew, my sister Guladys's fierce husband, even Gwennlew had to submit to him after their bitter quarrel. He who feared no other man alive feared him. Now Maelgwyn is dead. He died in the dun of Ros, of the yellow plague, in the selfsame visitation that took from us our priest Oran. Death makes strange bedfellows! He died: but his blood survives in this Byrdei, this Brude as you call him. O God our Heavenly Father, is there nowhere on earth—"

"Well," Connal said rising, "We are not afraid now here. This night at least we shall be safe and sleep in peace. We have a priest of our own blood with us, and that is something."

He wondered, tossing on his bed, if the rest did sleep in peace, or if they had such troubled dreams as he. And yet the pain he felt he was glad of: it was like the pain of a thawing limb.

XVII

THEY gathered to the celebration of the Sacrifice in a sheltered corner of the hill, a place between two rock walls. Lluan had, before the spoiling of Dunadd, hidden the abbot Oran's patten and cup wrapped in a linen cloth. She brought them out now in triumph, untarnished from the ground. It was in doubt whether they could find bread, but Lluan contrived to get grain enough and to grind it and to make what would suffice the congregation.

As strange a congregation as Colum had for long seen. There sat together the old and the young queen, and young dark-eyed pale-skinned bondmaids of the old stock of the people, one or two young men fretful with half-healed wounds, a gaunt chief from Loch Awe and three lustier princes from the Isles. It had taken time to confess some of them! Women in the anguish of war lying with any who came had nameless children to the dead, men had done evil things in raiding and in the savagery of battle, some of them boys in years. Many confessed to old practices, and more could no longer distinguish between old and new: they would turn their thumbs sunwise instead of signing themselves at prayer, cry "Deisuil!" for "Christ keep me." And yet the memory of their past teaching was not all gone away; they listened eagerly at the first litany for the name Oran. As Colum looked down on their faces, thin, famine blotched, yet hungry now for more than food or safety, he knew Christ's flock and was content to be one of them. When they remembered their many dead he had his own dead to remember, the young Oran who had on the Island given his blood to the ground. Their sin and his own weighed on him as one burden; but when he had bowed three times over the Oblation and raised it, he knew for both himself and them the vast mercy of God.

76

After the Sacrifice he called the princes and chiefs and their people together to eat the bread of peace.

"Connal is right," he said to them. "If you want to live and see Dalriada live you must be quiet. No raiding at all. Spend your time and energy in rebuilding what you still hold.

"Those of you from the far west and the Isles must send corn to the wasted places for a spring sowing."

"Sowing!" they echoed him. "Corn for seed! What's the use? What hope have we of reaping it?"

"Are we to plough and sow corn for our enemies?"

"Do as he says," the chief from Arran said, "I will send grain in my two longships, see that you get it sown. If the monks are to sow in spring on the Island we can sow anywhere in Dalriada."

"If he is rebuilding Oran's cashel we must rebuild Dunadd."

Connal said nothing to this, but as he was leaving the hall with Colum he said sadly, "It is a dream, father. If we rebuild and sow we shall incur Brude's anger again and draw his attack."

"It might be possible to obtain better terms from Brude. In the flush of victory men make hard treaties, but afterwards they grow more reasonable. Someone must intercede."

"Who can do that for us? Moluag of Lismor is kind to us as he is to all. but his work is among the Cruithnians up and down the western seaboard. I do not think he has dealings with Brude himself."

As Connal was arranging for the ship which was to sail from the Crinen Loch with him, Colum found the children, Connal's three with their mother, and one or two children from the neighbouring families. They had made horses of clay with tails of feathers, and they were making them hunt and race, and fight too. "We have these because we made them," Connad said, "Our men have lost their horses. My cousin Eogan wept because his bay horse was taken from him by the Cruithnians."

Colum down on his knees beside them would have taken a hand in the game, only the little girl made a horse of him, urging him on valiantly with heels drumming his sides.

"Colum," they said, "You're never going away? It's nice now in Dunadd, it's warm. You should spend the winter here at least. Winter is bad."

"Why are you going away? Have you a palace of your own to go to?"

"I have a little Island," he said proudly, "One which your father says he will give me for my own. No, there is no palace there. But there are little huts, cells, quite good; and I have men waiting for me."

"I know! Shaven men. Colum is king of the shaven men of the Island."

"May I come with you if I shave my head?"

"Better to stay here, where I can find you when I come again."

He left them to their clay horses; and went to the window seat where Connal's wife sat. "I have come to say good-bye."

"I wish you were staying here," she said sadly. "When you talk to us I lose my fear, and dream that all will be well again with Dalriada and this child of mine enter life to know security."

"But not for my sake only: but your own!—You do not mean to go only to your Island. I know. I see what is in your mind. You are going to throw your life away." She raised her face from the cloth of his habit, and said with trembling lips, "You are going to—"

"Sooner or later someone will have to go. Not only to get his sanction for my holding the Island, but who knows? to get better terms for us all. Don't be afraid. I will not go till I am ready, till I am sure the time is right. It will not be in winter, I must wait for spring."

Connal was coming in at the doorway, Artan ran to touch his sword. "Mother is crying because the priest Colum is going back to his Island."

She parted her lips to speak. But he stilled her, smiling and shaking his head; and said farewell cheerfully to Connal and herself, though on the children his eyes lingered, where they sat playing with their little horses of clay.

Journey
Towards Fear

XVIII

THE winter wind still moaned in the north of the Island, and the rocks were whitened by the surf. But its force was less. And on the rocks and on the pallid sands birds walked in companies, spreading their wings in the faint spring sun. Colum walking on the grassland with the young Cruithnian who was teaching him the language of Alba saw coming towards him in a great hurry his attendant Diarmaid. The boy ran stumbling over the tussocks and sandholes, too much excited to mind his feet.

"Lord Abbot! Look, father!—A curragh was coming round into the Sound to our harbour—and O sir, their voices! I knew they were men from Eire." He eyed the Cruithnian man. "It seems so long since we heard that speech. They've newly come to land, father. The ship that convoyed them isn't in yet."

Surely, up the Sound, staggered a ship, the onslaughts of the waves covering her over with spray. Catching excitement from the boy, and with deep intuition within himself, he climbed up the high dunes to see. Up the causeway from the harbour of the community were coming two figures: one man tall, one short, and a monk or two following them. It was Comgal and Cannich. Even at this distance he knew.

"Lord Abbot!" Diarmaid panted as Colum ran past him, on the track to the eastern gateway of the cashel wall. "Lord Abbot!" he went on as they leapt across over the mill stream, "No guest room or anything! The church scarcely built, and no gold over its door, and none but the books we brought with us to show your friends! Unless you can work a miracle, father, I doubt if there will be supper."

But Colum heard not a word, nor would he have heeded if he had. For Eire had sprung up all round him. The sea that moved to the left of him was not the Island Sound but Lough Foyle. His friends were coming to his cashel of Derry with its

Black Church thronged with men of Ailech, its schoolhouse loud with boys, its guest chambers full of scholars, its crowding cells, its shelter and peace.

They embraced one another with incredulous joy, scrutinising one another's faces. "So wild a journey, but Colum at the end of it!"

"So long a time, but Cannich and Comgal come!"

They had not got dry sandals on or sat down in the abbot cell before Cannich was opening the satchels their two attendant monks were carrying. "Here now, Colum. They may be damp a little, but I trust no sea water has got in. Here are books we have brought you. No, do not thank us! The most of them are from your men at Derry. It will take all night to give you all the news and messages they send with the gift."

"And there are two from Finbar," Congal added, "our old master. Yes, he is well, and busy always, though aged since you left Eire, I think. The numbers of his cashel still increase."

"Though not so fast as does Comgal's cashel at Bangor!"

"Here is what will please you," Comgal put in, denying himself the pleasure of talking of his Bangor. "Here in this box you will find colours and gold; not much, but something for you to be going on with when you're copying books. I doubt you may not find materials like this in Alba? Is the life here a privation for you?"

"But," Cannich said, standing looking out of the doorway, "This is a lovely isle. With grass enough and flat land and pasture and water for a mill. And it has an air about it—Is it your magic, Colum, or its own?"

"It is good enough," Colum answered, "and the right one evidently. It is the burial place of the royal kin of Dalriada, and the site of Oran's cashel, Oran of Latteragh. It is his causeway you have walked on coming up from the beach, and his rampart shelters us from the winds, or from most of them. Such a winter we have had! There was a sound as if of battle on the western side. Since Oran's time they have had no settled priest of their own in Dalriada. And indeed they need one! Moluag in the past has visited among them, but he is often away on journeys up and down the western seaboard with its crowding isles. Behind that mountain mass, look, across the Sound, that's where his Lismor lies, in the mouth of an ingoing sea. You must go and see him there since you have come so near.

" But get on these dry garments," he urged them, "And call your men to change." For they stood gazing with interest on all they saw, the small new cells within the enclosing rampart, the harbour and the bright Sound, and across it the smoke whirls from the fishermen's houses, the green grassland north of the cashel and the white white sands. " O I shall be proud to show you round. We have a roof on our church again luckily. The one we made in autumn blew away in a gale at Christmas."

" O the cold, sirs!" Diarmaid broke in, standing with a pile of their wet habits over his arm, " When you get up for mattins the wind stings your two ears."

"And we have finished making a granary and kiln, for we hope to be alive and in need of them in autum of this year. There is a good cowshed, at any rate the cows agree to sleep in it. But here are Grillan and Carnan who can tell you." Grillan from his farm work, Rus and Fechnus from the shore, Lugne from the moor, Baithene and Eochaid from their cells, Tochannu with his finger still in his book. " Yes, come and stare at them!" Colum said, " Our first men from Eire. Now they are warm and dry again we can sit together and hear their news of home. And for supper —the flounders from the Sound are so good," he boasted to his friends. " They quite spoil our fasting. You will think them too luxurious for a Lenten rule!"

" Come and see the whole Island now," he said to his two friends after supper, and led them away from the busy cashel and the curious eyes of the fishermen and of the young men. They took the track to the west side of the Island. Among the rocks the tides thundered; but along the shore of the great green machair it was calm and quiet and they could talk to their hearts' content.

" Well, Colum, we have told you how Finbar sends his love and blessing to you. Ever since you left Eire he has longed to go over to Alba after you. He longs to revisit the places he stayed at in his youth. If he was not himself able to go, his zeal kindled our own, and here we are, his envoys. He gave us messages for those in his old school of Teach Martain. And that is where we have just been. We had expected to be asked to help them in their work round there, south in Reged or in Strathclydd."

Cannich went on, " But on our arriving at Teach Martain we were told of the unrest in all the Brythons' lands. Not only do they face the constant threat of Saxon invasion but among the kings and chieftains there is strife and dissensions. Some are falling from Christian allegiance altogether and following the old religion. We heard of one who leagued himself with the Saxons against his own kin! Indeed so great is the fear of treachery that the good King Rederech of Strathclydd was hard put to it to safeguard his chaplain Cyndyrn and begged him to go south as far as Breconia."

"And so the brethren at Teach Martain considered it and then told us it would be best for us not to stay there in Strathclydd. They asked us instead to go into Cruithnian land. That was the mission field of Teach Martain, as you know, in the beginning, in Ninian's day. And in South Alba there is a settled faith, with cashels and cells and clerics travelling between—or so they hope. But with their own affairs so pressing and the times so troubled the mother church has lost contact with the Christians north of the Bannag, as they say. News comes scantily. And it is feared that from the North of Alba, which has lapsed into paganism, pressure is being brought to bear."

"It is so peaceful here," Cannich said, as their feet felt the softness of the clovered grass and the warm sand, and as they listened to the gentle sounds of the sea. "Who would think there was war or trouble anywhere? Has your kinsman the king of Dalriada granted you your right to hold the Island, Colum? Is the land across the Sound his domain?"

"He has certainly made over to me what right he had to it." Colum answered, saying to himself with an inward smile, "Poor Connal!" "But the fact is, nobody knows at the moment to whom the land across the Sound rightly belongs. It is both Connal's and the Cruithnian High King's. Nobody cares to decide. But, as for my little Island, I must make sure of my right to it. And since Connal for all his goodwill can give me only a doubtful right—"

Comgal, following up his own thoughts, was saying, "We are commissioned then to go into South Alba with messages to them from Teach Martain. We are hoping your King Connal will give us his favour and enable us to pass through his eastern borders into the Cruithnian province of Fortrin. That is what justified our visit to you: we had the overwhelming lure of our love for you, and needed only the excuse. They say it is stable throughout Alba. It is not only to find out the state of the Christians in the South that I hope to do. I long to go north, by the way Finbar went. How greatly I long to go back with news for him of the places he remembers but can never see more. From Fortrin we should have to strike the road north along the seacoast, through the province of Circind. There must be a number of Christian settlements, we can make our way from one to another, keeping northward always. I do not know how far north we may hope to get. They say it would be impossible to get past the province of Murav which is the native territory of the High King. For he is a staunch pagan and the tool of his Archdruid who hates the new way."

Cannich twitched Colum's sleeve. " Of course you are yourself too busy with this newfledged community, Colum, ever to dream of coming with us—part of the way, into the South, I mean?"

" I was about to tell you: I have to get the ear of this Cruithnian High King. I must as soon as possible obtain his sanction to my holding of this Island. It seems a forlorn errand. But I hope to achieve it, and at the same time to gain benefits for the sorely tried land. For it is not only in Strathclydd there is trouble. Dalriada, the land of my kindred, is crushed below the heel of this Brude. They are between the Cruithnians and the deep sea, they have no escape. Before I can do anything effective in the way of teaching I must get some measure of security for them."

" Come with us into Fortrin then," Comgal urged on the other side of him, " If you have a petition to make to the High King Brude, your best course is to approach the Christian kings of South Alba. It is only through their good offices you can have any hope of reaching him. Come with us to the South. Ah, how I long to go north and far north! To get as far as Dornaig where Finbar was, that is my dream."

On Easter Eve throughout the Island there was no light. The custom was that all should be put out until the blessing of the New Light.

Ernan at the door kindled it with ritual words. It wavered in the Island wind that blew round the little church, as if the dark fought against it. But as he cupped the flame in his hand it steadied, and when he brought it into the shelter of the church it rose tall and clear. Colum at the church door had his small lamp lit from it, and watched as his men and their guests lit theirs, one from the one before. Within the church and at the door the light grew and grew—each imprint of spade and hand appeared on the mud walls, so many memorials of victory over heavy-heartedness.

And he watched them as one by one they went away, carrying each his lamp with its Paschal flame, shielding it, nursing it, because of the eddying winds that made their attacks from all sides in the dark night; till there were only the three left, himself and Cannich and Comgal. He saw the New Light search either face, Cannich's smiling and aglow, Comgal's gaunt and ardent. As for him, his thoughts were already off on their journey. First to the island of Lismor, he said to himself, to get advice as to our route there.

XIX

COMGAL and Cannich walked down the long green slope to where they saw on the beach Colum with Lugne and Diarmaid and the Lismor sailors overhauling a boat. It was narrow and light. "Look at that!" Cannich whispered to his companion, "That is for carrying between those lochs."

"No wonder he has tried to escape us," Comgal replied. "He knows what we will say to this idea of his."

Colum straightened up to look at them. "I had to leave the cashel," he said very seriously while the Lismor men grinned. "I had started to envy Moluag. This long large island of his, with such abundant pasture, enough to nourish a score of communities! If only we had landed on Lismor and found the graves of our kings here—But alas! Moluag got in long before me. Where is he now, the wanderer? How I should have liked to ask him about the land of Alba: what the coast is like north of here, and—"

"And what trouble awaits those who try to take the route of this Great Glen! We have come to talk about that, Colum. So stand up. You shall not escape us. Are you serious in saying you think we should go that way into Alba?

"I have learned all about it," Colum replied. "The long narrow valley, with two smaller lochs and then the long long one. And how easy it is from the eastern end of it to reach the High King's palace. Lift it up now," he said to Lugne and Diarmaid, "till we see how many of us will be needed to carry it."

"It's called the hard and hungry way, sir," one of Moluag's sailors said, looking up with face smeared with the daubing pitch. "It lies through deep forest and desolate hills; in parts it is uninhabited. And you have to climb high mountains here and there to avoid the swamp."

87

"Are there no mountains to the east of Dalriada, if we go that way into Fortrin?"

"Ah, but that country is not wild like this. There are many wild beasts in the ancient forest, boars and wildcat, as well as the wolves."

"Don't say that to him!" Cannich said teasingly, "It will only inflame him the more to go."

"Well now, such dangers will affect us while we are on foot." Colum said. "But when we are on the lochs we shall go safely and speedily. There we can row our way or sail before God's good wind. I think four men can carry her? We can take turns.

"You may leave your attendants here if you will!" then he said to Cannich and Comgal, "But pick two of the strongest. I'll take Diarmaid and Lugne. And I have sent to Dunadd asking for guides."

"You will have to have a guide with you who can speak the older language of Alba, father," one of the sailors said, "Your knowledge of the Cruithnians' tongue will not help you much there. On the mountain slopes above the smaller lochs live the strange remote people, who are tributary to Brude though they never see his face."

"Colum." Comgal said, "Come back now to the cashel and listen patiently to what the seniors are telling us. It is not the dangers of the journey that concern them, so much as the danger of arriving uninvited at the court of the High King Brude."

So Colum went with them, with a backward glance or two at the beach. And the seniors came round them. "Indeed, Lord Abbot, it is scarcely to be thought of.

"At the King's court lives the Archdruid of the whole land. They say he is at the head of their religion, to the farthest south, to the Gallican Gulf. The High King is in his hands, for he fostered him. He controls the omens, and acts between gods and men or says he does. He presides over the College in the river valley near the King's dun, and from there as centre pupils trained by him go out into the length and breadth of the land. They know the secret counsels of every tribe, and they send reports to him secretly, and he informs the King. Nothing is hid from him. Even our talking now about him." .And the old monk crossed himself.

" Those two druid priests on our Island, father," Diarmaid said timidly, " we never saw them again. Maybe they went to tell him about our coming?"

Comgal and Cannich led Colum aside, " Come then, you are better persuaded? You will come with us the way we said? We will go all three together as we planned through Dalriada into Fortrin. Then, as we learn of the land and the way, we will strike up the flat coastal plain, the way Finbar took. There will be clerics to guide us much of the way and they will set us forward on our journey stage by stage. We shall go slowly but surely."

" But, Comgal, I must get quickly to him. I must make sure of my Island, my claim was not undisputed. And my people of Dalriada, their plight is desperate."

" Well but your quickest way is surely your safest?"

" It may be the longest that is least safe. Forgive me! I am not being headstrong. I think our best defence against danger is to walk straight into it. They say the Archdruid knows everything that goes on: let us give him the least time to act on his knowledge."

" You are right," Cannich said after a little while, " We take our lives in our hands wherever we go."

Comgal's pale face lit up, "Anything is possible to our God, of that I am sure. If He has work for us, I would pass through red martyrdom to do it."

XX

THE men of Lismor bowed to the King of Dalriada, and perhaps lower to the young man who was with him since he was Gauran's son. They led them up to the cashel, "The Abbot Colum is busy preparing the books they will take with them, and rugs and boat gear and food. They are making it up in bundles of man-loads, and securing the thongs of the book satchels."

"Colum, you are not really minded to make this journey?" Connal asked anxiously. "Going directly to his dun?"

"Have you brought the guides?"

"They are here." And he presented them, though still with doubtful look. "Here is Duncath who will help you with the boat on the lochs, he has some knowledge of them. And Fergal — his mother is of the old stock of the Cruithnians and he will help you should you pass through a place where they talk the old language. And Eogan has brought our most expert huntsman."

"Conn — he will stop at nothing. He has been known to catch a wolf and rend it with his bare hands."

Colum was acknowledging with his blessing the three men, "Duncath, Conn, Fergal," when Eogan burst angrily into speech. "I must go too! Am I to fail my blood a second time? I let Gauran die, but now for all Connal says I am going with this priest up into the Glen."

"Indeed," Colum said wryly, "Our thanks to you! It would be of great advantage to our cause with the High King to have Gauran's son!"

The young man drew in his breath in a long sigh. "I will have no more," Colum said gently, "but these three. And please God I shall bring them home safe, or send them home when they have put us on our way. I will have no young men losing their lives, if I can prevent it."

"Do not blame him," Connal said. "Some of your kindred should escort you. What shall I say to Donal of Ailech if I let you go and you never come back? His letters bade me protect you, with monstrous threats if I did not. He put me under bonds to keep your life with my own.

"But now it is not Donal of Ailech I fear, it is myself. I shall be shamed past cure if I let you go into this danger."

"I wonder," Colum said with a laugh for his troubled face, "How I ever survived before I knew you? I am not going solely on account of Dalriada, nor even of my Island. I am going with brother priests."

Connal said, "Priests! My cousin, it is not good land for priests. You are less safe than I would be on that account. They will call demons up against you. They will entrap you with spells. No, do not frown at me! It is not like Dalriada, not even like the west of Alba round here among the old gentle peoples. It is the Cruithnians of the east you will meet, who are wealthy and strong and who have their own gods."

"You and I," Colum said, putting a hand on his shoulder, "will have a talk about other gods when I come home again!"

Connal dropped on one knee taking the Abbot's hand, "It is not death I am afraid of, not even heathen spells. I do not think much of them. What keeps me from coming with you is the thought of my shaming. My dear, they will humiliate you. They will take your dignity from you. I cannot bear it."

"You and I both," Colum said then, "have great need of the sheltering prayer the men here are going to say as we go away. It is their abbot Moluag's Breastplate, they will gird it on us tomorrow."

Soon after the sun rose they knelt on the grass, Comgal and Cannich and Colum and the four monks who were going with them, and Duncath, Fergal and Conn, their Dalriadan guides. The monks of Lismor knelt in a ring round them; and they said over them Moluag's Breastplate of prayer. "By God the Creator, Preserver, Redeemer, Judge of all men: Brehon and Druid of the world, Abbot and Father of all living things . . . Against sword, against burning, against strangling, against falling, against drowning, against losing the way — against incantation, against magic spell, against shapeshifting. God be in the eyes of all who look on me, in the mouth of all who speak to me, in the hands that touch me, feet that guide me. May He be in my own heart, may He deliver me from the treachery of my own sin."

XXI

THEY took it in turn to carry the dripping curragh that smelt still of the sea, and laboured up a winding path from the beach as it skirted a swampy valley along the lower slopes of the hills.

"Where are we?" Colum asked Fergal, the most talkative of their three guides. "Is it Cruithnian country yet?"

"It is all debateable land, sir, round about here. It is ours one year and it is theirs the next. It is theirs now. The people themselves do not greatly care who claim the overlordship of them. But after the recent fighting there might be ill will from the chiefs. We must reach the forest by nightfall and keep under cover of it tomorrow."

"Aye, it's best if we are not seen," Duncath said, "or heard. We can speak the language after the Cruithnian fashion, and Fergal knows even the old language, but you and the other clerics, sir, have the accent of Eire. If we meet anyone on our journey you must please to be silent and let us speak."

"But," Cannich said smiling, "we are not of Dalriada, but of Eire."

"That might interest them a little afterwards. But they will strike first and ask later. That is the difficult thing."

"That is difficult," Colum agreed.

The wind blew colder. They were up high above sea level, nearing the trees. At first it was a matter of oak and beech, the young leaves tender with spring and smelling sweet. But after some time, as they were finding the carrying of the boat more burdensome, they found they were entering a sombre world of pine. It was dark and cold, and the wind made moaning sounds that troubled the ears. The men of Eire did not know which was the more desolate of aspect, the dark unearthly pines or the clearings where one caught dizzy glimpses of high towering

92

mountains, some with their heads in mist, and all sharp with bare rock. There were wailing bird cries, and it did not raise the spirits to hear the guides planning that as soon as they should stop to camp for the night they must build fires all round to keep off the wild beasts. "Hungry and lean after the winter still," they said, "wolves and boars; and though not so near the sea or inhabited places, the wild bear — you can hear its claws scratching on the rocks."

Yet the three guides seemed little perturbed by the thought of this, and that was a little comforting to the monks. They found a small clearing free of undergrowth, and well sheltered, and there they decided the party should spend the night. The high hills peered at them, the trees and the mountain torrents menaced them with sound, but they busied themselves helping their guides who scooped hollows in the floor of shining pine needles, and found fallen twigs and branches for the fires. Then Fergal drew out oat cakes and butter and cheese, still with the blessing of Lismor on them, and the memory of the quiet long green pastures. The other two, Conn and Duncath, went for water, taking with them the dippers for baling the boat. They would not have any of the monks with them, though Lugne and Diarmaid were all for going, lest by the bed of the stream nearby they should meet men of Alba who were bitter against Dalriada.

It was not long before they were back, without water, without even the dippers, and in great fear. When Colum and Cannich asked what ailed them, they shook their heads, reluctant to speak. But they whispered to Fergal in the old language and he, though also reluctant, told the monks what it was.

As the two men had gone over the forest slope, listening for the sound of the torrent, they had come to another clearing in the trees. On a high rock overhanging the confluence of two streams grew a solitary tree. It had caught their eyes, they could not pass it. The branches were like arms, crooked for attack. It was an ancient oak tree. Carved on its trunk—or rather peering from within—was the Eye.

Fergal said shivering, "They saw the Lord. It was his place. The Dark One, the old Horned King. We have lit our fires near his holy place, and he has seen us."

"The Eye," Conn was babbling to himself, "It looked at us. It followed us. It will follow us now everywhere we go."

"We must recover our dippers," Colum said, "Or we shall be thirsty tonight. And we cannot bale our boat when we come

to the lochs. Come on, I'll go with you. Take me to where you
saw this Eye. I will stare at it, and you will see it has no power
over us."

" In the morning!" they said, " In the daylight." And when
he pressed them, they turned angry " We have done enough
already to offend him."

" This is the old forest," they said, " there are Those in it
who do not love the new religion."

" Come," Comgal said to the monks, " It is time to say
evening prayer. They will remember the prayer we said on
Lismor and will trust that it brings safety."

But even the confident words of psalm and prayer did not
affect the terror of the Dalriadans. They crouched moaning,
sometimes bowing their foreheads to the ground, sometimes
raising themselves and peering through their fingers as children
do. When Colum came towards them, they shrank from him,
Conn saying openly he was adding to their guilt. On the floor
of pine needles that glittered softly in the firelight, they crouched
all night, while the monks slept, awakening at their accustomed
time for praying to hear the forest soughing all around them and
the torrent roaring from the high mountains.

Dawn came so slowly among the trees they were not sure
when it was really day. As they lay listening to the continuous
soughing, they heard a din that drowned it. Hunting horns rang
out, there was a clamour of shouting, a crashing through the
undergrowth. Far off among the trees men were running, naked
in the gloom. The monks got up to listen, the guides stood wary,
though Conn had in his confusion of the night before left his
knife somewhere on the ground.

Then with raucous squealing and grunting into their clearing, coming straight for them, rushed a gigantic boar, so immense
and uncouth they could not believe it was real. Barbs clung to
its blood-stained sides, it trailed hunting spears with it. In its
blind agony it charged right into their midst, its tusked mouth
ravening. Colum sprang forward in front of his men, but before
they could cry out to him, the huge beast stopped, whistled its
breath in and let it out in a groan, then fell dead on its side.

As they stayed still, dewed with the sweat of fear, the
hunters burst in upon them, and for a moment they stared aghast
at each other, the naked and the robed men. The hunters cried
out among each other in the old tongue, hallooed to their lean

94

dogs till they left off howling over the kill and came to their sides; then ran among the trees, leaving the monks standing with the great boar in their midst.

"God has preserved us from our first danger," Congal said gravely. But Cannich had already begun to smile. "From more than one danger!" he said, looking over at Colum. For Conn was kneeling by Colum's side, "What has happened? I had no knife on me—I had no knife—" and Duncath and Fergal were on the ground beside him, "The Lord Abbot simply made the holy sign, and the boar stopped immediately and it dropped dead."

They rolled the rugs up and put them in the boat. Calmly and without being bidden they went and came back with the lost dippers. They shouldered up the boat and looking at the clerics with trust and awe they told them to follow them. When they were asked they answered respectfully, Yes, they would go down to inhabited land soon — tomorrow. The people, they hoped, would be friendly disposed. But if not, the new god the Christ—

"We come of a Christian land, we folk of Dalriada," Fergal said virtuously.

XXII

WHEN the trees cleared and they were out in the open they saw houses low down in the steep-sided valley, lying in twilight though the sunset brilliance shone still on the tops of the eastern hills. They were little houses of mud and heather, set on the grass that ran in tongues among the rocks. On a slight eminence above them stood the nobleman's house of wood. How alluring it was, the smell of peat and woodsmoke! It was almost impossible to resist going down; the Dalriadan guides, though they pursed their lips, permitted it.

Indeed they might have spared themselves the anxiety. All was well. From the first to see them, a herdboy who leapt up from his flock and ran to them with the rush basket he was making still in his hand—to the nobleman he summoned from his chess, they could not have given kinder welcome in Eire. They set a table in the courtyard of the house, cooked food hot and appetising to mouths fasting from the forest; and the nobleman's wife herself, in her long dress with curious and many coloured patterns, touched their clothes exclaiming at the dampness of them. She called servants and they brought brushwood and pine twigs and made a fire at which they steamed off their clothes.

Much of what the people were saying the monks could not understand, but they could guess the questions that were being asked. " Where are you going?"

" That is easily answered," Colum said laughing to the guides. " Tell them we are going to their Paramount King Brude. I can think of no more respectable place to be going to."

But the guides paused, thinking; and at last they said, " They are holy men."

" Where have you come from? Are you druids from some very remote part of this country? Which kindred do you minister to?"

"Now for a tricky bit," Cannich said. "You had better let me speak. From Eire," he said to the people, "We are teachers of religion from Eire."

"Eire!" A torrent of speech came. "I know a pedlar who comes every second year to my sister's husband's dun from Eire. He brings fine cloth, and brave tales of the ancient heroes. Do you know many tales?"

"I suppose you have no wolf hounds with you?" the nobleman asked hopefully.

"What is it like in Eire? Do the women all have long golden hair, and turn into mermaids when the moon is full?"

"Eire is all one flat plain."

"I did not say they were Saxons, I asked you if they looked like Saxons."

"Saxons!" a woman cried, "That is a bad word to say. Take care, they may be Saxons from Eire."

"I assure you," Cannich said, "We are monks — religious men. There are no Saxons in our land."

"Nor in ours. We have troubles enough at times, but not that."

"Teachers of religion from Eire?" the nobleman said thoughtfully. "I wish our druid were at home, but he has gone on his rounds up the glen."

They spread dried bracken for beds, and got rugs of their own for the rugs the travellers had were damp with rain. "Where was it you said you were going? Did you say "Brude?" You do not mean our Paramount King? Surely he has not sent for you? Are you not going to the College of Druids near his dun? Our druid goes there once every year, and he tells us about his journeys. It is a long way."

"You are not from Dalriada?"

"We are, as we said, men of Eire. Only our guides are from Dalriada, innocent and unarmed men, as you see. They are with us to guide us."

"O that!" the people answered peaceably. "That is natural. We will shelter you all, for you seem harmless."

In the friendly company even the guides laid fears aside. They went about the homestead. Fergal and Duncath laughing with the young men and girls over their differences of speech.

Conn came to Colum's side as he sat dreaming in the firelight. "Father! That little copse of oaktrees—did you see it? It is their grove. And near it is their holy well."

Colum nodded, only half aware of what he was saying, for his mind was going on the next day's journey.

"They take no water from it. They use other water, from the stream or from another well on the moor."

Later as they settled down in shelters in the courtyard, Conn came to bid goodnight. "Father, I heard them saying it is their holy well. It is inhabited by a powerful spirit. They worship it at the four festivals, and at any other time if there is special need. I did not know the well was holy until I heard them talk about it."

Colum, rousing from sleep, heard an odd sound, as if a grown man were sobbing. There was a mutter of voices which swelled to a clamour. He got up quickly, and pulling his gown more tightly round himself against the night air went over the courtyard to where at the entrance to the other shelter a little crowd of the Alban folk stood talking to the Dalriadan guides inside.

"He did not know what it was," Duncath from the shelter was shouting, "It might have happened to any stranger who came. You should have warned us."

"It is obviously the habitation of a god," the Alban men shouted back at him, "Who would have imagined your companion would not have known?" And again, "What sort of men are you who do not recognise the sacred symbols when you see them?"

"But what is the matter?" He could not make out more than a few words, "He didn't drink it, only let it touch him." "No, but he stooped and put his hands in, he drew out water to wash himself."

And in the lulls of the talking, the hoarse sobbing. Colum put the men aside and got into the shelter to see. He found Conn lying twisting on his bed, his face hidden in his arm. He caught him by the arm and asked impatiently again, "What is the matter?"

"I am sick, I am sick, father!"

"You were well yesterday. What ails you?"

The man ran frenzied hands through his shaggy hair, "I have the yellow plague! I have the yellow plague! Look, on my hands, and on my arms, the yellow spots are coming. And my legs, my legs! It's because I splashed water on them. I was hot after the journey—and they never told me! They should have

warned us. Now I have the yellow plague, it is running through
me, all through me."

"Why then, it is unusually quick in coming!" Colum said,
"No fever or anything!"

The Alban men took him seriously. "The gods strike quick.
By noon, who knows? he will be dead of it. Poor man, he will
never see his home again!"

"Whatever shall we do with his body?"

"You will kill this man with fear," Colum sternly said. "Tell
me clearly what it is all about."

They were ready to explain. Their holy well, the habitation
of a god if not itself divine, had a power to protect itself against
anyone who defiled it by taking water from it for any ordinary
use. Anyone presumptuously washing himself at it would go
blind, or fall into decline, or catch the yellow plague.

"Have you ever seen this happen?"

"Not in our lifetime," they admitted. "No. For who would
dare? Our druid teaches us not to touch the well but to worship
it. They say a woman in our grandparents' time dipped her hands
in it, and they withered. A man, a stranger like your friend, took
a drink from it and he went blind."

"So your companion is sure to suffer some malady."

"Then I will suffer along with him," Colum said cheerfully.
"I'll go and put the matter to the proof. I will not only wash
hands and feet in it, but drink from it. A holy well should be for
the people's use."

Lugne and he pulled Conn up to his feet, and they all went,
the Alban people following, to the grove. It was dewy and cold
still with the night, but on the well the rising sun shone bright.
The people watched, whispering to one another.

Colum made the sign of the cross over the face of the well.
Then slowly he dipped water up from it and sprinkled it on
arms and feet; stooping, he took water up in his palm and drank;
it was cold and pleasant, tasting somewhat of iron. Cannich and
Comgal, Lugne, Diarmaid, they all drank after him, like a
strange communion.

The Alban men watched them as they walked away.

"This is wonderful! The well is harmless. To think we
were afraid! Either it is a kind god, a Bright One, or else the
god they pray to is stronger and will not let it do us harm."

"We must tell our druid, he should know. To think he was
so mistaken!"

XXIII

THE sky to westward flamed with colour, but the sunset was hidden by the mass of dark hills. They were very tired with the long journey, and as glad as astonished when they came to a village standing by the side of a gushing stream that flowed into the loch. They had come on it before they were aware, for it was in darkness.

It was not so much that the houses were few as that there were few people about the houses. None came to meet the strangers, to give either welcome or challenge. Only when they approached two men and asked if they might shelter for the night did they get word spoken. Yes, the men told them, they might stay here for the night. They might use one or two of the empty houses. Yes, they would bring them food.

The guides thankfully set the curragh down. They found a little hut by the stream, and laid it inside in case it filled with rain during the night. Duncath rubbed it with wax, grumbling at it, petting it, calling it the companion of their journey, their ready helper, their precious burden, for all the world like a mother bathing her child.

The other two set about preparing the larger hut that stood nearby. It had been swept already as if for their use, and there were heaps of heather waiting to be thrown on the floor for beds. Gladly they sat down, stretching their limbs luxuriously. The two men of the village brought them cooked fish, salmon, and pointed out the stream for them to take water from: but still they said no word, and they did not look much at the guests.

Comgal said he wished to pray in solitude, and that he would go to another house further away. Cannich and Colum felt the like desire. There was a house on the other side of the stream, and to it they three waded. Later, their prayer done, they found that Diarmaid and Lugne with the other two monks had joined them, saying it was time for vespers. And before that was done, the guides also had come over saying it was quiet and eerie in this place, they did not like it, and would like it less without company. Colum laughed saying they would be the warmer for being together; and since the guides had carried over the rugs they settled there to sleep. The dark hills loomed over them, but in the gaps the familiar friendly stars showed, Orion and the Great Bear.

. . . Colum was not surpised that Duncath was annoyed at being waked. But he shook the tired man by the shoulder calling him in a low voice until he had broken through his first heavy sleep. " Go across the stream, you and Fergal and Lugne, and get the curragh here. Pull it up on the bank this side of the stream."

Grumbling they rose, throwing off their rugs and blundering to the doorway. He heard them exclaim sharply as they went into the night chilled water, but he heard them splashing across, then after a silence splashing their way back slowly carrying the curragh. They dumped it down outside the doorway, dried their legs rubbing them warm again, then yawning lay down. Soon their deep breathing joined the others' in the room. Colum himself after a brief commendation to God of all of them lay down too and fell asleep.

. . . The light in the house was red, as if from a red dawn. Yet it flickered. Was it the Northern Lights? It was too near. Colum edged over to Diarmaid who, still his attendant, lay near him, and nudged him. " Lord Abbot?"

" Go to the door," Colum said, "And see what is happening to the houses where our curragh was."

One could see without going to the doorway. The night about them was made like daylight, for the houses were all in flames. There was a harsh crackling as dry rafters went on fire, a dull thud as one fell to the ground.

" O Lord Abbot! Fire!" Diarmaid in his headlong run went over the sleeping men, and they all rose calling out in alarm. Diarmaid showed them, " The houses are on fire!"

Though across the stream, the houses were so near they could feel the heat.

" The curragh! The curragh!"

The two guides who had fetched it in the night were very pleased with themselves, " Safe! We thought it wise to bring it over by us."

"My sons!" Colum said, half awed half laughing, "You give no credit to God. If He Himself had not waked me to call you, we should have lost our curragh."

Cannich cried out, "The people! The men of the village! If this fire spreads among their houses!"

They could see no one by the ravaged houses, could hear no lamenting cries such as one hears when homes go on fire. They called, over the crackling of the flames, but there was no answer.

"But we must go over and see," Cannich said, "In case. God help them! they are stifled in their sleep."

They forded the stream, and looking about for something to beat out flames, they approached the burning houses, the two they had used earlier and one or two more. There was no sign or vestige of human being. They went into the neighbouring houses, from which the two men had come. But there was no living soul anywhere. The village had been deserted before it had burned.

Colum called them together. "We must set out immediately though it is scarcely day, and get out of this territory."

To Comgal and Cannich only he said in Latin privately, "It was done deliberately. They planned to kill us, or at least to burn our curragh."

"We will trust in our Breastplate," Comgal said, "And push on towards the long loch. We must not let the young men see us look grave."

XXIV

THE Loch stretched out so long in front of them, one could not see the other end of it. Where the grass ended and the pebbled shore began the guides fell on their faces. They had picked up tales about it earlier on the journey, and now awed, terrified, they stared over the water patterned by the shadows of racing clouds.

A powerful goddess inhabited this Nesa. She might sometimes be seen, rising from the surface of the water—"Great eyes" —had come the drifts of whispered speech—"they draw you in. The goddess lusts for the lives of men. She takes whom she chooses, sucking them down. Their bodies are never seen again. Yet any man given in sacrifice she rejects. Whom she will she takes, whom she is given she rejects."

"Come," Colum said, "You are going to leave us and go back to Dalriada. Spare us your fears, and tell us what you really know about the Loch."

"It is true, father," Duncath said, "I've heard it many a time before, this Loch is known to be immensely deep. It cannot be fathomed. If any man dives down he never comes up again. There are underwater caves, too. Whoever goes in there never comes out. He is caught and taken—who would say where? The caves, some say, go under the land to the sea. But others say they pass into the druid hell—"

"Well, we do not propose to dive in. Tell us about the currents, my son, and the prevailing wind, and how long we can expect to take."

"There are strange currents in this Loch, and freakish winds. The wind may drive you along as quick as an arrow, or it may drop and hold you still. It does not welcome strangers."

And when the wind came strongly from the south and Colum gave the word for Lugne and Diarmaid to get ready for the voyage, Duncath fell on his knees, "Father, don't go further! Come back with us. It is impossible to make your way to the High King, and what if you did reach him? You would only be taken."

"Give us a push out, man!" Colum said, "And then all three of you go on your way. You have served us faithfully in bringing us to this point of our journey. Go back now with our blessing on you. Keep to the woods, without us and our books and the curragh you will pass unobserved. Remember that the eye of Christ is on you, watching out for you. Say to King Connal we hope soon to see the Paramount King, and ask him to send our love to our men on the Island."

The guides lamented as they pushed the curragh into the water, till Lugne could find depth. "I would go with you," Conn said, "Only I would be afraid to die in this dark valley. I was born in Dalriada, and for all I suffered in the war I would not face death anywhere but there."

The monks looked back at the three in blessing, at Conn and Duncath and Fergal. Then they turned their faces north and did not look back again.

The trouble was, there might indeed have been demons in the Loch, the water leapt so oddly on their keel, shaking the curragh.

When they hoisted sail, matters grew even worse; the boat would stop in her course and tremble helplessly, then start forwards as if thrown. "It's because of the wind channelled in the narrow glen," Comgal told them. Indeed sudden squalls of wind came in such strength it almost overturned them.

A kind of misery afflicted them. The dark depths beneath made them long for the clear water of the western sea. There one could see to the bottom when half a mile from shore. Diarmaid and Lugne could not quite forget the words of the guides, the goddess hungry for men in her secret lairs.

Comgal told them what he could remember of Finbar's talk of the site of a cell which Ninian had planted by this Lochside in earlier days. Where there was a high mountain on the western shore, he said, and a little bay set in a glen that runs west from the Great Glen. When therefore they passed opposite a bare mountain higher than the other slopes they kept a lookout, thinking they might come to land there and find friends.

A dun stood on a promontory, the figures of sentries outlined small and clear, even to the lances held in their right hands. Even their lances! "Keep beyond spear shot," Cannich said rather anxiously. But, "We will row in," said Colum, "For we must meet the folk later if not now. They will not harm us if we do not evade their challenge." And he pulled in under the very walls of the dun which rose straight up from the water, and he cried up into the faces peering down, "Greetings! We come in peace. Where is the holy place?"

Diarmaid bent his back, his arm shielding his head. But no spear whistled. Neither was any answer made. They rowed north across the little bay.

The bay was all a-glitter from the setting sun that sent its rays through the gap of the glen. It was rimmed with grassland and fields of rising crops, fertile and green below the dark of the woods. From the thriving farms people came down to the water's edge to watch as they crossed and approached the northern side. But no shout answered theirs, they could not hear the talk of the people among themselves. They were like imagined people in a bard's tale. The monks rowed over the bright water unwelcomed, unchallenged.

As they made in to shore those who lived nearest came to watch their landing, but there was silence still. Men in tunics of patterned stuff, women with great bronze necklets: when the monks tried to come towards them they shook their heads and went back from them.

The two younger men beached the curragh, Colum and Cannich and Comgal gathered up the books and rugs and oars, and went up into the hazelwood for shelter.

"Why are they so quiet? What do they mean to do with us? Will they come and attack us?"

"I think not," Colum said, "For it is of our own will we landed. But they do not seem to like us very much, in spite of Ninian and his cell!"

"You see, Colum," said Comgal, "Why I said we should have gone by Fortrin and the east! We need interpreters with the people, and a Christian king or chief to aid us in our approach to the High King." He spoke out, as the two young men were still at the Lochside busy with the curragh.

These came back into the hazelwood carrying food, cheese and butter and oatcake set out on a silver dish chased with intricate ornament and very beautiful. As they were coming up from the shore, they said, they had met a man who had laid this down beside them bowing low. They were very hungry and glad to see food. Comgal put a hand out to stop them. " —Poison?"—No, he answered, but by the manner of the giving, it was in all likelihood meat offered to idols. Diarmaid spat out what was in his mouth. And Lugne shivered, " I am afraid to eat in this strange land. They put this food in our way to make us eat it and pass into their possession."

" That is impossible," Colum sternly said. " We will say evening prayer and then you will go to sleep. You will not think such thoughts when it is morning."

But later as they lay on the mossy turf Cannich asked, ". Colum, are you asleep? I know it cannot be the enchantment of the food, and yet I feel as if my mind were no more part of me. My own identity is going out of me. O may Christ aid me! Surely they do not have the power to touch the mind or the spirit? They cannot take away a Christian man's faith and make him afraid? I know there are no other gods but one, and yet in this alien place—"

Comgal turned to them his haggard face, streaked with the shadow of the hazels in the faint moonlight. " Gods they are not, but there are evil forces abroad, they are laying siege to us. Now you see, Colum, why we should not have come by this way of the Great Glen. How are we without comfort of brethren and prayer to achieve anything? We cannot keep fear from our own hearts far less drive it from the hearts of this people."

" Colum, we might still go back? Even you are afraid. We are so alone."

Colum raised his head, though it was heavy like lead. " We are not really alone. It was for such a darkness as this they said their Lorica over us at Lismor. It is against our defeat now that they say prayers for us on the Island, and in Bangor and in Aghabo and in Derry. And somewhere here though we have not found it there was a Christian settlement in earlier days, there must still be a memory of it among the folk. Let us live out this night and wait for morning."

It was with agony that he prayed for it.

XXV

THE people would not come near them; their silence was as terrible as any attack could be. Colum walking between wood and shore saw only the small flowers in the grass, primroses still in bud and violets blue among their green leaves. He was astonished when a voice came to him. A man getting on in years was walking by his side, " Why do you ask to see our holy place? Is it our Mount of Judgement you mean? Our druids come here and judge cases on the Mount. Is it to receive or to give judgement the strange men have come?"

" That is not the holy place I mean," Colum answered him, speaking warily as if he were a bird that might be scared away. " Is there no other?"

The man looked at him sidelong out of dark eyes. " Whoever are you who know of another place?"

" We are Christian priests."

" Christian priests! I never thought to see them. We have not had Christian priests here since—Come with me. I'll show you."

He stooped and pulled back the trailing brambles, exposing a stone lodged in the ground. He walked round it sunwise before saying, " This they say was his foundation stone. The hole is where his centre beam was set up. Our druids do not know it, but sometimes in special need we come here and take the water that lies in the hole and it works cures. My father also knew a magic symbol to trace in the air before using the water. I have forgotten what it meant, if I ever knew. We have our own customs and our own gods. But I have some veneration for the stone, for when my son Uirolec was ill with fever and a twisting of his face, I gave him three drops of this water to drink and I think it was that cured him when the water with the druid's pebble in it did him no good. And if you have any cure for pains in the joints I would be glad to have it from you, Master, for I am sorely troubled in time of rain."

Colum sat by the stone that marked the place of the former cell and spread out the parchment sheet; he took water from the hollow in it to moisten his powder into ink. The new friend watched him as he wrote. "Is this a spell you are making? Master, do not let me see!"

"I am writing a letter. Whoever reads this will understand my message."

"Do not show me. I know no science. To whom is the stranger inscribing his message?"

"To your High King, Brude mac Maelchon."

"Do not name him aloud. The High King?"

"Is he at this time in his Palace?"

"He is so indeed. And they say he has kings with him, kings from the North and from the South. A fine thing it is for us, for we prepare their fir candles. But why are you sending a message to him?"

"To ask leave to approach him. And to tell him what my errand is. I come to request him to grant me a little island in the west to be my home."

"That is a strange errand."

"How can I get this letter into the hands of the High King?"

The man looked at him, frowning, without replying. Then he reluctantly put out his hand, "Give your letter to me. I cannot myself give it to His Excellency, but I might be able to let it fall into the hands of those who have access to him privily. I would not meddle in it were it not for the goodness of the water in the stone."

The
King's Gates

XXVI

THERE could be no harm in looking at him, thought Urpant who had come north in the retinue of prince Nechtan of Dunduirn: there could be no harm, when one was separated from him by kings and princes from the gods knew what provinces, in looking to one's heart's content at the High King. There he sat at the head of his hall, and light came in on him from the window which showed the little firths and the mountain they call Uivis, brindled still with its winter snow. Though he was bare of weapons there was that suggestion of armed force about him, it might be the set of his head, the stillness he had when he gazed. One could see the colour of his hair, not red like fire as the bards' tales had it, but reddish brown like bronze, silvering over the ears. One could almost discern the colour of his eyes, turning as they did now from speaker to speaker round the council table. They were brown with greenish flecks in them like an agate stone. He was not so very tall when he was standing, some of his picked men dwarfed him; only he was broad and strong as a bull, and as terrible! His right arm, lying now along the armrest of his chair, bulged with muscle, and when he stretched it out to take up a sword they were discussing one saw the sure close grasp.

Urpant remembered seeing that arm and that hand caked with dried blood. O it was a pleasure and no mistake to be sitting here in peace, with the quiet to study King Brude mac Maelchon as a man, watching him handle a sword whose edge one would not feel. Time was when there was strife between North and South: memories still might twitch like sleeping dogs in the brain. Men of the North coming riding down through the passes, roofs aflame, women screaming, cattle rushing madly away in a cloud of arrows, and pain, pain, blood flowing warm, and eyes dimming, and more pain. Those were old memories now, buried in the brain. It was not likely they would ever come on the South in like manner again, and the gods be praised for their mercy. For this Brude was Lord of South and North, High King of all the tribes of the Alban men. High King and champion.

Now his armed might went out against farther foes. And all power to him! He had driven the encroaching Dalriadan men back into the sea, delivering Fortrin and Fotla from their sneaking raids. There would be no more bundling up of cloaks and rugs to wrap round the children in the middle of the night, no leaving of hot supper pots before the fire for the invader to sit down to. The ploughed land now would be reaped by the rightful owner, one's good grain would not now make bread for Dalriadan throats.

He was trying too to put bonds on the pirate raiders from over the sea; most of them came from the far northern isles. His own sister, the Young Heiress, was fathered by the chief of those Orc kings, and it gave the High King such influence that a word from him would do what an army of men could not.

The Saxons even—Deisuil!—those foes beyond all foes, terrible even to the terrible, the dread of all who lived in Fortrin and Fibh—the Saxons were coming up in the High King's view. It was said he had secret spies far south deep into the territories they were occupying; that he sent messengers to the kings of the Far South from where his own father had come, and with them he laid plans how to face this foe, as if like any other they could be faced and routed.

A powerful fighting king! It was wonderful, and worth the journey, to sit here far from home, in the dun of Murav among the Northern men, in the company of the great among all the seven provinces, and not find anything more difficult to do than to watch the Paramount King, satisfying the hunger of one's mind about his arms and his hair, and guessing the thoughts of his inmost head.

They were Southern princes, men of the province of Fibh, who came near the end of the council to present their case before Brude. Theirs was a dispute over the succession; one was son of the sister of the deceased king, the other a brother's son; but the latter was the people's choice, he claimed, since he was tall and strong, apt for battle as was very necessary for a king of Fibh to be these days. From Fibh, Brude thought to himself as they wrangled, from that part of the shore of the Fortrin Sea straight across from the great hill town of Dunpelder. I

112

remember seeing the smoke of it in the sky floating above the rich fields. —It pleased him he could remember the South so well. — And west of Dunpelder, Dun Eidyn. It was said the King of Dun Eidyn was appealing for men, princes and young men skilled in war but not yet called to the responsibilities of rulers, who could give time to practise warfare together, to make one great united attack on the Saxons and drive them for good out of the land.

The silence drew his mind back. The two men had ceased their pleading and were waiting, eyeing each other sourly, whilst the High King's brehons murmured amongst themselves to find a verdict they could give to him.

The light was waning, council had lasted long. Some of the kings from the North were beginning to talk among themselves, impatient of a matter remote from their interest. Tarain of the Orc Isles, Brude's sister's father's brother, had a circle of grinning men round him. He was describing the slaves he had taken in raids off the coasts of Eire, the Far South and Dalriada. Beautiful girls, he said, the ones from Eire were, though at first much disfigured with weeping — he mimicked the sounds of screams and crying echoing in the round walls of his fortress. —Thin brows shaped like bent bows, he said, and black lashes, though their hair was yellow as corn. Their waists were narrow: smaller men, he said, than any now listening could put one arm quite round them. But their bosoms and their hips—

There were gusts of laughter in the very midst of the brehons' consultings, and Brude saw the displeasure in the Southern princes' faces, even Drost of Circind and the two Fotla men were frowning. And Brude himself was displeased on their behalf. He spoke a word sharply to his sister's uncle in the older language, and with one last guffaw Tarain stepped forward and by way of making amends promised to each of the suppliants a girl apiece to take their minds off their quarrel, as good as any brought as gifts to the royal palace, he swore, let them come and see.

They smiled uncertainly, eyes fixed still on the High King and his brehons. Decision was made in favour of the brother's son, and bowing they went away to their seats. The rest of the council rose, stretching, then stilled themselves to hear the palace druid's customary prayer at their dispersal: " O Sun and Moon, cause us to live safe and in health and in honour till we come together again."

One and another of the guest kings came up as if to have speech with him, but with a courteous look or murmured word Brude managed to slip by them all. For a kind of ecstasy was rising in him and he longed to be alone.

The little low door from the council hall into his private apartments gave under his hand, and he went along the passage that led out to the open air. He walked along the path that girded this eastern face of the royal hill, and there as he knew it would be lay his own Firth of Murav with the sunset colouring it. He went alone, glad to be by himself, to look down over the hill. So sheer down its side dropped one was like a bird over the hosting green and the fields of River silt where the palace grain was grown. The light was still clear in the air, and the people were only now leaving off their work and going home. Brude could see farmers shouldering up their hoes, fishing boats coming in with their catches of herring from the open sea, could hear the last hoarse shouts of captains dismissing their men. Life, human life—one could look down on it as if one were a god, the Sun or the Moon herself riding the vault of heaven. The smoke of the evening fires scented the air, one could fancy one smelt the cooking of food. Somewhere to the east where the temples were came a faint cry summoning to evening prayer. And the King, druid trained, lifted his arms towards the place. "Worship, O men and women! The Moon will appear."

The Moon will appear. She will lift up her potent beauty over the outer firth and shine on this inner one then on the inmost firth of Varrar. She will shine far and wide, catching the drifts of winter snow on Uivis, calling out strange shapes and shadows in the Great Glen. She will enfold in blessing my own kingdom of Murav. —So he had thought in the past, now it was otherwise. The Moon will appear and shine over all the provinces of Alba—over the far Northern Isles, their cliffs and their round towers, over the secret valleys of the West and their quiet inhabitants who speak the old tongue and follow the old ways, over the high mountains of Fotla, over the wide straths of Fortrin, over the seaboard of Circind and Fibh with its fish and its corn. Lost, smothered in her bright embrace will be the diversities of speech and custom, race and kindred. All Alba is one people sleeping under the Moon.

Around the firth below him the two promontories put their arms. And the King's arms went round his imagined Land. The emotion that came to him when he thought of its peace and safety had something more binding than the bond of family, more urgent than the body's desire and sweeter than its satisfaction, more precious than wealth, perhaps than fame and victory. To see the ordinary humdrum life of a people, plan its safety, keep it free from famine, plague or any calamity, so that it went on living: each sunrise the fires lit and the doors of houses opened and the day's work begun, each sunset the returning home, the children running out to meet uncles and brothers, women smiling over full pots on the hearths. For this one had to endure the perils of battle and the fatigues of council and the cares of diplomacy. For this small and great thing one performed all sorts of small and great things, ungrudging as a mother.

Like children's names the names of the provinces ran in his head: Ce, Cat, Fidach, Fotla, Fortrin, Circind, Fibh. The whole Land was his. It was, in moments like this, more; it was himself. Its rivers were his veins and arteries, its stone the stuff of his bone.

XXVII

YET even while the glow of the sunset still coloured the firth, the glow of his spirit faded. Someone was walking on a lower road on the slope of the hill, some lesser king strutting with his petty retinue, gaping at the walls and towers of the Palace in order to bring home great tales. Their presence undermined his visionary viewpoint as their unsubdued voices broke his blissful solitude. His mind filled again with all the tedious concerns, he ran over the small worries of the council—who had a grudge against whom, whose case had not rightly been judged, which of the Southern kings had taken offence at a rough word, a contemptuous act, of a Northerner, whether it were enough to sow a seed of disloyalty that might grow and disrupt this wonderful new unity of the Land. Well might he pray, " O Moon, keep me safe,"—it was not so much foes from outside, Dalriada or the Saxons, that one dreaded, it was ruin from within. To keep the Land safe he must assist the Moon.

An irreligious thought! He laughed sadly. A radiant mood did not last long. What was there of radiance in life that ever did? The moment after sexual satisfaction comes satiety, dis- taste even. Not even the holy exuberance of the Grove at Beltane and Lugnasa had power to thrill the body long.

Not even the fulness of victory can keep a king's heart rejoicing for ever. He comes from his slaughter and spoiling, and among his shouting people his own mouth is dumb for he is tired of the effort and tired by the triumph. His only joy now is to plan a new war. And for himself, now Gauran mac Domangart had fallen, there was little excitement even in that.

Was there nothing in life, he asked himself as he quickly retraced his steps along the path and turned his back on the sunset, nothing that stayed constant in delightfulness? Maybe men found a constant state when they found their god. —That young druid Morpet whom he had listened to, Morpet had spoken about his Bright One whom he called Bel, and when he spoke of him invariably a smile came over his lips.—His sentries stiffened and bowed as he entered.

In his inner chamber he half hoped he might find his wife but she must be helping his mother the Old Heiress see that all the preparations for the meal were in order. He smiled to himself thinking of all the guest kings and their appetites for food and drink. One would need to come of a rich province and have trade from overseas to entertain them.

His master of the robes and his expert hairdresser were awaiting him, and he sat for their ministrations. The keeper of the king's jewels was standing by—by the gods of night and day, what a business they made of it! He fidgeted with impatience. It took one man in a battle to carry the king's shield, and he carried his own sword!

But there were two men who held towels and oils and combs a little awkwardly. One was much sunburnt and his hair was a trifle shaggy for court. Brude leaned out and gave this man's sleeve a secret pull, and as he was washed and combed and anointed with sweet oil from Gaul or who knows where this man came and went at his ear and told his news. Conducting a war can train a king in secret ways.

"No sign of rebellion, Exalted One, in the village where the brehons exacted the fine for the killing of hostages. They eat less, but they do not complain. A quarrel arose today between the chief—"

Brude pointed to the blue robe and stood to let his servant put it over his head. He emerged to listen to his spy. "Nothing else of note? Nothing unusual?"

"Nothing, Exalted One. Perhaps only this — that in the Glen the people are talking of the coming of strangers. They came by boat up the two lesser lochs and took to the water again and are half way up Loch Nesa."

"Strangers?"

"They are not men of Alba. Three, who acted as their guides and interpreters, were men of Dalriada. They have left them and gone home. The men who have come on—"

"You do not tell me that spies were able to proceed so far on their way? Has no one stopped them?"

"It appears the people did not take them for spies. They travel by day, openly. They are men of Eire."

"Pedlars? Or bards, are they? The women will like to have them come."

"Sire, they are neither. Yet they wish to come to the Palace. They have tried to speak with the people and have asked advice how they should gain audience with the Exalted One."

"Audience with me? Ah! They must be a delegation from Dalriada, from that poor Connal. He has found helpers to send to beg delay in paying his tribute. I can hardly imagine they have come bringing any!"

"It may be, sire. Yet so far as people have understood them, they say it is one of their number who has a request to make to the Exalted One. Some request for a piece of land. — Sire, they are Christian clerics!"

"Christian clerics! Coming to see me?—Why are you not replying? It's safe to speak here."

"It is very strange they have approached the King this way. One would have thought they would come by the coast land, and make request through one of the southern kings. Yet they have come confidently straight up the desolate Glen to the High King. The leaders of the party are three, sire. And one of them is tall and bright haired—"

"I am not afraid, my good raven!" Brude said with a sudden smile, "I am not likely to suffer enchantment here, in the centre of the old faith with an Archdruid to watch over me who is indeed like the sacred ravens."

"No, sire. — But it is strange these men should not be afraid."

"Do they state their names and origin?"

"Freely, if asked. The tall fair stranger is called Colum mac Felim. He is of the kings of Ailech, cousin of the powerful Donal. He is also, though it is less to his credit, kin to Connal."

"Royal, eh!"

"None of them look it, sire, not even he. They travel like poor men, they row the boat themselves and help to carry it over land. They are dressed in plain grey cloth, and are tonsured like druids. Only they are not like our druids. They carry books, out of which by their science they can read words. I do not think they should be permitted to come any nearer to the Palace. The Exalted One must refuse them permission to approach."

"That I am almost sorry to do. You have roused my curiosity. I have not so often talked to men of Eire, unless in Dalriada, when I did not find much to say. And Christian clerics! A cleric who is of the family of kings!—I shall grant their request to visit me if they make it."

"Sire, they have made it. They have sent a letter to you, a message traced on a sheet of parchment with some dark water."

"They sent it? Where is it?"

"Sire, it is here." And reluctantly the shaggy man fumbled in the breast of his tunic and brought out the letter rolled round and covered with hazel leaves. "I have carried it to you. But do not touch it! It is certain to be enchanted. Coming so boldly—and none stopping them. Though in one place they fired the village they were in yet they still came on."

"Where are they now?"

"At Airchardtan, where there was once a shrine of the new religion. The people there are at a loss what to do with them. They are anxious not to offend . . ."

"I will see to it," Brude said dismissing the man. And as his attendants put his bracelets and his gold neck torque upon him, he eyed the parchment letter lying on the floor. Beside it, by chance, lay the shoulder brooch he had taken from Connal. He never could bear wearing it; it was best to do one's spoiling in heat at the time of battle. Moreover he had finer workmanship of his own.

XXVIII

A DISCREET cough at his door. Brude would have liked to be alone. Strange to be so lonely in the inmost heart, and yet never be free of company! He looked up with a scowl at his doorkeeper who was trying to attract his attention, asking if it were permitted to let a visitor come in. Why did a guest come now to trouble him, before he was dressed?

Then he saw who it was, Nechtan, his sister's lover. To be sure, he had sent for him. He smiled and with his eyes bade the young man be admitted. He limped slightly coming into the room; and there on his left leg below the knee was that triangular scar from his last summer's wound, the skin still raised and discoloured. Brude felt a surge of affection for him. He had fought well, this boy: animated no doubt by his wrath at the encroachments of Dalriadan raiders into the glen of Dunduirn, but also by sheer pleasure. He was daring but skilful, his men liked him. His wide grin never left his face even in the midst of a fight. Brude looked with curiosity at his face now, short nose and a multitude of freckles spread over it, and the usual wide grin.

" Well! " he said, " How goes it with the father of my heir?" That is, he thought in to himself, as far as we now can judge. My sister may choose another mate.

Indulgently, father himself, he listened to the surprising flow of talk that came from the young warrior's lips, all about the gain in weight and the development in skills of the infant Derile; though since Nechtan had not been north since his birth his talk was but an echo of the grianan. He let the young man run on, thinking his own thoughts. Whom would the child Derile take after? Would the heir, the Sister's Son, of Brude mac Maelchon, have just this short nose and wide-mouthed grin? A High King's heir—would he indeed inherit this great united realm of North and South?

120

Suddenly he interrupted Nechtan. " Is it true that kings in the South can read words and even write them, so that without speaking through a messenger they can communicate?"

Nechtan looked up surprised, then back came his grin. " Kings? No, sir, I don't think that could be said of kings. What time have they for that sort of thing? It's true that some of royal rank have an idea of it, though, those who have been fostered in the monastic schools. —Yes, there's my own brother, you met him on our journey through the pass of Loch Awe, Drost, if your Excellency remembers him? He can, I believe, still write words that another man could understand, and he can read—once he knew some of the language of the Romans. It seems to be easier to write than our own. He was taught — indeed I was too—in the monks' community below my uncle's palace of Dunduirn. Only Drost stayed in and listened whereas I ran off and fished on the loch. It looked at one time as if he would stay in the community; yes, become a disciple, take vows and shave his head. But no. The men of Dalriada spoiled that, for when they came into our valley he changed his mind. And the abbot Fillan blessed him to be a king and told him to rule men well and do justice without fear and avoid hurting the weak—that sort of thing. They used to speak a lot to us about ruling well, and read us stories from Roman bards. My father was relieved, I tell you, when the talk of head shaving ceased! For as you know my mother is heiress, and my brother or I likely to succeed." He looked at the King and found him as if still willing to listen.

" My father used to laugh at it, my uncle the king too, but only when they had taken wine. When my uncle went down to pray at Fillan's church, even when he went past it, he dared not laugh. There is a sort of authority about the place. I cannot explain what I mean. As if there were some hidden king and his laws were binding on these men as if they had drunk his mead. My father did not go often to pray, it is true, but he had been baptised — initiated by a water rite, I mean. And he let our uncle have us children baptised too, though I do not remember it. If he laughed he would not let anyone else laugh. My uncle gave gifts of cattle and corn, and no raider could attack the community without first rasing Dunduirn!"

" So then you are of the new religion?"

" I scarcely think about it, sir. Simply I have a fondness for Fillan's cashel. When I got this wound and thought I was

121

dying, down in the churned mud among the horses' feet, I held
on to the thought of it in my mind. I could hear the abbot's
bell in my ears, and I suppose I prayed. —I am not the only
one, Highness. There are others of Circind and of Fibh who
are of the new way. We are none the less your men."

Brude smiled at the anxiety on the young man's face.
Strange to see the man of battle suddenly timid.

"I did not doubt your loyalty. But I confess I hoped you
could read. For just before you came in I got this letter." And
he directed Nechtan's eyes to it, where it lay on the floor among
the mess of leaves the spy had wrapped round it to keep ill
luck away. "An unusual piece of news is that a party of Christian clerics have made their way up the Great Glen, and are
now halted at Airchardtan waiting permission to approach me.
One of them has sent that letter. What in heaven or hell does
he think I can make of it? The spies say his name is Colum mac
Felim."

"There is an abbot Colum in Marr, will it be he? Scarcely,
if he is coming from the west."

"This man, they say, is from Eire, of the royal blood, kinsman of Donal of Ailech."

"It is the abbot Colum of Derry then maybe, our abbot
Fillan sometimes spoke of him. But how should he be in Alba?"

"Whoever they are, it is odd enough to have them try to
come to the very Palace. Christian kings I have known, but I
have never had speech with your priests. How should I know
how to speak to them? If you are a disciple of Fillan's, can you
not tell me of their beliefs? You worship one god, I know, and
he is a Bright One. He is manifest in three forms. —You see I
have at times turned disciple too. It was when I was in Circind
before King Gallan's death. What's the matter?" He looked
at Nechtan and Nechtan looked back at him, the grin quite
gone from his face. "What's the matter?" Brude was going to
ask again, but he refrained, unwilling to hear what a truthful
reply would be. "It is not lucky to talk religion with the High
King."

Once more he wondered about Gallan's mysterious death.
Although it had been to his advantage, making him sole High
King, Paramount over all kings, princes and nobles of Alba,
yet it left a shadow of fear on the mind. There was the young
druid too, Morpet, of whom he kept thinking. —It was at
Dornaig Morpet had lived, a rural druid in charge of preaching

and school. There as in other places, this Airchardtan
the spies had mentioned, one might speak to folk who had some
dim memory of a system of belief, a word or two of a strange
hymn, a pattern of prayer. —But Morpet had gone, vanished;
he had never understood what his end had been. He sighed.

And here before him was Nechtan wearing that anxious
look. " I hope, sir, I have not said too much? Perhaps I should
not have spoken about Fillan at Dunduirn? I should not have
pronounced the names, either, of those princes in Circind and
— —".

" You said nothing," Brude answered with a bleak smile.
" You are the father of my heir and you are afraid of me."

" I am only afraid when I am here. —Brude, I fancied that
your Archdruid Broichan was greatly displeased with me. We
did not ask his counsel, your sister and I, when—— It was
only your command and my desire to see her and the child that
made me come North again."

"You need not be afraid. Well, if neither you nor any
Southerner can read my letter, I shall have to take it to the
Druids' College and have it deciphered there."

" But I am forgetting the state banquet. The labour of
the day is far from done. We must sit and eat too much and
drink and talk in order of precedence and conduct ourselves so
as to please our gods and our women."

XXIX

THE candles were of bog fir and shone luminous but fitful on the walls. The carving of the Lord of Life sprang in and out of sight. It had been set there in her brother's time—as if he knew, the Old Heiress pondered, as if her brother the king of Murav knew that a greater hour than his own was to come, and his heir, her little son Brudean, to be King of both North and South. Her eyes, so used to dwelling with awe and delight on the Lord with his upward curving horns of power and on the beasts that surrounded him—the wolf and the boar and the cat and the deer—her eyes left the pictured wall; for there below, not in wood but in quick flesh was the parallel. Brude sat, with head erect and gold banded, and his lords sat on either side of him; the Wolf from Fodla in the mountains, the Boar from the Northern Isles of Orc, the Cat.— It was by no means the first time that the likeness had struck her, for Brude had gathered the South and the North to council many times in the three years he had held the paramountcy. Yet the sight was not dull to her yet, but a glowing in the eyes and in the mind.

It was her own traditional task to stand a moment or two before the beginning of the evening feasting to see that all were seated and served, a task of responsibility, since one had to arbitrate in disputes about precedence or put in a word to allay animosities. Though her back might ache, for her age was creeping upon her, she was unwilling to give up this duty to any of the younger womenfolk: to Roith her son Brude's royal wife, who would no doubt do it well, calm and untroubled as she was about all that did not too nearly concern the safety of Brude: or to Leiven her daughter, Brude's half sister and now mother of an heir. Leiven would surely please both North and South, and with her sweet beauty charm away any rancours among the kings and chiefs—so long as she did not charm too much.

124

It might have been good, had the gods so willed it, that
the quiet woman should have held the Seed in her body, not
this quick wilful rash one. She herself in her days of young
love and creativeness had been something between these two. But
even then, even then she had high purpose in her heart and
had willed that Brudean should succeed without harm or accident to the Kingship of Murav, and after that to the High
Kingship of all the Land.

Her eyes examined Brude again, not this time loving and
gloating but observing and criticising. Were his habiliments all
as they should be, no spot, no dullness, nothing lacking? Tarain
of Orc, the two princes from Circind — the fame of the High
King would go as if on winds over all the seven provinces when
this time of council was over and the guests back in their homes.
His sons — the eldest Uirgain was in handsome robe indeed,
almost too handsome for a boy who could not succeed. He had
been a fair child, but now, but now, she thought, watching his
sullen face, he was not shaping to be a comely man. Had his
tutor so failed in his teaching of him that he had not made it
plain it was honour enough to take one's life from a great king
even if one might therefore never reign? He must content himself with his mother's brother's little place in the far West.

She forgot Uirgain, dropping him from her mind like a
garment picked up by mistake. His mother Roith too. These
were things that were a comfort to Brude, but nothing in themselves. It was upon her daughter Leiven that her eyes stayed.
The child should be content. She had borne a male child and
given her brother his heir; she had thus justified her title of
Young Princess. Now she had no more to think of than the
bearing of a female child who in due time should bear the new
heir. Life passes on like a stream. Her thin face had filled out
a little with her maternity, her large restless eyes held more
often a look of wellbeing and peace. She had her hands now
absently over her breasts filling with milk. A nice way to behave
at the High King's table! Well that she had settled on a mate
at all, the restless one, even if she had not taken the one they
had planned for her! She could still take him, another child or
two would ensure the succession, one had to choose the best out
of several heirs.

My life is fulfilled, the Old Heiress thought as the last king
was seated, I have accomplished what my fate was to do. For
I have borne the Heir, I have raised him to a height of king-

liness; and having set him on high I hold him there, him and
all that is his—sister and heir, wife and sons, lords and friends.
I am creator and succourer of the Land, like one of the Immortal Ones.

They were shouting and laughing over the food, but her
mood had changed, as if a candle within her had been blown
out. I am wrong in taking credit to myself, may the gods
pardon me! May they not have heard my presumptuousness.
Life hangs on a thread. It is like a house of straws. One
builds a fine house high over one's head, honour and riches
and power: then sickness comes, a fever, a pain in the head—
or one's foot slips and one falls—and the house is gone, gone
like straws in the wind. It is the gods who have power, and
the Priest of the gods who comprehends their ways. Whatever
I have done in making or keeping, I have done with the help
of the Archdruid. With the help and favour of the Archdruid!
she almost said the words aloud, so anxious was she to placate.

The Archdruid was not present in the hall. His carved
seat was set back against the wall to warn the unwary of the
impiety of sitting in it. High business often kept him from the
Palace, even at council time. His ways were secret, one must
not try to follow them. Last night he had come to the feasting:
the door of the druids' apartment had opened and he had
entered in his many coloured robe of state and with his amulet
glittering on the breast of it. The waiting company had drawn
in their breath and turned their eyes away from him in his
holiness and splendour. The lords of the South indeed had not
quite looked up again the whole evening. They were not used
to the sight of the greatest Wise Master, Archdruid of all the
druids in Alba, and beyond it to lands across the Gallican Gulf.

But the Old Heiress had not been able to keep her gaze
from his face, so anxious was she to judge of his state of mind
with regard to the Family. Through all the offering of food
and drink she watched him covertly. Had there lately been a
cloud of displeasure? Ah surely not, they had done nothing to
offend? Had they? Brude, great warrior as he was, was tender
of conscience, obedient to the gods, swift to be guided in
obedience by his Archdruid. It had been wise to have him
fostered by him when he was a child.

If there had been any cloud on his face, could it be on
account of Leiven—her lover from Fortrin who had come north
to see his babe? How had she eluded them, and conceived

before her mating was arranged by the Archdruid? Had His
Holiness forgiven that rash act, done at the fierce bidding of
youth? Or, counting it disobedience, could he be storing up
anger? A pity the young man should have come here flaunting
their marriage.

One must obey. As if by an arrow now her whole heart
was transfixed. The old grief had such power over her that,
disciplined as she was, it was all she could do to keep it from
showing in her face. Deep deep within her consciousness she
was filled with crying. She saw a blue gown, the girl leaning
out from the coppice her hands on two trees, her eager coaxing
frightened half understanding face. It was Drusticca. There in
the heart she stood forever, even to the untidy hair . . . The
Old Heiress pressed meat to her lips to keep herself from moaning, remembering the height and the depth of her own obedience to the Holy Ones. For was it not her obedience, though
the Master had helped her . . . ? Blacker than night the trees
were. She followed the track of the moon. In to the inmost
shrine, the indigenous holy place . . . the moon shone on the
upright stones casting shadows of them like fingers pointing to
her . . . *At the heart of the spirit's life is sacrifice. In this pure
and awful place devotion is weighed — For the safety of the
Land and its High King . . . You have a virgin daughter . . .*
She saw his bare feet pale in the moonlight on the grass, but
the thoughts were her own . . . Virgin like the new snow . . .
The broad flat stone shone, terribly, as if with inward light, or
as if wet.

Her breath whistled through her fingers for she could not
take them from her mouth. Other girls will live and love and
have sons, sons and daughters' sons to be their heirs. But this
one girl will never live, except in my mind, always in my mind!

Beside her, touching her, was not Drusticca but Brude.
The guests had left the hall for their small sleeping chambers
round the courtyard.

" Mother? I asked if you knew where the Archdruid is?"

She cried with a vehemence which startled them both,
" What do you want with him?"

" Has he gone to the Valley of Science?"

" I think so, my son." She was her accustomed self again,
tall, upright, splendid, and the painted tracery on her face con-
cealed the lines of age. " You must wait till he comes here
again."

"I cannot wait," he was going to say, but he thought better of it. The less one told the better, even to those nearest one's life. Instead he said, indifferently, "It is a small matter," and smiled at her. Her mouth softened though her eyes still held their secret pain.

XXX

THE sunlight clothed the two slopes of the Valley of Science, and in the fresh morning air was the smell of grass and moss and roots of heather. From the students' houses came a drift of peat smoke. The King got off his horse throwing his attendant the reins and stood a moment looking down on the place once so familiar to him. Then he walked to the entrance of the Precincts alone.

He turned his thumbs sunwise and said his prayer of obeisance as he stooped to the doorway made from three ancient stones and he took a long stride to avoid touching the threshold at which in past ages men had given their lives to the ground. Whether it was something palpable in the air, the sour smell of the courtyard of the Grove maybe, or a disgust he had felt since ever the young druid Morpet had opened his mind to the ugliness of the rites of sacrifice, he could not tell; only now the breath stood in his nostrils and he could not swallow.

And then, alleviating the painful mood, came childhood memories — gentle old men in robe and tonsure who had left their rites and incantations to play with him, taken leave of their philosophy to carve him a little horse and chariot in wood; and Broichan his fosterfather, in his prime, before the high office of Archdruid fell on him, running races with him barefoot, showing him the pools in the Nairn river where he could swim.

But now to get on! He had set off from the Palace at dawn, stealing time from other affairs. He must find somebody who could read the letter. He walked through the alleys of the Precincts wondering to which house it was best to go. Not many, master druids or students, looked a second time at him, for he had left his royal clothing at home and come in tunic and mantle of grey like their own.

He passed the bards' school. When first he had come to the kingship of Murav he had listened avidly to bards' songs about himself. It was like strongest wine to him. Now as Paramount King of North and South, when he listened to such songs, he was afflicted by a curious sense of emptiness. So much glory and high passion — for what? He walked on quickly to another house, the faculty of theology. He knew that no one unlearned in science should go near it; except when he was a young child he had never been as far as the door. Yet Morpet that memorable summer had taken him inside and let him stay while he lectured on his idea of the Sun God, the warmth of his love for Him filling the hearts of the hearers as if indeed with sunshine—" He is more powerful than the dark gods." He had made man and He loved him. He would redeem him. Where was the mouth now that had said words that lived on in the brain?

O! to get on with this business of the letter. Forget past things. The voice of a lecturer came through the slats of the wall, the King stole near to listen but it seemed dull stuff. " Error creeps in. Because of some devious tendency in human life. The standard belief and practice must be constantly checked with the norm. Therefore country druids must be sure they come regularly to the College for teaching and to the Grove. They must scent out any eccentric notion, track down—." The King said " Hist!" to a druid sitting near the door and he came out startled. Had he been asleep?

But he was wakeful when the King disclosed a corner of the letter.

" I? No! I cannot. Highest One, Excellency!—There is no one here who could."

On to the next school. Stillness here. The King stopped as if cold air had touched his face. The still room of the magic art. One voice was speaking: Whether a cure is real, or in the mind? " Take this pebble. Now, when it floats in water, is its floating actual or apparent? Does it float in the world of nature or in the world of the spirit of the believing sick man?"

But from them as from all others the one answer. " I cannot! Only the Archdruid, Excellency, can read your letter. Will you wait for him? He is at the Holy Grove. Excellency—"

Mixed with the smell of trees, innocent and fresh, the smell of death and of captivity. Brude had for long been used to it, it was part of the childhood world. It was only lately, coming

hère with Morpet, that he had come to dislike it. It was bad
enough when the stench of animal entrails and blood made him
think of the battlefield when the crisis of danger and delight
is over; it was worse on the one or two occasions when no
animals had been in evidence, and he had heard the gibbering
of human men or women made inhuman by utter terror, the
terror of the human being waiting for death with hands bound.
It was not fitting that a King should think of such things.
Justice must be done, and evil purged from under the gaze of
of the pure Sun.

So now he went with firm step to the outer court of the
Shrine. The priest druids seemed as if afraid to pause in their
exacting task of finding an auspicious omen. As soon as one
cock was slaughtered and the steaming entrails thrown upon the
ground, they shouted for a new one, and their assistants ran to
them with the flapping birds held at arm's length from the face.
Could they not influence the result by a calculated throw? Why
not! It was all out-moded stuff anyhow, in the South it would
be laughed at. There are good times and bad times, safety and
danger, however the entrails go. So anyone knows who is not
simple.

"Another!" the priest called. But no assistant came this
time with a cock. "Another! Another! do you hear?" Still no
cock was brought him. He looked up, to see the assistants,
empty handed, gaping at a stalwart figure, a man wrapped in
a grey mantle, standing right inside the courtyard among all the
cages and feathers. The priest with an exclamation went to
drive out the intruder, but his colleague caught him by his wide
sleeve. "Take care! It is— — the High King."

They both looked silently at the figure. The King? As if
to dispel their doubt the man for a moment let his mantle fall
away from his body. Before he gathered it to himself again
they had seen that it was Brude indeed. His thick arms with
the reddish hairs, the golden bracelet above one elbow, the lines
the grey gown took over thigh and knee. The priests went down
on one knee "Royal Lord?"

"If the Archdruid my fosterfather is here," the king said
in a quiet tone, "Tell him I have come to have speech with
him."

"Yes, Excellency.—No, sire, it cannot be! Forgive us. But
the holy Briochan is performing the morning rite within the
Grove."

"I can wait," said the King, calmly enough, though the priests saw a pulse beating in his throat. "Though I do not think I shall have to. His Holiness is coming."

The priests had a secret and depraved sense of pleasure watching the coming encounter. But as the white robe came nearer, glimmering through the trees, they covered their faces with their hands, curiosity smothered in apprehension that they might be implicated in any blame.

The Archdruid as he approached seemed to be adorned with light, though he wore no jewels but the one amulet flashing on the breast of his white gown. He seemed to glide towards the King on his bare feet. Brude found himself unable to look up, only the bare feet on the ground might he look at. It was when the familiar shape of that one great toe thawed his icy dread that he looked up again.

The voice was familiar too, yet unfamiliar in the tone it used, a gasping tone as of a man lately come from viewing the secrets of the gods. "Brude! My son! What have you come for?" Before the King could reply, he said with some sternness, "You may not satisfy your lust here, it is not a due season. You must stay in the Palace, and—"

As the King frowned and still made no reply, he laid a thin hand on his arm, "What is wrong, Brude? Out of what need have you come to me without warning?"

"Nothing is wrong," the King answered composedly. "There is no special need. But there is a small matter on which I should like your help."

"Go!" the Archdruid said, "Go to my house and wait for me. I will come to you when I have divested myself of this ceremonial clothing. Go slowly, and I will overtake you."

The King eyed him, as together they walked towards the Archdruid's house on the crest of the northern slope which commanded a view northwestwards to the Palace: yes to the Palace!

"Why are you staring at me?" Broichan asked. "It is I who should stare at you, for your conduct is highly irregular. You must not come into the holy courtyard unless I send for you, or at the stated times."

"You are well, fosterfather? In the shadow of the trees I could not judge, even supposing I had dared to look directly at you. Here in the sunshine I think you look—" He did not know whether to say, tired or old or ill. And with prudence learned earlier in his life he left the word unsaid.

The Archdruid looked sharply at him. "Do not presume on our former familiarity." But then he smiled his aloof wintry smile. Yet the King was displeased, guessing the thoughts that might be in his mind: "Such a plain honest face he has, this son of the fierce Maelchon and the Princess of Murav! He has no subtlety to mean anything more than he says. He is so like a farmer or a craftsman. Who but a man of science would ever have guessed he would have made a great king?" Well, fair enough. He himself remembered what a small thin child he had at one time been. He had had to hold his fosterfather's hand on a windy day. Then how he had grown and broadened and reached to his heritage! And one by one the obstacles had fallen that barred his way to the kingship, and then his fame got beyond the North and they accepted him when Gallan died as Paramount King, Lord of the North and South and of the West and of the far Islands, the strong quiet terrible Keeper of the Alban Land. I am his creation. And he turned towards the Archdruid with a boyish gesture. On the whole he had been a good child, docile, obedient to his holy fosterfather, only on occasion showing resistance to his will.

"My Brude!" Broichan said now with answering tenderness, "If you have come for counsel, if something is weighing on your mind, you will tell me and I will show you the way out. No need to fret. So now let us eat together."

The servants brought a trestle table and set it in the porch which caught the early summer sun. They set food before them, hot roasted chickens (though the King remembered at sight of them the outer court of the Shrine), and broiled river trout. Broichan said graciously, "The fulness of the Land to the Land's King."

He watched the King as the meal progressed, to judge of his state of mind from his manner of eating. And Brude cast secretly in his mind whether he should pretend it was on some other affair, some quarrel among the vassal kings, some slander in the grianans, some rude word from the boy Uirgain which had sparked off a brawl with steward or guest. When at the end of the meal the servant brought wine, however, he set his beaker some distance from the edge of the table, carefully. "Though there is no trouble there is a matter—"

"Some spiritual matter, do you mean? Well, I am glad you have ceased asking others! If you have questions regarding the service of the gods you may come to me."

"How do we know the gods we serve?" the King asked suddenly. "How can we know them?"

The Archdruid laid his hand beside the King's hand where it lay by his beaker of wine. "How do we know the gods, Brudean! It is not necessary. The gods know us, my son. That is, the gods know ordinary men. In the case of those in science it is true that they may be said to know the gods seeing they understand how to worship and please them, and they learn their craft and can in some measure predict their will. But for you, as for lesser laymen, the favour of the gods is enough, and that is gained for you by the orderly succession of anciently established rites and sacrifices."

"Why do you look at me so hungrily?"

"I have everything I desired, victory, power, a good name. And yet I am dissatisfied. Is it not possible for me to know some god as an inmost friend—"

Broichan looked at him smiling tenderly, "You have a fine and lofty nature of yourself, my son. And I think the sacredness of your state as High King has interpenetrated your substance with a substance divine. I feel sure that in your next life you will be reborn as a man of science. As a Wise Master, —who knows? as my successor as Archdruid."

The King said slowly, "But it is possible here and now to be reborn, not by death, in this life, now: to possess a sort of life so that one can never really be said to die or to have to be reborn."

"Here is doctrine!" cried Broichan. "Who has been teaching you things of this sort? Not that you seem to have mastered the lesson very well, you were always slow. I hope you have not recently been asking advice in the wrong places?"

"It was while I was in the South over the Dalriadan campaign. I spoke with one or two men there, one on the night before a battle. They were of the new religion, so it scarcely mattered what they had to say.

"But the matter I have come about," he said taking a drink, "is this." He did not see the Archdruid's eyes widen, and he drew out from the breast of his gown the letter, and laid it gingerly down on the table between them. Broichan stood up suddenly so that the trestle table shook and the wine jumped in their cups. Recovering himself he sat down again, though out of breath.

"You are surprised, father, as I was to get it. It is not often I receive a message written. I do not think I have ever before had one. You will not guess who has sent it."

"I do not guess, my son."

"Strangers are coming up through the Great Glen, men of Eire. One of them, who they say is called Colum Mac Felim, wrote this letter being familiar with the art, and sent it to me at the Palace."

The Archdruid smiling nodded his head, "But I know. I have known of their coming for some time now. I have watched their progress through our land with the eyes that serve me. I am sorry your spies have troubled you with this. It is for me if it is for anyone."

The King's hand stopped him as he made to push the letter off the table. "Fosterfather, a moment please. This man Colum is some kinsman to Connal. I ought to know why he has written, why he is coming to me."

"It might be interesting," Broichan signed to his servant to fill the King's beaker again, "To know why he is coming when most men of Connal's are only too anxious to run away! But of no great interest surely?"

"I would like you to decipher it and let me know what request he makes."

"I will see to it. Now tell me, Brudean, what news the kings from Fortrin had of the latest incursion of the Saxons? The gods have blessed us here—"

XXXI

BRUDE went roaming through the paved courtyards of his Palace. He saw two girls making for an open doorway, one walking lightly on slender feet had her gilt sandals swinging from her hand, the other carried a baby wrapped against the morning chill in a fur rug; and he went himself to the doorway over which were set the symbols of comb and mirror. He looked, with a desire for comfort, into the grianan. And there in the light of the doorway matching threads for weaving were his mother and his wife. His sister Leiven the Young Heiress was putting her little son Derile down by his cradle to kick on a rug at her feet. They looked up as he darkened the doorway, and cried out to him, " Brude! Brudean! Come in. You're not going away again?"

" You are restless these days, my son," said his mother. " Too remote from us even for a High King. What ails you?" Brude looked not at her so much as at his silent wife, to whom through all his loves he had returned, stretching out his left hand secretly to her in answer to her own troubled look. " Is there bickering between North and South? Or—"

His sister the Heiress came to the doorway, matching crimson to crimson and she chattered to him. " What were the men saying, Brude, last night at the feasting? They were at it again this morning, and I could not get my girls near enough to overhear. Something about foreign men coming to us on a visit. What sort of men are they? You should know everything! Singers, I hope; or no, better, pedlars with silk cloth from the Mediterranean Sea. No? They are of gentle blood? Why don't you say for sure?

" I wonder what they will bring as gifts for us. A harp with a gold frame maybe, like the one mother has. She got it from a bard who came with your father from the far South. I hope it won't be a few old swords for you. O I know they were Roman!"

"I have heard," said his mother, "that they are from Eire? At first they were thought to come from Dalriada. It surprised me. After the defeat you inflicted on their King Connal."

And Leiven laughed so merrily she made the baby laugh too. "That poor fat king! He could not get up from his knees. One of his followers had to take him below the armpits and heave him up. He was like a man stunned. How we laughed at him. I saw the sweat shine on his face."

Then suddenly her mood changed. Her eyes, brown like Brude's own, took on a look that made them as different from his in expression as it was possible for them to be. The look of a girl's eyes as she dreams of a lover. "I know the gift you are wanting," he said contemptuously, "Strange love, and a new heir for me with the blood of Eire in him—your child a cousin of King Connal!"

Her eyes stabbed him, she muttered with petulance kept in bounds only by awe of his status, and stooping caught up Derile from his rug and cradled him in her arms, gazing over his wool wrapped little body as if to place herself in the protection of the future king And restored to good temper by having shaken his sister's, Brude prodded the baby with a finger till it crowed at him. Then he said to his sister, "I see no reason why this young one's father should not also be the father of his sister. These men fiom Eire will not interest you, my dear. As well as having an unsavoury connecton with recollections of Connal, they are men of religion, Christian clerics, and it is not their custom to marry, far less to think of such princesses as you."

His mother followed him beyond the doorway as he left it. "Brude! It seems to me the Archdruid is disturbed like yourself. There is no rift between you? You have not displeased him?" Her eyes spoke on to him after she had finished speaking, and Roith in her silence spoke no less urgently.

He turned away from them. He wondered whether it were possible for them to read his remembering mind.

. . . The silence had stirred up in him all his childhood dread, but he had ventured: "Why will your Holiness not tell me what was in that letter? The guests of my Palace ask; the womenfolk too. Tell me, so that I may answer, even if I must refuse any request he makes."

Silence still; but he had persisted, "It is strange a man connected with Connal of Dalriada should dare to come straight

through the Great Glen directly to me! I understand from——
I understand he is really from Eire, kinsman of Donal of
Ailech. They are overlords of Dalriada, the Ailech kings, though
they do not send them aid."

"He has come from Dalriada, and deserves no notice whatever. You are wasting your time, not to speak of your dignity.

"Come, Brudean! I will explain to you. Whether they are
from Eire or from Dalriada, those men who are trying to come
to you are Christian clerics. They have come here in an attempt
to pervert the purity of worship and belief in this land."

"I do not see how they can harm us. There are many such
in the Southern Provinces. I have spoken to them in the course
of the campaign. Every man is entitled to his belief."

"Sir! That is blasphemy. You have learnt much in the
South indeed if you have learnt disloyalty to your ancient faith.
Listen to me! In the Southern Provinces, as you say, the new
religion increases and spreads. It is not in your power, High
King though you are, to quench it suddenly. It will take us long
years. But at least in the North—"

"The new religion was once known and practised here.
There were churches."

"That is over. We stamp on the smouldering fires, and
there is no new blaze. No, and there will not be! For you stand
like a champion maintaining the ancient purity of the faith.
Yours is high privilege, for you are aware that to us now other
lands look for guidance and inspiration, even Gaul and lands
beyond it far south of the Gallican Gulf.

"Ah my son! evil is subtle. I say that the new religion in
this Northern Land of ours is no more than a smouldering fire.
But here and there a small glowing shows in the embers. One
comes upon a mood, a belief that is not orthodox. There is a
thinning of the reverence due to hallowed custom and our
mothers' gods. Error makes itself visible in unlooked for places.
Yes, Brude mac Maelchon, it can invade even the heart of the
High King! You show less than your proper and wonted respect
for me, who am the interpreter of the will of the Holy Ones.
In scanting respect for me you scant respect for Them." The
King himself had been silent now under the reproof. "Take
good care! The gods who lift up a mortal man can cast him
down.

"I do not wish to threaten you, my dear. I will not recount
to you the penalties disobedience to the gods can bring. You

have heard of common men who felt their wrath—some intimate
with you have felt it recently. Interdiction — no word at the
well, no mill for the corn, no fire to replenish fire, no marriage
for daughter or son, no vengeance allowed for injury. Do you
think such punishment is not for the noble? It does not touch
the High King? It is the other way. If you should offend, you
the mate of the Land, your suffering would be greater in pro-
portion to your grandeur. You would suffer in the mind—care
and anxiety always, unreprieved by hope, failure to command
respect from your followers, loneliness—"

"I am lonely enough already," the King had said sullenly.

"That is inevitable because of your high position. But it
is a quiet thing. It does not fret your flesh from off your bones.
Are you aware, I wonder, of the sacrifices that your family
have in times past made for you? Do you know what your
mother gave, to build up your security? I do not think you
are clearly aware of it, and it is not my purpose to tell you
unless you drive me. If you should—deisuil, deisuil!—incur the
anger of the most potent gods, ruin would not fall only on
yourself it would fall on them. Your sister has borne a male
child to be your heir. Your wife has borne you royal sons and
you have the children of other loves. I will not ask you to
picture your wife's body stricken by disfiguring disease, your son
Uirgain mutilated in battle, the child afflicted so that you
would be ashamed to call the thing your heir."

. . . His mother and Roith were still gazing at him anxiously. His sister busy with her colours still was teasing all
three: "He needs a war to take his attention up! When his
fighting is over he does not know what to do. Maybe the
coming of these men, as far as they have come, will be pro-
vocation for a war next year, and you will make a complete end
of that wretched Connal."

XXXII

THE River ran swift and sparkling in the sunshine. The King, riding up its course with Nechtan and Urpant and the Circind men, was for a moment distracted from his vexed thoughts by it. He longed briefly for his boyhood when he could kick off his sandals and wade into it upon the smooth slippery stones. Time was when he knew every deep and every shallow, and the salmon lurking in its brown pools. Urpant, whose home was on the River Tay, was speaking about the fish there and he listened with what patience he could muster. So broad and swift the River ran here who would say it went in its higher reaches through those dark woods that made its waters black as jet?

He paused to look over at the opposite bank where were the river lodges, small holiday houses which in these later years he had been too busy to enjoy. They stood in shelter of the long sandy ridge which in far distant ages, tradition said, the old gods had placed in the middle of the fertile River valley. He pointed it out to his guests. But soon they left houses and ridge behind and took the slope rising to the moor.

In a little they would gain the crest of it, and then suddenly, he knew, suddenly the Long Loch would flash upon the sight like a vision, stretching herself long and slim between the hills, her end lying in mists as if at the end of the world. So he had thought as a boy; now as a man he knew the truth and it was still more full of wonder—the Loch ended in the Western Territory where people remote from himself in speech and custom nevertheless knew his name and called him Lord. He had taken Roith from there.

Fronting the beauty of the long expanse of water was a shrine, set in a circle of ancient stones, for countless generations in awe and reverence had worshipped here. But Drost of Circind was saying eagerly, " Where will their camp be? When

140

shall we see them?" and the High King determined not to stop
to turn in there but to go on, ride fast down to loch level and
once and for all see those clerics and have done.

He could not believe his horse was slowing his pace, still
less that it was his own hand that was reining him in. Nechtan
and Talorg had galloped on before him, ignorant of his check-
ing pace. Angry as if at a servant's disobedience he reproved
himself for leaping to the ground. . . . Drost caught his reins
from him, astonished, "Excellency?" . . . He saw his own feet
going straight over a field and could not stop them, could only
mutter a prayer of contrition at his treading upon the rising
grain. He felt his followers' perplexed gaze, but he left them
behind. He went faster as he got nearer to the little grove of
trees that hid the shrine.

But he knew he could do no other. He raised his head to
look for the Archdruid. There he stood, indeed, in the entrance
of the shrine between the two upright stones. The stones were
carved in patterns in honour of the central figure, the Boar,
his own ancestral emblem. He was afraid, he felt himself to
be a stranger, though he could touch his own protective stones.

The Archdruid said nothing, forcing the King to speak.
And he said flippantly like a rude child, "This is as much a
surprise as a pleasure! I am glad to see your Holiness free from
duties at the College."

"Where were you going?" then the Archdruid asked.

And the King plunged into a reply without thinking further about it, the way when the hour has come a man plunges
into batttle. "I am going to see from a distance those men
of Eire we have spoken about."

"From a distance! Do you dare to stand and tell me lies?
I forbade you to answer their message. Now the High King
takes an answer himself."

"I had not intended to meet them or to speak."

"You are telling me a lie, and it is not worth your while;
for I see your heart. You were going with those that would
speak."

"Why may I not receive them?"

"Suffice it that I your adviser and priest decide against it."

"I must decide for myself!"

Broichan turned his head away, unmoved by the King's
anger. When he next spoke it was in a calm thin tone like a
voice in the air. "I have warned you."

"You have threatened me. But I am not afraid."

"Not for yourself. Not yet. But for your family?"

"No, not for them. The gods do with us as they please, whether we do this or that. How can it offend Them that I give audience to these men? It is our tradition to honour peaceful strangers. Did not my own father come to the North as a guest, and see with what honour they received him! It is to the welcome my mother gave him that I owe my being!"

"These men are not innocent. Have you lost your reason? They come to undermine the faith of the simple people. They may already have perverted those they met on their way. They have come to teach their new religion. It is natural they should, as it should be natural for you to abhor it."

"But in the South—"

The Archdruid's voice was like a thin flame. "In the South the vengeance of the gods is already begun. Why was it that the King who shared the High Kingship with you lived after but one year? Can you tell me why he died and you lived on? Why did the paramountcy pass to the North? Your Southern land is now in peril of invasion from the Brythons south of the Sea of Fortrin, as they themselves stand in dire peril of the Saxons. Are you so blind you cannot see that the Saxons are the punishment of the gods against apostasy? But death by the sword is not the worst evil that can befall mortal men. You say you are not afraid—not of the yellow plague? The father you speak of, whose flesh you wear, he died of plague. For all his armies and his skill in swordplay he died unclean and shunned. But think of it in terms of a whole land—it has visited the far South, it has visited Strathclydd, it has visited Eire. But not your own land, not the North. Why? Why, because both King and people walked in the ancient ways, both the Land and the Land's Mate were pure of deviation in worship and belief. Here we are blessed with peace and food.

"You may fear nothing—I wonder!—for yourself or your family. But are you so base you do not fear for your Land, for the innocent men and the women and the wordless children? Will you bring famine on them, the wailing of mouths that crave food, the agony of mothers who cannot feed their young, or floods, or the Saxons in their savage cruelty, or filthiness of plague? You do not know what you do, you who know only death in war! The gods who bless your land can curse it too."

" I have done no wrong," the King said gasping, " No
wrong yet. Only in my desire—I do not know why I so much
wanted to see these strangers."

" But I know! It is a new kind of warfare by Dalriada.
Because you stopped them from stealing away your land, and
drove them back, and crushed their nationhood and degraded
their king, they are planning a most secret and cunning vengeance. They cannot send against you armed men, so they are
sending influences, spirits of the air, that have invaded even the
very thoughts of your mind. They are working to bring down
on you the displeasure of the gods, and with you to destroy all
your broad lands. They would make you the agent of your own
doom—O Brude, the instrument of your people's! You would
be shamed through all your lives, the shaming of Connal would
be as nothing to it."

Now the King sank down upon his knees, bowing his face
on the palms of his hands. " Intercede for us! Placate the gods
for me. If you have any love or pity for me do not take the glory
from my Land! Do not let them bring famine or plague on my
people. I will do anything."

" Then turn your horse's head, and ride home.

" They will either, when they have no message from you, give
up their project and go back where they should be, or they will
come on to your Palace. In either case you will not see or hear
them. For you will shut your gate. Shut it and bolt it. It is a
holy gate. Remember the devoted in past ages who there gave
their lives to the ground. And she whom your mother does not
name aloud, her blood is there, a potent sacrifice for she gave
youth, virginity and all. And I will call my druid priests together
— they are waiting at the palace — and we will place around
your walls the invisible Fence. No one shall come in, and woe
to him who tries to come!

" There is scarcely need for you to lock the gate at all. Only
as a sign of repentance and of new obedience, give strict orders
to all guards and gate-keepers."

The wind whistled by his ears as he rode along the river to
the palace. Nechtan and Talorg and Drost did not ride so fast
as he did.

XXXIII

FROM the ramparts of the Palace Brude looked longingly out towards the fortress that stood on the outmost spur of the opposite range of hills. Fronting the firths as the Palace itself did, and from a better point of vantage, it had been fortified by the men of old against the expected attack of the Roman legions. They raised walls of stone and lit great peat fires over them so that the stone ran together in a solid mass. There were bards' songs still of the greatness of the fires they made, the air dancing a mile away. Now, if it came to a siege — say the Saxons raided as far north as Murav — But it would be no case simply of standing a siege! They would from the two points hurl back the invader, chase them away or kill them where they stood. They would not come a second time to the citadel of Brude mac Maelchon.

The yellow plague blast the whole swarm of them, how many there were crowded all together in the courtyards so that one shouldered one and stood on the feet of another! There was no privacy anywhere. Their voices too! Talking, talking, talking. His inmost thoughts were like deer fleeing before the hounds of their tongues.

"Ask him if it's really true," Tarain of the Orc Islands was saying to Uncath who was Brude's fosterbrother, a son of Maelchon by a Palace slave. "My own armour-bearer says he was told it by the chief gate-keeper himself. Stringent orders, he said, not to let anybody go out or come in. And special guard to stand by him. Now by all the dark powers what's it all about? I wanted to go hunting in the woods yonder, there's just the right kind of moon — "

"Are you talking about the orders to shut the great gate?" one of the Fortrin princes Urpant asked loudly, annoyed at their using the old language which himself could not clearly understand. "It is true. Those with homes anywhere near the Palace had permission to go to them, but for us guests, sir, it's a case of staying in. And I find I have certain business tonight. Why is it the moment a man's shut in he wants to go out as he wants nothing else at all?"

"Ask him why," Tarain urged his nephew who was half-brother to the Young Heiress, " Go on, man, ask him. Ask Brude."

" Indeed and I know better!" answered he. " Brude's in a bad mood. It's not so often that he gets into a passion, but when he does—when he puts on (deisuil!) the look his father Maelchon had!—Look now, do you see?"

Brude was in a bad mood, it was true. He could not endure them. Uncath, his fosterbrother, against whom childish resentments welled up suddenly again, and Uirgain his eldest son with his hoarse breaking voice and reedy laughter — he attended council now, swaggering before his mother Roith's admiring eyes, he would take little encouragement to air his views—and Tarain of Orc blundering up and down on the paved floor, talking about girls. By all the gods of death and life, they were like nothing so much as a bunch of horses led by their grooms up and down for exercise. He roared at a servant, watching his anxious look reflected on most of the kingly faces, and it made him feel better.

It was Nechtan of Dunduirn, husband of the Young Heiress, who saw his chance and came out with it. " The great gate is shortly to be shut, Brudean? Why and for how long? Is it a measure for testing the bolts—or is there some other reason?"

The King looked stonily at him. " The order comes from the Archdruid. Do you care to ask his Holiness about it?"

"Ah, that's another thing I want to know," Orc said, leaning on the young man's shoulder, his breath in his ear, " Why's the Archdruid at the Palace again today, and a host of the College with him? It's like a grove at time of festival. I must say I find it cheerier without so many men of religion."

Brude walked rapidly away, before he should say or do anything unworthy of kingship. He looked over the wall towards the fortress again, trying to keep his mind away from the present time and place. They had fortified the rock yonder against the Romans, and the Romans never came . . . The men's voices were like hornets, buzzing, buzzing.

" Who are they, why should we be afraid of them?"

"Afraid!"

" Yes. If we shut our gate against them, and they unarmed men, there must be something about them—"

" I don't know who they are or why we should be afraid of them, if we are afraid. But it is intolerable that the life of the Palace should be disturbed for them."

"I'll call out a few men, and we'll go and cut them down."
That was Tarain!

"No! No!" Nechtan cried, and with him in one breath most of the Southern princes, Talorg and Drostan and Urpant. "No! Never! They are holy men."

"We should not only spare them, we should receive them with honour. We should be going out now to meet them and bring them in. That is the way in the South."

"I tell you what it is," Uncath was menacing the Southerners, "You people are too close to the Banag Hills to have much notion of where you belong. You get yourselves muddled up with all the bits of nations round about you. I think you lack loyalty to our Alban land."

"That's it. They have thrown over our mothers' faith for the new religion. Nechtan, the father of our heir—I think we buy new blood at too high a price."

And now, Brude said to himself, as he heard Nechtan's furious cry, we shall have a killing on our hands, here in the very courtyards of the Palace, and my sister will mope. And he stepped towards them, watching their passions still themselves for fear of him. "My own father came from the Far South," he said to Uncath, "Keep the peace!"

He heard his son Uirgain's uncertain voice raised even while he was speaking, "Let's have them in! Why don't we have them in? Don't you remember when we had in Connal? Let's have Connal's holy men in!"

Tarain shouted, "There are enough druids around. We have our own druids. Who'll come out with me, and catch them as they come, and make an end of them?"

"I'll make an end of you first! I will not see it done. Come to me, all who—"

They will fight in the Palace of my realm! Brude said to himself. They will split the Land. Ah! Now I see it was good advice I had from my Archdruid. This is a trick of Connal. If those men come in here they will divide us like a watershed.

And at thought of such craft and daring his anger came up over him like a tide of fire, it was like battle fury. Yet when he spoke to his vassal kings his voice was calm. "Do not mind me! Brawl in my presence! I thought the council might have tired you, but you have women's tongues! The great gate is being shut now, there is nothing to say about it. And you will remain inside with as much grace as you please."

XXXIV

"NOW then, come in if you're coming," the gateman said to the pedlars. "For we're shutting this up in a minute."

"Shutting up the great gate? Now? And why?"

"It's the High King's gate, isn't it? And he has the best right to say when it's to be shut, hasn't he?"

"Holy fire, what are you shutting it up for at this time of day? It wants two hours of sunset."

"That's the King's business. The Palace is his. And if he wants it stood on its head or tumbled into the River, it's for him to say. Don't you stand there giving lip about the High King, but come in if you want to yourself and all your rubbish. Come on in."

"Rubbish!" they said bridling, "Here's silks from Gaul and over the great mountains—brought here through all the storms of the sea, and carried north — beautiful stuff that none but a High King should look at, and he calls it rubbish! Whoever heard of shutting up the great gate of a palace in broad daylight?"

The gateman and his assistant pressed on the lever, and the gate went slowly slowly on its grooves. The pedlars lifted in their stuff, with an oath as one of the halves of the gate bruised a bale of cloth. "It's a time of peace, isn't it? Nothing's happened suddenly, has it? Aren't all the kings at peace? Never a trace of a marching army did we see on our journey and we've come from Dumpelder and the Fortrin Sea."

"I daresay not," replied the gateman, running his hand lovingly over the iron studded face of the gate, "I daresay you have noticed nothing at all. A land may look safe and snug, and a war be going on below the surface. There's folks about that badly want to get in here, folks that have little business with us, folks our High King is not going to see. What do I mean? Lord

147

of Light, it's not to talk politics or druidcraft I'm paid for! Uinguist! Come and lend us a hand. The bolts are too heavy for me to push in alone, though time was — There's important people within, kings from south and north and the Isles, a nice batch of royalty here for council. And we've to guard them from dangers you might well be unable to see."

"You are great people for magic," one of the pedlars grumbled, smoothing the injured bale. "I thought this gate of yours needed no bolting. It's what once you told me."

"It's true of it today," Uinguist pressed forward to tell them, "For besides its ancient power — the holy ones that gave their life to the ground — it is most strongly fenced by our Archdruid and by all his druids of the College; they have said Words and set their symbols over it; it is so sure today that never a bolting would it need."

"Hurry you up!" the gateman cried, "Do you want to get us into trouble? I had such orders from his Holiness and from the King! Go you along, and sell your stuff if you can. It might be a good time for you, seeing they will want to take presents home."

"We do our best trade with the women," the pedlars said, "We'll go along to the grianan, shall we, as we always do?"

"Not to the Old Heiress!" the gateman called after them, "Not today. And not the King's wife, and not the young Princess — They are not in the mood. It's like as if we were all expecting a thunderstorm. Best sell your cheaper stuff, if you have any, to the attendants and retinues. I'll give you a hen and her twelve chicks for a mantle-length."

The pedlars made their way over the paved courtyards, peering down the alleys and into a doorway or two, but too uncertain to shout their wares. As they went they heard the squeaking of the bolts in the staples of the great gate.

The
Opening

XXXV

THEY had come to the head of the Loch. Passing the bay where the shore was broad and rosy with its granite stones they had come to the narrow part from which the River ran eastwards to Brude's capital. They had thought they might be intercepted at the dun which commanded the head, but they set their camp by the houses there and lived ten days, and were not molested. Not much encouraged either! For they saw the sun rise and set over the alien land, ten times, and yet there was no word sent, in answer to Colum's letter, from the High King. Those of the people who came near enough for them to speak to could not or would not understand their speech. To any question of the King or of the propriety of approaching him there was never an answer.

When they had rolled up their rugs and taken up their book satchels, and were ready to push off, they found themselves stealing one last look back over the way they had come. South-westward through the gap of hills lay Dalriada where their own tongue was spoken, and Lismor with its green slopes and quiet busy days, and Eire over the sea. Eire! It was like looking back at life, painful and sweet and never dearer than when men have to be leaving it   But westwards behind them, above all, were the steadfast prayer and the strong faith; and they felt less alone.

The first reach of the River was a long pool. Here the water was dark and still, untroubled by waves but awful in its mystery and quietude. There were no houses here, only trees, willow and alder by the water's edge, but above them oak and hazel; and as they rowed by they looked up a clearing and saw on the crest of land a circle of stones and the domed roof of a shrine. And they saw two pale-robed men standing as if watching them, and they could not forbear to cross themselves.

For they heard a sound like incantation. But as, teeth set, they rowed on they found it was the singing of the River that opened out of the pool and began to run bright and restless over

151

its stones. Its currents caught them. They were shaken and drenched with flung spray. "It's dangerous," Lugne at the rudder gasped, "Father, shall we pull for the bank and see if we can go on on foot?"

The curragh reeled and shipped water. "The current is too swift! We shall founder."

"Oh no! Not till we have seen this King!" Colum said clapping him on the shoulder. "Ease your stroke," he said to Diarmaid and one of Cannich's men. "You can have a holiday and let the river take us."

They looked at him with mingled relief and resentment. He was almost ashamed at the surge of joy in his heart. His desire rushed onwards like the curragh on the River. This River was racing to the Eastern Sea where lay conflict, agony, encounter. He sat crouched in the bowsprit, and the shed water leapt up into his face and helped to hide its jubilation.

People stood along the River brink watching them. But what struck their eyes with a shock of excitement was a seagull hovering white in the air. The sea, and the High King's dun, and for good or ill their journey's end.

And now rounding a curve of the broad swift river they were coming to cultivated land on either side, green with rising grain. They passed houses that had nets and fishing tackle at the doors, and men busy with them, and they wondered if they would be hailed or called to stop. But no one checked their course, and the River took them on with it. The fields spread out broad on the left hand against a spur of hills, broken only by a high mound shaped like a longship. And had they had leisure they would have greatly admired the beauty of that fertile plain. Colum's heart beat an insistent rhythm within him, "When shall I see a church go up? When shall I see a church here?" And looking at Cannich and Comgal he saw his longing mirrored in their faces.

It was when they came to a very rapid part of the River where its waters divided to form islands, swirling between, that the scent of peat smoke thickened in the air, and they knew they were approaching a township. Then as they rounded that curve they saw men and women crossing on a ford, some riding, some in chariots, many on foot; and as they neared the ford they drew in to the right bank where a paved road ascended a gentle slope at the end of the long ridge.

As they beached the curragh a voice spoke in Colum's ear, and looking sidelong up without moving his head he saw their one friend from Airdchartan. "Do not look at me, and do not speak. Those to whom I gave your letter delivered it. But it is of no good your going on." He passed into the crowds — the crowds who were eyeing them, but in such silence it was as if they had come to a town of the dumb. It was more terrifying than anything to read a sort of expectancy in the pallid faces, with here and there on a woman's face a sort of pity.

But they made their curragh fast, and left it, and picked up the books and the abbots' staffs; and then on the smooth road they saw their own feet walking, gaping sandals and all. As the way ascended they saw down the course of the River they had left to the small blue shimmer of the sea. Then as it still ascended they drew in their breaths for below them on the left hand opened the linked firths and then the widening mouth of the Eastern Sea. And before them looking over it the high walls and towers of the great Palace, with shouts of guards in the air and sounds of trumpets from a hosting ground somewhere below. And in the summer sunshine they were cold.

They saw their feet going on, step after step. The people were coming to the doors of their houses lining the royal way. They nudged each other, pointed, grimacing with eagerness as people do who settle to listen to a good tale. They saw their own feet going on, step after step of the smooth way.

The way ran straight up to a gateway, the only opening in the high wall.

And the gates were shut, quite shut: one with the wall. The wood was patterned all over with ironwork, the sun made it glitter. And they might have admired the beauty of it, if it had not stood obdurate to their entry.

The eyes of watchers multiplied around them, some closing in at a distance behind them muttering what seemed like threats in their older language. But for the most part the people were still, watching in silence, and the air was still as it is still before the breakng of a thunderstorm.

"Father!" Diarmaid said on a gasp, "They have seen us from the ramparts. I think they have barred the gates against us."

"What shall we do now? Can we turn and go back—"

"We'll go on till we stand at the gates. If we get in it must be God's doing not our own."

And there were their feet walking towards the shut gates.

Walk with us, Ciaran: walk with us, Brendan: Finbar, Moluag, Ninian and his master Martain! Walk with us, Jesus our Lord, put foot on the earth again. Walk with us now, walk with us.

The feet walking, and the shut gates.

XXXVI

THE swineherd and the mason of the Palace sat holding their ribs with their hands, comfortably looking down the slope of the royal hill. It was safe enough in the open, and there was plenty of company for the road was thronged. It was better than the best bard's tale to see the strangers come as they had been expecting. The swineherd thoughtfully gave a call to his womenfolk, and they came out, even to the bondslave carrying the youngest of the children; and the neighbours hearing their excited voices came out of their houses too.

The strangers came slowly, so that the time was nice and long. They were tired, just as if they had been up all night with the beasts or working night and day to finish a guesthouse for sudden use. Their feet were as dusty and their faces as white as any man's in Alba. It was interesting to observe their odd cut of hair, rather like a druid's (deisuil!) only with some difference. They wore no jewels, which would have been dull if it had not been so unusual. But they carried satchels of hide slung on their shoulders—and if there are spells being made, let us go back at once into our houses, and cover the child's face from them, for it is beautiful.

They did not seem much put out by the staring and the muttering — had they some secret power? — But the short man had a kindly face, as he glanced this way and that at the watching people: though for the most part all of the holy strangers kept their eyes on the ground.

What was so exquisitely pleasant, a thing to roll in the mind, was that they were gazing down at the road before them, surely expecting to find an open gate. And the gates were shut! As shut as they could be . . . Shut in every way, seen and unseen. It was delicious and very like a bard's tale, known already but enjoyed afresh in the telling, to see the shut gates on the one hand and the hopeful men on the other.

What will they do when they see the shut gates? Will they falter and turn away before going right up to them? Will they go right up, and knock — and knock and knock? Will they speak to us, ask any of us to help them to gain admittance? What will we do if they ask our aid? Cry out at them, they are unwelcome to our King, that they are all against them, all the powers of the Palace, and the holy Grove, that they will be lucky to get home with their lives!

Tell them that with our hands! Fall upon them! Fall upon them with swords and knives if we have them, or with pitchforks and hammers and with clubs, with anything. Their lives are as little worth as a puff of smoke in the air, rising from my kitchen. No question will be asked concerning their deaths, no reckoning to druid or chief. They are strangers, far far from home, kingless and undefended.

Their hands groped for weapons, their mouths lengthened; but they did not interrupt their trance-like stare.

It was a thing to take in the breath for, that first smiting of the strangers' eyes by the shut gates. Shut! Stay out! You are despised, hated. You will not enter here. The strangers stopped on the track, and turned as if to take counsel with one another. The younger ones behind looked into the faces of the older three. When they looked at the crowds now it was with eyes that had no hold, as men's eyes stare unseeing when they are deep in thought. Then one, the tallest, with the bright hair, stepped on and his companions and their attendants followed on close to him. They came on their way as if nothing were there to discourage them. Yet the gates were shut. What would they do? What? Unless their power were supreme.—

Pigeons sat on the top of the gateway, preening their radiant feathers, their voices so soft as to add silence to the silent air. Quiet and undisturbed they sat preening their feathers, after their little diet of scattered grain.

The strangers had reached the gates. They stepped right up to them, then the tall one traced some symbol in the air, and laid his hand on the face of the gates and pushed gently, as if it were the door of a friend.

Then suddenly the birds were all up in the air. And the silence was rent by the crash of great bolts going back, one and another. Before the incredulous eyes of the Palace servants the gate swung slowly back. A vista of the courtyard showed in the space, blue sky and part of a wall and the paved floor.

156

The men and women and children ran back into their houses, huddling far from the door. A few bolder ones, however, advanced to the gaping gateway and peered in. One or two even made bold to enter, but it was not long before they were out again and leaping for their houses. They shook their heads for only answer to those that questioned them. When they got their breath back they tried to tell: " The Archdruid himself—quite near — I saw his face. But I am not to blame! I have done nothing. It was with the strangers he was angry, with them surely? Only with them?"

XXXVII

THEIR eyes could see nothing for a while. They were
blinded by the sudden change from sunshine to shade,
their minds dazed with the suddenness of their own
entry. The shaft of light from the open gateway shone
on a house, revealed a bronze Eye over the door. Then it faded.
The gate had been hastily swung back again, the gatekeepers
standing with arms spread over it, holding the huge bolts,
wailing like women at a burial.

There was a commotion of people. Shapes moved in the
dimness, only gradually becoming clear as men, soldiers and
servants, noblemen and slaves, and women too. They ran out
from doorways, they swirled round, advancing then retreating
into the lanes between the houses. It seemed unreal, dreamlike.
Almost the monks had to overcome a lassitude, unable to act
or think.

"Where is the King?" then Colum called in a loud voice,
changing the human patterns of movement, for many wheeled
round where they stood. A kind of silence fell and he seized
his chance and called loudly again. "Where is the High King?"
There were so many men of noble rank, with torques and
jewelled belts and coloured clothing.

But though they began to shout to each other, asking
questions in anger or dismay, none paid any attention to his
question. And they swirled round, keeping their faces to the
strangers but not answering him.

One nobleman, burly and tall, of ferocious aspect, caught
Colum's questing eye. Could this be Brude? But when he
called, "Are you the High King?" the man stepped back,
answered in the tongue not known to the monks, and violently
shook his head.

Then out from the crowd came a young boy with a thin gold
coronet on his dark red hair. Leaning forward to them, his

jaw outthrust, his lips pouting as if to spit on them, he mocked
them in a high unstable voice in the language they knew.
"Beggars! Royal men in broken shoes! Envoys from Connal!
Do you think anyone will take you to the presence of the High
King Brude?"

Through his cackling laughter a woman's voice cried, "Take
care, Uirgain! Take care. Come back from them." But he
laughed shrilly and went on shouting in his voice that went up
and down, "Look at them in the court dress of Dalriada! These
are Dunadd fashions." And grown men joined in the laughter,
"Are they Connal's soldiers, do you think? His bodyguard? The
spoilers will not find much on them."

Their laughter brought others round. From lanes and doorways they came to join the crowds in the courtyard. How shall
we ever find the High King?

There was one house, with the symbol of a wild boar above
its door, and it was guarded by ten men with spears at the
ready. Colum made his way over to it as best he might. As he
got near it men dressed differently from all the others sprang up
in his path, men in pale robes with coloured collars and with
tonsured heads. The druids of Alba. Comgal and Cannich put
their arms over the bent heads of their boys. Colum went on
to the doorway signing it with the cross, inwardly imploring.
One of the druids in that unknown tongue called sharply out to
the guards who trained their spears on him. There was a whistling sound as the crowd of warriors behind them drew their
swords from their sheaths. The monks stood stockstill waiting
for them to fall.

But in the doorway of the King's house a man stood. The
elevation of three steps made him visible, with his broad
shoulders and dark red hair. His voice called a command.
Swords were sheathed though a low grumbling of balked
warriors followed the action. Through the low hum could be
heard the voice now shrill, now gruff, of the mocking boy. The
King in the doorway made a small gesture with his left hand,
and the voice ceased.

"Give me audience!" Colum cried, "I have come to make
request." But already, like a foreglimpse of a birth not yet
accomplished, the High King had withdrawn out of sight. A
company of druids now stood around the door defending and
hiding him. They too vanished. The doorway stood empty. The
armed guards alone stood motionless on either side of it.

The crowd were moving back, deep silence had followed the din, and stillness the swirling movement.

A steward came towards them, speaking slowly in the language of Eire. "Tell me what you seek here?"

"I seek audience with the High King Brude mac Maelchon."

"You may not approach him now. He is busy. But His Excellency says, you may stay this night in the Palace. I am come to lead you to your appointed guest house."

"A strange bed we shall have," Lugne sobbed through his teeth, then made to smile as Cannich wryly agreed, "And maybe a cold one. But we shall sleep in God's hands."

They followed the High King's steward to a guest house lower on the royal hill. Shaken with confusion, dazed themselves at the apparently miraculous entry, as well as oppressed by the hatred and danger, they knelt on the stone floor. Even the peering of eyes through the window and doorway could not stop them from satisfying their hunger for prayer.

XXXVIII

THE two attendants peered in at a chink in the guest house door. Then they threw the door open and tossed their armfuls of rugs in the direction of the beds. As they blundered away back down the alley they ran right into the water carriers. "Will you look what you're doing?" one of these cried in natural exasperation. "What way is this to behave in the palace of the Paramount King?"

"Wet to the skin!" lamented the other. "As if it isn't enough to be told to carry—"

"Wheesht you, keep quiet," cried one of the guest house attendants, "Am I not wet too?"

"That's some comfort. Lucky for yourselves it was not this fellow you ran into." For along the alley came a slave with a brazier. "It would have been a lesson to you if you singed your silly legs."

"All very well for you to complain. You haven't been to the guest house."

"Why? What are they doing? What happened to you? Was it fear drove you?"

There was no answer. "Come on, tell us! What did they do to scare the pair of you?"

"Just go yourselves and see. You have to give them water to wash their travel off, haven't you? Go in with it, then you'll see."

"You'll have to tell us what to expect."

"No. You go on. We'll see if you'll come out so quiet and nice."

"What's this all about?" asked the slave with the brazier. His hands were beginning to shake, and the fragments of glowing charcoal spilled out of it. "It isn't fair scaring the wits out of a man, and I'm in a bad way as it is, for I've been hearing the questioning of the gatekeepers . . . May the gods I have served, my mother's gods, preserve me, deisuil! Are they raving? And will I get drawn in?"

"Raving? No. Quiet as mice. Kneeling upon their knees and as still as thieves."

"In a trance, is it?"

"A trance maybe. Glad am I not to have to go in there again."

"Clear the way, will you?" cried two food servers who now came on the scene. "What's the crowd for? As if it isn't hard enough to carry platters all this way—"

"Who's harming you?—Is this the supper they're to have? God of Light, here's a lovely feast. Are they giving them all this because they've appetites more than mortal men? I would not dare, would I, to—?"

"Keep your hands off! Hindering us in the serving."

"Go on," they all said politely. "Let us not hinder you. Go you on; the rest of us will come after you and see. We'll see if they can eat like men although they came through the shut gates."

"Deisuil! Don't speak of that."

"It was all eye tricking anyway. Aren't the holy druids going throughout the Palace explaining it? They only seemed to come through, if I understood it. It was all a bit of tricking."

"Maybe it's tricking then that they're in the guest house where we've just been? We'll come up softly now behind you, and we'll see what happens when you go in with the meal."

"By all the gods my mother loved," said one of the water carriers. "If it's water to wash them they want they can fetch it themselves. I'll leave it outside the door."

"That's it," said the slave with the brazier, "I'll leave my fire outside too. One of us can raise a shout to tell them it's there. What need in any case have they of fire who have most likely the heat of the Sun Himself running in their veins?"

"We won't disturb them either," the food servers then said. "It may not be to their liking and it may only anger them. We poor folk get it always, every way. It's holy druids should be ministering to the like of them, if you ask me what I think."

"Man, they're too busy consulting all together. Making up strong prayers and spells they are for the protection of the palace. And indeed we have need. For if we're scared of these foreign men of science when they are in one place quiet together, what will it be when they take it into their heads to walk here and there? Coming upon us when we are asleep, when we least expect them."

XXXIX

I F the evening were fair or ill Brude did not see. He sat still
in his private room, his hands grasping his knees; and his
doorway was guarded, his sentries with spears at ready. It
was great peace to be here, unapproachable, alone.
He had escaped the women, his wife Roith's wild arms clinging and his sister's swift torrents of speech; even his mother the
Old Heiress, he had eluded her and seen her go to restore order
in the clamorous grianans. He wanted none of them, though
a woman's flesh might comfort.

He had half a mind to send for Nechtan, but he had seen
Nechtan from his window, walking like a drunk man round and
round, babbling of impiety and casting furious looks at any of
the Northern kings. They were all astir in the courtyards and
alleys of the palace, moving restlessly, wrangling bitterly. He
was well off here. Yet it was not wrangling men he had fled
from but from—from—from astonishment that had struck him
like a blow. It was the druids who had covered his retreat,
closing in behind him, impelling him down the passage to this
remote place, guarding the passage after him; as a bodyguard in
stress of battle set their shields above their king's head.

In the dim light he sat playing chess with his attendant
slave, a red headed fellow like himself, one whose virtue apart
from a knowledge of the game was an ability to keep silent and
still. They played a dull slow game, and the King's hands shook
on the board chinking the jewelled chessmen.

There was an unfamiliar sound in the air. He frowned
trying to catch the drift of it, what it meant. He got up and
went to his door, throwing it open, startling the sentries.
Clear light flowed from the passage into the room, illuminating
the gold-embroidered hangings that curtained the round wall,
touching with brightness the polished bronze water jar. The
sound was still in the air, and louder. The words he could not

discern, but the cadences — he remembered the scent of whin and saw suddenly before his mind's eye the small shrine at Arbirlot, the priests of the new religion that Drostan had taken him to hear. After their service they had been presented to him —or he to them was it? Such love, such veneration, shone in Drostan's face when he looked at them. And once in Fortrin—

It must be the stranger monks praying! God of Light, here in his own courtyards! It might be the guest house they had been put in was below this room on the slope of the hill, and the wind blowing from them to him. Or it might be they were foot-loose wandering at will — he went back into the room spreading his hands to the brazier in the middle of it.

Then he was thinking of Morpet the young druid again. Warming his mind, as the brazier's glow warmed his hands, came Morpet's well remembered but half understood words. *God is one, and benign. Light is so powerful it is not worth a man's while to think of the dark gods at all. Not by rebirth, in some unrealised kingdom, but now, now in this life, one can enter a life where joy does not come to an end.* Morpet is dead. I shall never again hear him call eagerly, "Where is the King?" But someone is calling me—

Now into the air came another, more familiar sound: the druid call to prayer at moonrise. "Come, come, men and women. The moon will appear." The hymn swelled into full volume, so fraught with holy associations for him that he raised his two hands in a little worship in the close room. Loud it swelled.— Loud, loud, till it filled all his brain. "You may shut the door," he said to the slave. But even when the door was shut he heard the druid hymn.

When they paused, changing the mode, he heard again the chanting of the stranger priests. How could the sound be as loud as this? Is he making his way to me? He is fighting his way through all my men, not through my guards but through my druids? He still cries out, "Where is the King?" and he means to find me.

How else in this remote and enclosed room could he hear so clearly, not the sound of one set of voices but both! When one paused the other came through. It was a battle of sounds, a battle of wills.

A battle of wills in me! The King walked fretfully round the brazier, irked by the narrowness of the room. A battle of desires, a battle of beliefs.

He tipped the water jar over the cup and drank the last drops, and still his throat was dry. His mind was a battlefield over which two armies made their attacks. First he heard the sound of the druid hymn and then the Christian, and he did not know whether the sounds were in the air or only in his mind.

"Keep the door guarded, let me not be taken by surprise," he bade the slave. "I will stay and sleep the night here."

And when the fellow had spread the rugs and cushions he lay down and kept still. But the slave on the floor at his feet was sleeping before he could sleep.

The King, sleeping now and the more deeply for his long waking, rose on an elbow. The slave was quiet at his feet, but someone else was in the room. Still half asleep out of the depth of dreaming he said confused things: "Forgive me. Do not misjudge us when you speak of it in your land." But waking properly he found he was being scrutinised by the Archdruid, and he exclaimed in dismay at the white drawn face. "These agents of Dalriada, these practisers of an alien religion, these Christian clerics—will you lie here and permit them to wander at will over the Palace? They are speaking to our people. It is those Southern kings—but more than one of the Northern kings and chiefs have sought them out. Are you content to lie here?"

"O," said the King with a contemptuous look, "It was you yourself who bade me retire here. I have long since given up the leadership."

"Why did you in the first place let them in? Put them out!" He could say no more for gasping. The slave had risen to his knees, his mouth wide open with fright.

"I cannot put them out if I have let them in. It would be inhospitable."

"You did not let them in. They came in, forcing their way."

"That is just it. They forced a way in, the gods know how They have power above our power."

"They have power! What do you, a mere fighting man, know of such things?"

"I think they have great power. For I gave orders for the gates to be closed and bolted, and yet these clerics came in, as easily as a girl comes through the curtain of the grianan. How? How?"

"There is an explanation, though it is not flattering to the King. The gates were locked——"

" And guarded."

"And guarded; if you will. But were your guards guarded? Who had access to the guards the morning of yesterday?"

The slave was sobbing, crouched with his head between his knees. Brude went over to him, and pushed him with the side of his foot towards the door. He said to the Archdruid, "I was not there to see."

"I have had the guards tortured again. And they reveal that the bolts had been interfered with."

"Men in pain will say anything."

"Why then did you believe them the first time?"

The King shrugged. He gathered together his chess men and rattled them between his two hands. Broichan watched him, drawing rapid breaths as if to speak. Brude thrust the chess men into the slave's hands and pushed him out of the door, he shut it behind him and returned to the Archdruid's side. He said calmly, "The fact remains, the men got in. And now that they are in I must let them stay. It was, when all is said, a victory for them. One has to abide by the code of fighting men."

The Archdruid's jaw trembled. "You talk like a boy. You think like a boy. Have you no sense of responsibility and you a grown man? These priests constitute the direst peril to our state. Will you the High King and Guardian of the people smile at it? If you are so concerned for your kingly honour, then the reception they have already had here is enough. They will have spent a night here, fed and sheltered by a gentle king, one with a high sense of honour truly, perhaps too high for his Land's good. Now let them go, unscathed if you will; but they will go without seeing the face of the High King, and they will go at the earliest light, now, with no further delay. The eyes of the Bright One, the Holy, must not see them here; no more alien prayers and hymns will rise on the wind to anger the gods we worship. Brude mac Maelchon, are you not afraid? Where is the insight that recently made you realise their coming is a danger to Alba? You have fallen away from the obedience you showed. Brude, are you not afraid?"

The King went from him, stepping slowly over the paved floor, looking at his feet.

The Archdruid said softly, "You are never so taken by their spells, surely, as to think you can afford not to be afraid? For the sake of the Land and its peace—"

The King looked at him, and he said nothing, but made a tiny movement of the head as if one part of him would say, " I am not afraid."

Broichan smoothed the rugs on the bed, making them neat in the manner of a woman. " In any case," he said after that pause, " They themselves do not wish to stay. They declare they wish to go north to Dornaig. Do they imagine they will find flourishing Christian churches up and down our Northern domain? Anyhow, let them go if so they wish."

" One of them, Colum mac Felim, desires first to speak with me. I said on the —— the occasion of their coming in that I would give him audience. That I must do."

" Let him go north first, on his way back he may speak with you."

" I do not wish to offend you, Master. But I will have it the other way round."

" Brude!" the Archdruid cried out as if the King had struck him. " My dear!" then he said, " Do you not understand? They are setting you and me against one another. Why did you not let your guards cut them down? " The rushlight was paling in the faint light of day that had found its way into the shut room. King and druid stared at one another. " I do not know," Brude sighed. " It would have saved some trouble, I will allow. I could not, that is all. They had something about them that charmed me. There was no need for any further spell. In any case, I left them to your Holiness. I took it for your business. The gates had your fencing over them. I know you had all the druids of the grove and Palace consulting on it, you should have made it strong. Why when they made to open the gates did you not intervene?"

" I will intervene when I choose, when the gods tell me the time has come. And when the time comes for their destruction these clerics may well wish they had been cut down! "

" Let me give audience to this Colum. He comes on some personal errand, with some request. I will hear it, whether or not I will accede to it."

"Very well, Brudean, very well. You may give your letter writer audience. But I shall be present with you. And you will admit him to your presence alone, without friend or even such retinue as he has with him. He is Connal's cousin, and you will make him stand before your royal seat."

" But he came in through our gates——"

"Think no more about that!"

"They say he is a great man in his own land."

"He has left his own land. His land is Dalriada now, the land of your foes. Perhaps it is good that you should see him waiting. He must show meekness, it is enjoined on his kind. He must come and stand in all humility before you, and wait for an answer. You may amuse yourself, more than you did with Connal. O I know all about him. He is proud, and impatient too. Yes, who knows, you may do more to humble Dalriada through this Christian priest than even through their King."

XL

THEY were still at Lauds in the guest house when they heard a murmur at their door, then into the room came a palace steward, grand as a king himself in coloured robe and mantle. Speaking slowly so that they could understand he said the High King would now give audience to the man whose name was Colum. He must enter the King's presence alone without any of the rest as retinue.

"No! Not alone! Either we go, father, or you stay with us here. We may as well stay here, what can they do worse than kill us?"

"Father, at least you shall not go without me."

But Colum with rueful smile undid the fingers of Diarmaid from his grey habit, and spoke to his young attendants. "My sons, have you so soon forgotten the deliverance of God? If He opened the way for us through the gate, He can preserve us now we are within." And he bowed to the blessing of Cannich and Comgal, and to the younger men who stood with moving lips to see him go . . .

Along the corridor were doors of little chambers. At more than one, as he passed, he saw a man stand, prince or palace official, from this or from other provinces he did not know. They watched him pass in silence with neither greeting nor taunt, their eyes dwelling on him. And he wondered in that rich land at such hunger in men's eyes.

Over the High King's door stood his emblem of the Boar and the crossed slanting rods that were symbol of his state. The door opened, and he went walking up the council chamber till he stood before a figure seated on a raised throne. The man he had only glimpsed before in the dream-like time after their entry, him he now saw clear. Brude mac Maelchon was a man in his prime, about his own age maybe; broad if perhaps not very tall,

169

with powerful arms lying on the supports of the throne. His head held high on his thick neck had hair the colour of bronze, greying at the sides. His eyes, sober, aloof, regarded the incomer. There was no other person in the great room; only at the right side of the throne stood a screen of silverwork over crimson silk, and there was a hint of someone or some persons behind it, hidden advisers of the King.

Colum made a sign of blessing with his right hand. But the King on the throne did not rise and kneel as Ainmir, as Donal of Ailech, as Connal would have done. True, he started in his seat, but he sat still thereafter and did not even incline his head. So, without reverence done him, Colum made his own reverence to the King, bowing his head to the slayer of Gauran. Blood rushed to his face, burning, burning. Burning memories rushed into his mind. Lluan grief-crazed, children coughing in the night, and men disputing with dogs over a morsel of bread.

It was an obeisance which he found costly, yet the King took it with indifference. He spoke abruptly, in a deep voice: "You have a petition. Is it from Connal?"

"It is my own. I have come to ask you, Gentle King, for a small island off the great Isle of Mula."

"That is Connal's land, and Connal's affair. Ask him."

"I have asked him. I have his consent."

"Then why do you trouble me?"

All the hunger and homelessness of the journey, uncertainty, dread of failure, and the keen eating care on account of the men who had come with him — all of that added themselves to the burden of discouragement and of shame. He forced the words out: "I must ask you, for you are our overlord. Without your permission I cannot hold the Island secure."

"What right have you to hold it in the first place?"

This was the room, with its glowing curtains and screens, its beautiful carvings, this was the room where Connal was shamed. It had been full enough that day with men, for Brude's warriors had crowded to it to witness their enemy's degrading; the corridor was lined with laughing men who saw him go in a king and come out a fourth grade prince. Connal had told him, gasping for breath, his words heavy with pain. But he prayed for quietness, no anger. And he said, patiently, ' No more right maybe than mortal man has to anything. It is the burial isle of a line of kings, and a settlement of Oran, a Christian priest."

At that the King called out loudly, "If you are going to speak of religious matters!" He half rose from his seat. From the screen beside him came a pale sleeve; a pale wrinkled hand was laid upon his arm. And he turned his head a little as if to hear words softly spoken for his ear. Then he said, calm again, contemptuous, "How can you hope that I will grant anything to my country's foe?"

Then Colum answered, "It seems strange indeed. Yet I have come from far in hope of it. Far indeed! Far not only from peace and safety, but from dignity. May Christ my Lord hold me."

He said in the few words he could muster, cheerfully, "I think the High King must grant my petition."

There was such murmuring from behind the screen now that the King turned from his suppliant altogether to listen.

Then he turned towards him again. One would almost have thought there was a slight movement of the brawny arm that shook off the aged hand.

"You must go out of the palace, you and all your clerics. But do not go away, stay near at hand until I send you my answer."

"Sir, will you answer?"

"I will send you an answer, I swear by the word of a king." There was a movement behind the screen, seen dimly through its silk and beautiful silver patterns. "Whether it be yes or no I cannot tell you yet."

But Colum bowed, "I am content to wait."

The King rose, burly if not tall, and clapped his hands. As if out of the floor a servant appeared. "Senguist, this stranger and his company are to be given dwelling at the fishing lodge of the fourth mile."

"It is done already, Exalted One."

To the eager questions of his friends he did not know what reply to make. The King was clement, if not friendly, and seemed honourable. But of the Island, and the plight of Dalriada there was no hope yet, and no chance of his permitting Cannich and Comgal access to Dornaig, if indeed any place of Christian worship any more existed there. After the seeming miracle of their entry, delay was perplexing, but they must bear it with patience.

XLI

IT was plain that their guards were friendly towards them, their protectors not their captors. Even the roof and the walls of the river lodge seemed friendly to them, affording sanctuary from scorn and danger. There were no swords on the wall, only hunting spears and bows and fishing tackle. It was a place of leisure and peace.

The people too, who brought them their morning meal, smiled at them though warily, and spoke greetings in the speech so like their own. As they ate in the doorway they could look out and watch the journeyings of women to the nearby well, a fisher or two returning from the river with a string of fish, and they could hear the sound of children laughing and calling as they played.

After the storm, calm. After the pain of danger, the blissful relaxation of safety and rest.

But when, with a little commotion at the gate, the King's messenger entered with a summons to Colum to come and speak with the Kigh King, the spell was broken. Now into the mind crowded misgivings bred by sinister memories. They had come unbidden to a High King, alien, their enemy; they had by some sort of miracle forced a way in to him, disobeying the clear injunction of his shut gate. They had set him at odds with his Archdruid, a foe for them more formidable than any King.

The two messengers, in Palace livery and with a ring of state to prove their authenticity—it had on it the likeness of the Boar, the King's ensign—the two messengers told them that Colum was expected by the King at the Palace. They went away without offering escort, but saying the way led by the ferry across the river.

They made ready to go with Colum, tying sandals on, taking the cross and the Gospels in its satchel of hide.

They walked over meadow land, green and flowered, and approached the River where the ferry was.

But they had not reached it, not yet come within distance of its sound and glitter, when they heard shrill piping and the beat of drums, mingled with the wailing of human voices. It was a noise not tending to increase their courage. And yet to see some dramatic event is a hunger with men, and some of them were well enough content to go on and see what was afoot; in any case it lay in their way.

It was a funeral. The little company was threading its way from the River's brink, the pipes and drums leading and the mourners behind. Before the monks were near them, the people halted and, turning back towards the River, fell on their faces as if in worship. They seemed divided indeed between worship and their task of burial.

The look on their faces, when they raised their heads, was less one of sorrow than of sharp dismay. The body they had laid down was covered entirely with a deerskin, no part of it was visible.

Colum went forward and in words he had learned asked gently what person it was and how death had come. For answer, one of the Alban men pulled away the deerskin—and for all his leechcraft Colum cried out at what lay revealed. A man, young or old could not now be said so disfigured was the body, parts of it torn away, hideous, without scarcely human shape at all. The injuries seemed too awful for men to have made.

"The River!" the people kept saying, "The River!" wailing.

Dangling from the dead man's back was a hook embedded in spine and flesh. The people were trying to explain, so filled with horror now as to be indifferent to both worship or burial. The story emerged. — Fishers had seen this man swimming out to his nets in mid stream. Suddenly there was a dreadful roar. Those who stood their ground saw a—saw—saw the Spirit of the River, a fearsome monster, disclosing itself from the water. It came upon the man, and savagely gashed him with its teeth. His screams could be heard faintly through the roaring of the beast.

When the monster had gone away, after some time the man's uncle and a fisher friend of his went rowing through the water that was soiled with blood, and had hastily caught the body up with their boat hooks and dragged it after their boat to shore. Better to free the River from the pollution, some of the people said. Others said they had done wrong to disturb it in its enjoyment of blood. All were agreed they must now say special prayers to placate the god of the River if it were possible. — They turned and did obeisance again. They must bury him, quickly, quickly, they said; hide his ill-omened body from the sun. The kinsmen of the dead and his wife or mother, lamenting, begged for burial in holy ground among the ancient stones on the rising land. It was being granted, but on condition they would summon druids to cleanse this reach of the River and the houses nearby.

"Lord Abbot, we can go to the Palace by walking along the course of the River," his men said to Colum, "It may take longer, but we must walk along its course and cross at the ford at the foot of the Palace road. There are many people there, there will be do danger."

But Colum said, "The road is on the other side. It is quick walking and leads directly to the Palace. I must take the shortest way since I am summoned to Brude."

"But—cross the River at this point—?" Their faces were filled with incredulous dismay.

Even the people stayed to advise them. "Keep away from the River, if you wish to live! It may well be it was on your account the god was angry. Perhaps he made a mistake in taking this poor Uile, he took him for one of you."

"In any case, there is no boat," one of the young monks said with relief, "Our own curragh is being mended, and there is no other boat here—none except—and it is filthied with the blood—"

"There is the punt yonder, the ferry boat, we will go across in that."

"No, father. We cannot. There is no one on the other bank, the ferryman is here."

"Then it must be brought across."

There was a silence, they looked at the ferryman but he was engrossed in his prayer, his face to the ground.

Colum said softly, "You are our best swimmer, Lugne. Will you swim over and bring the ferry punt here?"

If for the time of an eyeblink Lugne paused, one could hardly tell. Quietly and without looking at the Abbot he took off his sandals and pulled his robe over his head, standing in his white inner tunic. The light breeze blew it about his knees. The next moment it clung wet upon him as he went into the River. His arms flashed pale in the broken water. Only his head raised above the level looked strong and human, the rest of him oddly weak and helpless, distorted by the current.

"It has tasted blood!" the people were whispering, "It will come again. It will come again now for his blood."

"Are you trying to placate the god? Are you giving one of your men as an expiation for Uile?" They watched, as if all eyes, the head and dim body of the swimmer.

Though they were half expecting it, it came with a suddenness that made them cry out. A huge shape—what looked like a fantastic wet and dripping head rose from the water near Lugne, and with a roar like a bull's the river beast perceived what had disturbed its lair. It glided swift as wind towards Lugne. None could cry out to him, their throats were dry. As if spellbound, none could move. Then Colum leapt down the bank, and threw up his arm as if to make the sign of the cross, and cried out hoarsely, "Don't touch him!" There was no more than the length of a punt pole between beast and man when the beast disappeared as if jerked away by a rope.

They were standing so still that it was the sound of splashing from Lugne's punt pole that first made them look up. There he was, standing strong and straight upon the ferry punt, slender in his wet garment, poling across as if nothing had been amiss.

They rushed to the brink and drew the boat in, the monks lifting him out on to the bank, the Alban men crowding round to touch him, to exclaim.

Only when the people had taken up the corpse and gone off carrying it to the burial place on the rising land and the monks were left to themselves did they begin to wonder whether anything had indeed appeared out of the River at all. So sudden had the appearing and the disappearing been; and Lugne stood there unharmed in body or mind—perplexed indeed by their concern for him.

Soon they were all perplexed. "Have we listened too long to our guides' tales of the Loch?" Cannich asked, "Have we let fear into our minds? Did we imagine it?"

But the people had believed—and such terrible mutilations —and did we not all of us see the dark dripping shape and hear its evil roar—all but Lugne himself?

Colum raised his head. "We were meant to believe it. There is great power of evil in this land. Where are the messengers I am to follow? I must go quickly to the King."

But the messengers were nowhere to be seen.

XLII

IN the people who came about the lodge they recognised some of the mourners at the ferry. Comgal's eyes glistened as he and Cannich with their two men turned to go with them. " I begin to find myself at home here!" Comgal cried. And Cannich caught up a child with fingers and mouth stained with raspberries, the first child his hands had touched for so long.

"Colum, you are not coming to their houses?" the two abbots asked him as they turned away. For Colum was speaking to two riders who had leapt down at the gate. They were again pulling out a ring with the emblem of the Boar on it. " The High King is waiting. You are to come to him."

"O father, no!" Diarmaid cried. "It is another snare laid for you. And this time it may succeed."

But Colum had mounted the horse they had brought for him and was leaning over to wave to his two boys; and though they followed a few steps protesting he was off with his escort—escort or assassins they did not know which.

For before they had come to the ford on the River at which the road to the Palace led uphill, a company of riders came to meet them, closing in around them. All were wrapped in mantles with hoods which covered the most part of their faces, and sword hilts showed through the mantle cloth. They led the way over grassy spaces to the ridge of hills on whose edge a fortress stood high on its crags. Up they climbed, the horses sure footed as if they knew the track, through the rocks and crags that formed the outer defences, and then along the passage of the walls that man had made.

The sentries challenged. And at this the men drew off their hoods. And out came dark auburn hair to glint like bronze in the sun—Brude mac Maelchon! The King himself at last! Colum said to himself, and with heart mounting like his mounting feet he followed over ditch and rampart to the great rockbound

176

citadel. On the one hand lay the fields and the broad River curving between, on the other the firths lay and beyond them a mountain streaked still with winter snow.

They entered a chamber with stone seats round the wall. The King sat down and with a gesture invited the Abbot to sit by him. "You and your small company are still alive! For a man in the midst of his foes you show an astonishing disregard for danger." And Colum smiled in answer to the hint of a smile: "The safest place is in the middle of danger."

"What will you do with this island, if I grant it to you?"

"I will make it into a sort of fortress. Only the enemies we fight will not be men; we will fight all manner of wrong, sin and trouble of which the King knows there is much everywhere —unseen enemies within ourselves and within those who come for our help. I and my men, we will be a sort of soldiers.." And the King's face encouraging him, "We will support ourselves and have enough to give where there is need by farming and fishing like any other men. And some of us have skill in medicine and will tend the sick and injured. It is not for myself that I ask the Island, but for the great God whom I serve as king. I am myself only his servant. That is why I come dressed in this way without colour or ornament and with my head shaved."

The King nodded warily. "You are another kind of druid, a Christian such as exist in my Southern kingdom. I have heard of the settlements there and can imagine what you mean. I know you are a holy man, and I would have no quarrel with you, believe it, were it not that you come from Dalriada. Your care will be to benefit Connal's people."

"The benefits we have to offer are for all nations, for any man at all who is in need. I am myself by birth neither of Alba nor Dalriada."

"It is true then you come from Eire. Are you as they say of the family of Donal and Fergus the kings of Ailech?"

"It is true. I am so by birth. And I could have wished to live in Eire all my days. I would have asked for nothing better than to live and work there always. Always. Only—by the calling of my God I must be a man who comes from no land and goes to no land. I have turned my back on Eire."

The King stared at him, as if trying to understand. Then he said gently enough, "They say you are of the 'true family.' I know your custom of succession. You are the son of Felim, an heir who might have been chosen king; the right descends to the son from the natural father, and not as with us to the sister's son. But they say you were of the blood of the kings of Laighen by your mother. Indeed, that you might, had you succeeded to kingship, succeeded to the High Kingship at Tara. I have asked and heard much about you. They say you were become a danger to the security of the High King, leading your kinsmen to victory against him.—Is it not true? You turn your head away—I have never in my life met the High King of Eire, Diarmaid. It would have been something to have met his rival at anyrate!

"What freak of fate it was for you to have come near kingship and yet not possessed it!"

"I did not desire it."

"Not desire it! But it is what men of our rank most prize. How can you be of the kings of Eire and not prize kingship?"

"I prize it indeed in other men. I know that on royal kings and princes the safety and happiness of the common people depend. But for myself I wanted other things, things that lay beyond even kingship."

"And I!" cried the King suddenly, "And I! I hold Alba, Paramount King of the North and South, what has never been one before. I have won my wars; I look, for worthy rivals, to the very Saxons that men say are invincible, I have yet to see. And yet I look for something, something—Was it to excel in science that you gave up claim to kingship? I am told you were one of the foremost druids in Eire. And indeed I believe no less, for you came through my gate when I had given strict orders for its closing."

"I have no power in myself, there too I am like a servant. My power is lent by God."

"God—and gods. Who can understand divinity? All I know is that my druids failed, even—even—" He glanced at his men standing still as stone beside the stone walls, then looked uneasily out through a slit window towards the east. "Even my Archdruid."

"All men fail. But there is a Druid above all druids whose power is supreme."

The sun's rays fell long over the countryside, lighting tracks of bright green over the grown corn not yet in ear. The King like a weary but still obedient child lifted his arms to it. "It is not the sun," Colum said to him, "It is the Creator of the sun who is bright beyond all beholding. And yet he is like a king, to see and to serve; and for us his people he wins all wars. It is knowledge of Him that you long for, it is what all men long for. And it is this knowledge I have come to bring you. My asking the Island was the least part of our errand."

Brude rose and stood before him. "I think I knew that at the first moment that I saw you. You have come to grant and not to ask a boon." He sighed and drew his mantle close about him again. "The sun will soon set. There are ceremonies. I must return to the palace. I hold the power to make bond or free, and yet I am not free as other men are free.

"Come to me again. When I am able to meet you I will send escort as I did today." He smiled whimsically, "I must disguise myself. And you coming humble and a stranger, you disguise yourself too."

179

XLIII

TWO noblemen came to the High King's apartments to attend him at his hunting. But the sentry on duty there said, "No, the Exalted One is not in. He has gone out. Where? Who can say. Hunting with some other guest? Not likely, since his dogs are here. Yes, he was gone yesterday for a long time, and people asking for him. What can I do?"

The noblemen went to ask a steward, fearing to displease the King if he still wanted their company. And he said, "Wait. I will inquire for you." And he himself went to the women's grianan and made request at the door to see the Old Heiress or the consort Roith or the Young Princess. His voice held something in it that made Roith rise to her feet and come to him. "Where is the King? He slept the night here. But now he is not with me. Why do you ask for him?"

—"Why do they ask?" she said in a whisper to Leiven, who sat drawing her long auburn plaits through her fingers, too listless to do anything. "They are always asking where is the King? these days. It makes me uneasy. And I miss him too."

"You are luckier than I am. You need not complain. For you have the King my brother here except when there is a war. But I—it is only once or twice in the year that I see Nechtan. When shall I have another child? Some day I will go to his Southern Land. I might even go to the wars with him, as the bards say women did in the old days. At anyrate I am tired of this palace, especially with all this in the air.—Go and ask my mother if you want to know about Brudean."

—"It is not for us to follow the doings of the King," the Old Heiress reproved her, "The King's life is secret at the best of times. Our part as women is to bear the Seed, or tend the King's family; not to ask always, Where is he? Whom is he with?—And another thing, my daughter, do not let anxiety appear so plainly in your face. However much your heart misgives you, never show it, for you are royal."

But as soon as the younger woman had turned away, her own face lost its untroubled look. Lines sprang up around her mouth. She sat still awhile, moving her thumbs, praying. And then she wrapped a cloak round her and went out of the grianan, calling a single lady to attend her. The people in the courtyards saluted her yet let her pass in silence, since it was her prerogative to be first to speak. She made her way towards the House of the Druids. They were preparing the space around it for sunset prayer.

Once she went near, but turned away, and wandered round it in a wide circle, going sunwise to make it seem it was in worship. And indeed as she went she prayed. "I gave you Drusticca! Spare my son now, my hope, my fulfilment." To her ears as she went here and there came small sounds from the House: Did she hear or did she imagine the voice rustling with anger?

When the Archdruid appeared in the doorway, though it appalled her, it gave her courage. She signed to her lady to remain behind, and she herself alone went to the door. She did not speak first there, but stood like a suppliant before him. And to some god going farther and farther from her soul she went on praying, Spare him. Spare him. I gave you much. Spare Brude.

"You have come to worship in place of Maelchon's son?" She shuddered at the coldness of the tone.—not Maelchon's but her son!

"The King is busy. He was called away."

"I know who called him!"

"It is because he is Lord of the South as well as of the North. He wishes to know everything that affects his other people. He wishes to find out—it is only that—it is a passing whim. Master, forgive it."

Her eyes met Broichan's. For a moment she said to herself, "He is a man. And hungry for Brude's love." Then she came to herself, for here was the Holy One, vested for worship, thronged by unseen powers.

"You are right, Lady. It is a passing whim. He has suffered momentary fits of apostasy before today, and has returned to his proper frame.

"Only, if he should stray too far—! If he should take any decisive step—"

"Ah no, how could he? Do not be angry with him. You are his fosterfather, you are of his father's stock, so they say, you know him, you love him. Do not be angry with him. I gave—I gave—" Her voice ran into sobs, she put her hands over her cheeks, yet angrily repulsed the lady in waiting who made to come to comfort her. Through her tears falling between her hands, she pled with him. " My son is bewitched. It is no fault of his. They are druids of great craft. They came through our gates! They have gone into the King's heart, bewitching him. Have pity on him, do not be angry with him."

" Do not trouble yourself," the words in the thin tone said comfort but gave none. "As the King offends he shall pay the penalty.

" But it is on the one who seduces him I will take utter vengeance! You say they are of great craft. But this priest from Eire is very human for all that. I know humankind. It will be strange if I can find no means against him."

An outcry of dogs sounded from the main gateway. And the Old Heiress said to herself, " Brude has come in." But the sunset worship began, and she stood alone watching while the Arch-druid moved in the ritual and said the solemn words.

XLIV

"*In nomine Patris, et Filii, et Spiritus Sancti*" . . .
"*In the name of the Father and of the Son and of the
Holy Spirit.*"

Over the sound of the River currents the fishers heard
another sound. But for some moments they did not look up,
only along the surface of the water where strange reflections
wavered. Pale-robed men, moving — When they looked they
found the real shapes stranger than the reflected ones. They
were wading into the River, not far from where the fishers' nets
were spread. By all the dark and the bright gods! It was those
Christian priests who had burst their way through the King's
locked gate—

"Be still! Don't cry out. Don't let them hear and see us,
don't get mixed up in this! They are performing some ritual,
chanting, moving—Turn the other way. Don't look at them."

"What are they doing, splashing in the water? Will you be
brave and turn round, Urpant, and see?"

"They have some man in the midst of them, the tall priest
is putting river water on him."

"They are going away, wading back to the shore.— But now
they'll have taken all the fish from here by their potent presence.
We might as well give up—They are chanting their hymns again,
and the man that's with them—" A glint of white slid over the
water's face. "They are putting a white tunic on him. There he
is, drawing it down from his head."

They stared in silence, their nets trailing. Each tried not
to be first to speak. "Surely it cannot be? In the white tunic—
It is Brude himself, or else too like him to be natural. They have
changed shapes with him. How else could it be he should stand
quiet beside them, without an ornament to neck or arm, or robe
of state?

183

"God of life and death, Horned One, I will give you my silver brooch and the next three catches of fish—they are looking this way, O let them not see us and practise on us."

"Hush up you!" Urpant said, "It is indeed the King. How could they get him so much like life? And he is not quite all alone, One of his princes from the South is standing by, and another. And there's a man, see—dressed like a small farmer or a herd maybe—he's coming up to kneel and take the King's hand. The tall priest's putting his hand on his head—and he not minding, smiling."

They watched as the company passed alongside them on the River bank, turning towards the royal way where it went from River to Palace.

"The King is smiling too. How odd the way he's smiling. I have never seen him smile that way before. Though look, his clothes are dry, but his head's wet—his hair was never so dark in colour. Come on, pull the nets in. We don't get a sight like this every day."

"I can't see!" wailed the swineherd of the palace as the crowd pressed in front of him, "I can't see. I don't even know what it is we're looking at. Is it the tall priest from Eire breaking in to see the High King again?"

"Mind where you put your elbow. Man, it is the High King. He and the priests together."

"Let me see, let me see!"

"They say they have performed some sacred rite in the River. The King is their god's now, body and soul.—I can see him! I can see the top of his head. That's Brude mac Maelchon. I wonder has it changed his looks? I can see his face."

"What's the matter with it then? Can you see? What is he like now?"

"He's just the same. Only he's smiling, that's all.—What are they pushing for, that lot behind? I was just getting a good look at him.—Will you stop pushing? You'll have us all down in the dust."

But the people in the crowd behind them pushed more violently than before, and then they screamed, for horsemen were coming thundering down the royal way and would ride straight into their midst. Those who were caught went down among the grinding hoofs. With their hands over their faces they had

184

glimpses of tossing manes, wide nostrils; and higher, flying mantles and bright sword hilts sticking out above the hips.

"Gods!" cried the swineherd who had luckily got to the side, "Have they taken leave of their senses? Riding by as if they were entering Dalriada."

And on all sides the people were asking, "What are they doing? Are they going to attack the High King?"

"No, but they've come to rescue him."

"What are we to do, Tarain?" one of the nobles from the Orc Isles shouted to his leader, above the clamour, "What do you want us to do? The King has his hand in the hand of the of the tall priest from Eire. How can we cut him down and not harm the King?"

Uncath, Brude's half-brother, reared his horse round in their path, "Take care! Don't hurt the King. Wait till he comes out from the midst of the clerics. Keep back, don't hurt the King."

"The King's trying to speak!" one of the Fortrin princes cried to them, "Be still till we hear. How can we hear him in this din?"

"He's smiling, look! He hasn't smiled like that for many a day. Can we not hear what he's saying? Look at him standing in his stirrups to shout to us. There's Nechtan of Dunduirn getting through to his side. He's leaping from his horse and getting down on one knee—he's turning up his face to speak to the priest—it's as if he was of the new religion. Did you know he was of the new religion like Drost and Talorgan?"

"What are we to do, Uncath?" one of the princes from Fortrin asked, "How can we rescue a man that does not want rescue? Who sent us here to protect him anyhow?"

"I don't know who sent us. Somebody said to me the King was in danger. Maybe it was the Young Heiress, or was it the Mother. I'm not clear. I thought the King was in danger."

"One of the druids in the Palace it was who said it to me. But I can't see any danger, I'm going to his side as Nechtan did."

"And so am I. We'll give him escort, then they'll think it was for that we rode here."

"Look at them all, drawing to the King's side!" the people said, "Look at them drawing in behind them, King and clerics and all, as merry as can be! All the bother that there was over shutting the gate, and there they are all riding up to go through it! I never understood the ways of kings."

"The worst is still to come!" Brude said to Colum as together they rode in through the gates, the gateman gaping after them. "The women and the druids — We have won the first attack, but not the war."

Roused by the noise of the company that came pouring in at the gates the Palace folk were peering from tops of walls and windows, and from the grianans women were running, from the waiting women to the queens.

Brude's eyes met his sister's, and slowly she smiled in answer to his smiling face, and she went to Nechtan and let him draw her to the monk's side, while Brude took Roith's hand, "Here are guests you have seen before," he said to her, "But have not welcomed. Welcome them now for my sake, and perhaps later for their own."

Roith let Colum bless her, bending her dark head, murmuring in her fear words of the older language. Brude said to her in the same speech, "Where are our sons?" But before she could summon their eldest son Uirgain, who was standing moodily apart and would not come to them, Leiven called to her woman and she brought the infant Derile still asleep from his cradle in the grianan. "Here is my son. Bless him too—bless him first. If you have a spell of safety lay it over him. For he is Brude's heir and his life is perilous."

"Sir!" an attendant, despairing of catching the King's eye, had to speak, "The Royal Lady."

The Old Heiress stood, her hands clutching the breast of her patterned gown. "What have you done, my son! What have you done! Entering openly, in broad daylight. Brude, you have lost all fear! Why do you look at me like that, as if heedless of your plight? You are smiling!" Her lips trembled as he put his arms on hers, and kissed her forehead. "You are bewitched.

"He shall not touch the heir!" And she snatched up Derile from his nurse, so that he woke and cried lustily. "Thank the immortal ones that he has cried! He has withstood the Eye they have put on him. Carry him into the inmost grianan.—I gave up so much to secure you the paramountcy!" she said very bitterly to Brude. "Will you make it in vain? How shall I find an offering to placate the gods for such apostasy as this?"

"Come, mother!" Brude took her hands in his, "There is less to fear than you think."

"If only the Archdriud did not know of this!"

"Where is the Archdruid?"

"At the Grove, I daresay, making sacrifices and supplication"

"He is in the Palace," Leiven said. "For he asked today if you would give him one of your slavegirls, one that my uncle brought you. We were glad enough to give her if it contented him."

"Why should he want her? For a servant—I hope—" And he looked over at the priest Colum who was gazing everywhere around. "He has eyes of war!" Brude said to himself. "He will open one gate after another." And he remembered his confession at the River, and grimaced, thinking of his men and some of their ways.

The
Slavegirl

XLV

COLUM, looking down the long slope of the royal way from the palace gate, was half amused, half impressed at the escort of Comgal and Cannich: with so many men of the Cruithnians to accompany them on their way north they seemed like Alban princes. It was all fluttering mantles and trotting horses. Their desire to explore along the north east coast, and find the old settlements Finbar had spoken of to them in their student days, had been met not only with consent but with encouragement. Even the druid advisers of the King had sanctioned it, and sent their own messengers together with the King's to prepare the way. It was the King himself who had given the guides and the escort, the King, who for long had loved the way of the Lord and had not known.

Now like leaves and flowers breaking their buds after a long winter, hidden followers were springing up here and there; in a hut below the palace smithy, in the guardroom, in the grianan, questions would be asked and the answers listened to with intentness. He had grown so used to the lean pale-skinned faces and the dark eyes he might have been born and lived all his days among them. He could judge their need from the accents of their speech as for years ever since his priesting he had been able to judge of human need in Eire.

And yet so much was yet to be explored. His friends with their company were going along the broad River, they were crossing it near its entry into the firth; he could from the height of the Palace still see a flutter of bright colours and a sober contrast of grey! They were turning west to skirt the inmost firth of Varrar, before they should strike north. Colum's prayer went after them, on their journey. They might find men with the faith of Christ still in their hearts, and establish them. They might find the faith lost altogether, and kindle it again. The new fire—Well might they hope to kindle it and not see it go out in adverse winds, since the Paramount King, Brude mac Maelchon, their guardian, was himself of the New Way. Their

road would run into country new and unknown but touched with
promise and hope. And he might have envied it them. But his
road ran into the heart of the King, unknown till recently and
now not much more than half known.

His mind forsook his friends with one last hurried blessing
on their mission, and filled with thought of Brude and his court
and his councillors. He re-entered the great gate, hallowed for
him yet by their miraculous entry through it the first time; past
the gateman and sentries there who grinned at him. He was to
go to the King's chamber where the symbols over the door were
grown familiar. He had to pass the great hall. From within it,
enticingly, a strain of music rose into the air like water from a
fountain. Though it was no more than a bard tuning harpstrings
it sounded angelic. And then came the full song caught up from
one bard to another, the melody hummed here and there by those
listening till it seemed that all the world were singing.

Smiling, he entered the hall and looked round. Before his
delighted eyes the pattern of its dwellers formed this way then
that, changing in colours as in shape. There were now battle-
pages laughing together, then girls with sweet merry faces clustered over some woven stuff, then the two groups merged as the
young men came to tease. Nobles passed by giving orders, their
servants coming forward and retreating with a reverence, slaves
on the outskirts of the groups, sweeping rushes aside to lay a
fresh supply.

His eyes lit on one of the women slaves sweeping rushes with
the rest. Although her drab garment obscured its outlines, her
body moved like that of a young girl. Her head, bent in her
task, was of a bright brown colour. He had often in his life seen
hair of that hue, but not here, not now—He knew by instinct
deep within him that she was of different race from all others
in the hall.

"Did you see her? Who can she be?"

Diarmaid turned to him, "Who, father?"

"A young slavegirl. She had bright hair. Didn't you see
her? Who can she be?"

"Father, don't ask too much about the court here. Their
customs are different. Don't ask. It's best not to know."

But Colum was threading his way across the hall between
the pages and princes and bards, his reluctant young men after
him.

"Where did she go?"

There was a curtain over a wall embrasure to keep slaves out of sight when their labour was not needed. He caught the curtain impatiently and wrenched it aside. From the embrasure came a stale smell of sweat and of sickness.

"Father, do come away! There are bad things in this land. We cannot make it all right in a few days. It's not our business. They will resent it. Come away!"

The Abbot caught one of his men by the wrist. "There, do you not see, Lugne?" He peered into the glom. "Do you not see? There's a girl there, on the floor. I think she must be from Eire."

"No, no, father! Why should she be? It's only fancy. There must be many women in Alba with golden hair. In any case—"

The Abbot bent and went in. He went down on the ground beside her. "My daughter?" he said in the Cruithnian manner. She did not speak or cry, but shrank away, moving her head stiffly to look at him. In her white face her eyes were black as jet. He saw that the pupils were dilated so that all the irises were covered.

"My daughter!" he said again, this time in the speech of Eire. She swallowed dryly, and drew her scanty garment up over her pointed breasts. She might have been about fifteen.

The abbot said gently, "I mean no harm to you. I am a priest. Who are you? Where have you come from?"

He almost hoped he might not hear her answer him in their own tongue, lest his guess prove true. Indeed when she spoke he could not make words out, for suddenly she cried out and flung herself on her knees at his feet, clinging to his gown, laughing and weeping and speaking all together. Her body was hot as fire against his. He did not have to put his hand on her to know she had high fever. He stroked her hair. "Where do you come from, little daughter?"

"From Eire! From Eire, father! From Eire too. O you are the Christian priest they spoke of who came through the shut gate! O have you come to take me? It's what I prayed for. But I did not dare dream it would happen!" She lifted her face to him, flushed with the sudden hope, almost for the moment beautiful though stained with her tears. The hair round her forehead was dark with sweat, on one cheek an old bruise stood out on the fair skin.

Colum said trembling, "Poor little woman — What has happened to you? How do you come to be here?"

Men came from the sea, she answered all in a rush. From Alba. In longships. Her home was on the coast of Laighen. It happened suddenly, it was like a dream. They were busy with the harvest, singing songs, dressing the "maiden" with flowers. Her father was slain where he stood. Her brothers—she had seen them last defending their house wall. We are noble! Her sister-in-law, who was with child—she cried out loudly and put her arm over her eyes. It was only the virgins they wanted.

"Come along, tell me!"

Herself and her sister with a woman servant dragged to the ships. Then seasickness, mountainous seas! They told her her sister had leapt overboard. Then everything unreal — Loud drunken laughter and the reeling ship, blows, caresses worse than blows—

She shivered, huddling into herself, hiding her face in the cloth of his habit. "And then?"

A far cold island, where she could not tell—a round tower—men's faces hot beside her, prying hands—no one whose speech she could understand. And always prying hands.

Then to sea again, and she was here. So far as she could understand it was a great King's palace. If only she might be allowed to sweep rushes here, or serve the women, but—

"Whose slave are you now then?" Colum asked. "Have you been given to the High King? Whether you are his or another's, I will ask for you. Don't be afraid any more. I will have you set free."

She seemed scarcely to be listening, saying as if to herself, "I did not think I should see anyone from Eire again. And a priest! O father, give me pardon, it was not my wish! It was not my wish—but I am sick, I have no strength to resist.."

"Ah, so that is what they have done to you, that is what makes you so afraid?" And now her returning beauty and her youthfulness stood out like so many more disfigurements on her face. "But don't be afraid now. They shall not hurt you again, they shall not take you against your will. Poor child, and you are sick! You have a fever. And no one to tend you, no one to tend you. Why if you are the King's does no steward look after you? Is it their custom to let their slaves die?"

He felt the shaking of her body at his knees. When she raised her head he saw the pupils of her eyes grown large again.

She said wailing, "I am no longer a palace slave. I have been given,—My master now is Broichan the Archdruid." Her

voice rose to a shriek, "I am afraid of their Grove! I am afraid
of their Grove!"

He gazed at her, for a moment his heart invaded by her
own horror. To calm himself and her he asked a question in an
even tone. "What is your name, my daughter?"

"Muirne, daughter of Alain son of Conn," and at the
memory of home she wept.

"Be still," Colum bade her. "Weep if you must, but be comforted. I will ask your freedom from both King and Archdruid.
Have patience and you will see your home again."

XLVI

H E was not out of the great hall before he found one of the druids standing watching, and he went up to him and asked if the Archdruid Broichan might be found at leisure. The man answered courteously enough and readily, " His Holiness is indeed n the Palace. He is close by, in an adjoining room, conferring with one or two of our order before he has audience with the King. I will go and see if he has time now to speak with the cleric from Eire."

He was back in a moment, beckoning to Colum to follow him. He parted a curtain of cloth woven with pictures of animals of the chase. Colum had not yet met the Archdruid alone and face to face, and his heart beat with something like apprehension.

The Archdruid was sitting in a chair high-backed like a throne, light falling from a window upon him. His white mantle was flecked all over with spots of colour, and was clasped below his chin with a golden brooch. His grey hair was caught back by a fillet of gold thread. He was in consultation with one or two of his order, as had been said. But as he heard the Abbot's entry he turned from them and looked at him.

His face was quite mild, he seemed a gentle old man. The eyes though large and luminous held blandness not domination. Almost Colum was reminded of his old teacher, Finbar, seated and waiting for a boy's request. But he said nothing by way of welcome.

" Sir! " Colum said, " Sir, I should be glad to speak with you, if you have leisure."

" Indeed?' Broichan replied, " I have not as yet had such a privilege. I think perhaps you are happier speaking with Kings? Well, I am at leisure now, for a little, before I see my fosterson."

" You have in your possession a certain slavegirl, Muirne."

" Have I?" the Archdruid said and smiled. " It cannot be so trifling a circumstance that you wished to talk of? I confess I hoped you were ready for a discussion on spiritual things."

"This girl is sick, she has at the moment a high fever. But more than that, she is sick of heart, lonely and terrified, unable to bear captivity."

The Archdruid still wore his smile, attending for courtesy's sake with half his mind; his eyes strayed to the door as if he were expecting the King's coming. And Colum might have been swayed by a sudden sense of hopelessness from his purpose, had he not remembered the girl shaking at his knees and the clutching of her hands.

"I beg for her release. I beg you to give her to me so that I may send her back to her home in Laighen."

"You are good at asking," the Archdruid observed, speaking so softly it still seemed to be in courtesy. "I am sorry I cannot comply with the request."

"Have pity on her! She has done no wrong to anyone. It was for no fault of hers she was snatched from her home and taken so far into a country unknown to her. Have pity and let her go. You do not love me, and might think it just to refuse my request. But out of humanity, let her go."

"Out of humanity?" The Archdruid pondered the word, equable and smiling still. "Out of humanity!—Ah, if we were humane we would perhaps not have slaves at all. We would perhaps use no domestic animals, since to do so is to make them a sort of slaves. I believe deeply spiritual souls feel pain at causing harm to the veriest insect—fleas and lice even."

"Sir—"

"If you yourself are so humane, do not stop at one girl, ask to free all. At least that all slaves taken from Eire to this country be freed, for I think it is her nationhood that has excited your interest, rather than any peculiar suffering?"

"But she does suffer!"

"So do all captives, I am afraid. In every land. And most of them are innocent. Ah, my brother, it is the immemorial problem of suffering we face here. This girl you speak of is, I imagine, guiltless of mortal crime; it cannot be said to be as a punishment the gods have brought this fate upon her. This sort of thing has been a riddle obsessing the mind of countless generations. I should like to hear your Christian views on it."

"Then you will set her free?"

"It may of course be her parents' sin. The God of Light, whom I imagine even you believe in, he who regards the whole world and the whole life—and who can escape his scrutiny?—He

may have found evil where men see none. She may come of
parents who have offended his pure Eye, their sin is being visited
on her innocent head. Of her parentage and background you are
yourself the better judge, since she is of your land, and you
appear to have had extensive speech with her."

"You will let me send her back?"

"I should really be most interested to discuss sometime with
you—for at this moment I have not the leisure—this baffling
problem of unmerited suffering. Or should I not rather say,
apparently unmerited, out of reverence to those immortal ones
whose eyes alone see all and understand? Which of us, even of us
men of science, can claim to see into the heart's inmost depth?
We must trust — Your pardon! — We must bow our heads and
trust in those higher than ourselves. That was what you were
going to tell me?

"I do not know whether you hold, as we do, that the soul
is migratory, inhabiting various bodies in various earthly mani-
festations? If not, sir, I commend it to your consideraton. You
might even stay to hear about the belief here, and teach it to
your student priests on your return to Eire. For it makes justice
of the apparent injustice in the universe. There is no doubt in
my mind that in some former life, since not in this one, your
slavegirl, poor child, was guilty of great evil not until now
atoned for."

"Archdruid Broichan—"

"I think I know what you are going to say! You are going
to object that if the sin be lost to the memory the punishment is
without redemptive purpose. And that it has redemptive purpose
must be our human hope, if it cannot be a belief. No, but I do
not agree!—Will you not sit down?—The personality of man is
so complex. Though forgetful of past sin in the conscious mind
he may nevertheless in the hidden depths of his soul remember it
—remember it and concur in the punishment. Nay, even delight
in it! For in a future life, which as I told you is a future
manifestation of the undying spirit, it works his release.

"Have no fear, sir. If you are stirred by pity, as I see you
most strongly are, for this young captive slavegirl, take comfort in
the thought that her spirit will be all the happier the next time
it visits this mortal scene for all the sufferings you have so
feelingly described to me—fever, was it? and homesickness for
your motherland Eire."

"Archdruid Broichan, I demand this girl's release."

But the Archdruid was not listening at all now. The smile played upon his lips and he was looking at the doorway at which the High King had come in.

As the King came towards them Broichan's eyes were on him in affection, and he stretched out his left hand in intimate greeting. But Colum looked with alien regard on the man he had been instructing not half an hour back. Brude watched his face, and Broichan watched the King's.

"Exalted One! This august stranger whom you have been pleased to welcome into our midst"—The King looked at his Archdruid now—"suggests that out of humanity I hand over to him one of my slavegirls, who it seems has excited his pity. I ask him whether out of humanity I am to free all my slaves, whether perhaps your Excellency is to free all his captives taken from other lands. You could certainly make a worthwhile release to Dalriada. It is a praiseworthy suggestion, if only the economy of the country could bear it. Who is to take the places of these workers of ours when they are free? Is his Worship perhaps ready to arrange an exchange of captives between our countries? It might be to our advantage if for our captives we could get back the land of Dalriada that belongs to us."

A laugh came from one of the attendant lords who had followed the King in, then laughter from one and another, though as the King remained sober it was stilled.

"What slavegirl are you talking about, fosterfather?"

"One that belongs to me."

"I do not understand. If she belongs to your Holiness, how has our guest seen her?"

"Because she is in the Palace. It is one of the captive girls your Excellency has recently been pleased to give me."

"I gave her?"

"Certainly. With other two. And I value the gift as I value all from so beloved a giver.

"But the trouble is, this girl happens to have been taken from Eire. And this man of Eire is all on fire with zeal for her sake. And so he has asked me for her."

"Fosterfather, if our guest has asked a favour — I will give you another girl for her."

"Our guest does not ask a favour, Exalted One, he demands as a right."

"The right of a priest of God!" Colum said in a low shaking voice. "Do not gainsay it.'

"Ah, doubtless she took sanctuary!" Broichan said. A shiver
of delighted amusement now went round his druid colleagues
though they forbore to laugh outright. " He, being the personage
he is, carries his own climate, as it were, around with him. His
own land's customs come into force wherever he is. Such a pity
we do not share his point of view."

"What is it all about?" Brude asked with a puzzled frown,
" What girl is it? I do not recollect them. But for one slave, this
is a lot of trouble. I'll give you two girls for her—virgins still if
that is what you want."

"You are kind to offer," the Archdruid said. " Perhaps more
kind than wise. But whatever offer is made I do not have to
accept it. We have law in our country. There is no statute among
the brehons that a man's property may be taken away from him
if he is a freeman. And the girl is my property, given to me by
the King. Whatever her value to me or any other man, I may
keep her. And keep her I will."

"Do not make him angry," the King said to his Archdruid in
the older language. Broichan answered loudly in the newer
tongue. " It is not my concern to make him angry or not angry.
Let him be angry or not angry as he will. I am not going to give
my slave to him for all his asking, or for yours if you so far forget
yourself."

He drew gasping breaths. " If the High King of Alba so far
forgets himself as to deny his Archdruid the simple rights of a
freeman as well as the honour he ought to pay him—Take that
girl," he called in a thin high voice to his attendant druids, "And
put chains on her feet and hands. She will be sorry for your
intervention."

Colum said, gasping like the Archdruid, " Son of my God!"
And to the harassed King, " Will you permit this? You who have
embraced the Lord's mercy, will you not see mercy done to this
hapless girl? The water of baptism is not dry on you."

The Archdruid interposed, " What can the King do? The
girl is mine, he himself gave her to me. Can a King take back
his gift? It may be so in Dalriada but not here."

The King spoke urgently in their older language "Why do
you flout him so? He is a person I esteem. Give him the slavegirl, and I will give you as many slaves as you ask for."

And the Archdruid replied to him briefly in the same
language. " No. " Then to Colum in the newer tongue, he said
softly, " It is a pity you are not in Eire now. You would find men

200

there to gratify your whim. You might even start a war on those
who did not, as it is said that you have done before. You might
lead men in rebellion against this High King too, if you had men
behind you. But the men around you now are mine! And you
have none; even your greyrobed friends are gone from you.

"Are you afraid of this priest of the new religion, fosterson?
You are easily made afraid. You see I do not fear him, though
he is cunning in magic I will not deny it to him. But to those
who know science it is a little matter, an illusion of the eyes
caused by certain ways of lighting. I could teach you how it is
done, if you cared to know. Such tricks do not make a man
terrible. My poor Brudean! You were quite under his spell. The
man is an imposter, and a hypocrite. He teaches you, does he, of
a merciful God; a wonderful Bright One, one you must serve with
mercy and gentleness like his own. O he would have you univers-
ally mild and forgiving, ' forgive your enemies especially the poor
folk of Dalriada! Was that the way of it? But he himself is
filled with fury. Look at his face! Look at him shaking with
uncontrollable anger, the teacher of mercy! I think his Bright
One is no brighter than any of our own.

" What do you say to that, sir, if you can bring words out?"
Colum took his fists down from either side of his face. " I
have no right to be angry," he said to Archdruid and King, " I
am no longer in Eire, as you say, and have no men to protect my
rights or make war for me. And well for me that it is so! But
God can do all He will. And I declare to you, Archdruid Broichan,
that your life is in God's hands. You are of His making, and
subject to the hazards of life like any other man. If you do not
release to me, safe and unharmed, this captive stranger before I
leave this province, you will fall sick and die."

Then with no greeting to the King he went slow and sad
down the room and out by the palace gate. The King stared
unhappily after him. But Broichan met the eyes of his colleagues
laughing merrily. " It is as good a threat as any. We must admit
our holy rival came out of this situation with as much dignity
as he could, if not with much success."

201

XLVII

"**F**ATHER, Diarmaid said to the Abbot, "We must get away. The men who guard our lodge are obeying the King's orders. When they hear of what has happened they will fall upon us." And Lugne joined in the persuasion.

"Even if the King is favourable, father—though who is to say he is? It is hard for him to break with his customs and his fosterfather. Even if he takes our part what can he do against the power of his Archdruid? And him you have mortally offended. We must go, Colum. We'll wait till the darkness falls and then we will slip away."

"And if it's the other abbots and their men you are thinking of, they are in less danger than ourselves. They will get wind of what has happened and make their way south without ever coming near the Palace. In any case, the Abbot Comgal has a look of these Cruithnian folk about him. He will not rouse their anger."

"Will you not come away? For it's not your own safety we are thinking of, but the errand you came on, father. Let's go before things get any worse. After all, you have the permission of the King to hold the Island and work among the folk there who may be his. However his mind goes now toward us and the Christian faith, he is a King, he cannot break his pledged word. And hasn't he promised to be at peace with Dalriada if they do not make incursions into his territories? Well, what more need we wait for? You have won what you came for. Let us get safe home now if we can."

"We shall not go today," he replied patiently, "I will know when it is time to go. I do not think it is yet. But I shall see. There is a man in the house yonder who has a poisoned wound. I promised to send a paste of herbs for him. Will you go now with it? For I am weary, and do not want to speak."

So he got rid of them, and went alone and silent to the River bank, and went walking by himself, the River only a companion. It ran as ever, shining and strong, swiftly down to the sea. Remembering his elation when he first rowed down it his heart was heavy. He would have exchanged that time of dread and uncertainty for this present time. He had entered the stronghold, its gates had yielded before them, how they did not know; it was as if God intervened. And like the gate the King's heart had opened and the light of the knowledge of Christ's salvation had gone in. But if it were a battle, he had both won and lost it. The name of the God of mercy had been mocked at openly, and the King had heard and had had no strength yet with which to defend it. And as for himself—it was in the sin of his own nature that the blasphemy had found its root. A man of anger. The words of the Archdruid Broichan had been true. He was no servant of the Holy One and had no light to lead the King by.

Ah but he still was angry! For more than anything, more than his self abasement or his disappointment over the good regenerated King, the thought of the captive girl still in their hands stuck in his memory like an arrow stuck festering in a wound. As he walked here safe and well, where was she? What were they doing to her? Again about his knees he felt the shaking of her body and her clutching hands, and saw the gold hair dark with sweat round her face. O if God had not let me see her! Since I can do nothing, why did He let me see her? I woke hope in her and it is in vain. I have only added to her suffering. How can a God of mercy—

He had forgotten where he was, and what river this was that ran by him. It surprised him to see the strange faces of the people walking beside him, their dark hair and their patterned cloaks and bronze clasps and armlets. But it surprised him more to hear the gentle tones of their speech. He could understand them in spite of his lethargy for they spoke slowly and in their language which he had learned.

"The man from the West is sick? It was a long journey, it is not to be wondered. And you are not used to our kinds of food maybe. In your land of Eire is it true they eat the flesh of wolves?"

Another asked, "Where do you feel the pain?"

He smiled at them; they were the River folk who had been about when Lugne swam across to fetch the ferry and that Thing had appeared from the River or they thought it had appeared. They were as friendly as people are who share a secret. :

"You should lie down," a woman said, "If you are sick. Why do you walk about like this, up and down, up and down? We have watched you for a long time, walking, walking," Imitating him she made her neighbours laugh.

"Sit and rest," they bade him, "and tell us one of those stories your friend told us on the funeral day." And when he sat down they came round him, touching his clothes curiously. "You have cured more than one person since you came; we do not like to see yourself sick."

"I think it was to seek a cure you came to the River now?" an old man asked then. "You have been walking up and down looking for a Stone?"

They saw he did not understand.

"Do you not have power to bless a Stone and make it powerful? If you know how to get through a locked gate!"

"Have you not cured people in your own land in that way?"

He shook his head, his burdened mind unclear.

"You use herbs only? There are different ways. Some of our druids cure by a Stone. It is really wonderful. They pick out the right one from the River and say a wise spell over it, and it will cure many kinds of sickness or injury, so long as the sick person is not very wicked, that is."

"My son was gored by our bull. A good boy, if unlucky. And he took a drink from the water when the Stone was floating, and the blood stopped and he felt no more pain."

"Our druid here has a white pebble, very precious to him. He will not give it out of his own hand. You must send for him and he will bring it."

After they had gone, he went walking by the River again. The water ran swift and bright over its stones. He stood still, prayer moistening his heart once more. It was not the slavegirl he saw it was the Archdruid. His own words to him echoed in his ears, "You will fall sick."

He went to the brink of the River and stepped down into the water, meeting its chill, and waded here and there. His thoughts were held in prayer, but he could scan the river bottom of pebbles and sand. He saw a round white stone, in the current it was striking and bright. He rolled his sleeve up and put his arm deep in up to the shoulder, and got hold of it. It lay, less bright, but cold and white and round in the palm of his hand.

He waded to the bank again and stepped on to the grass. And with a light step now he went to their lodge. The two boys came to meet him, " Father, where have you been, Colum? Your robe is wet."

" Look at this stone," he said opening his hand.

" It is rather beautiful, white and round."

" I took it from the River."

" Yes, father.—Why?"

" It's like a druid's Stone. You know, the magic stones they say they heal by." They looked at him doubtfully, and he closed his fingers over the stone again.

XLVIII

URGART and Young Uirb his sister's son were removing the dried bracken from the box and lifting out the precious glassware. "Where did it come from?" Urgart marvelled, "Where would even the Archdruid find such lovely stuff as this? It's likely he got it sent from over the Gallican Gulf. I've never seen its equal anywhere." Uirb's fingers at this shook so much that he dropped a beaker back into the box, but by the mercy of the Bright One it fell on bracken and was not even cracked.

"Mind what you're doing!" cried the steward Uinguist in a twitter of nerves, "You are not handling clay. Glass when it's broken cannot be mended again. If you had broken this and it the property of no less a person—'"

"I'm scared to touch it," Uirb said whimpering; and his uncle upheld him, "It's to mind the High King's stuff I'm commanded: let the Archdruid send his own servants to handle his gear."

The steward had to take it out of the box for them. He set them to polish the bronze cups for the lesser noblity while he himself went off to see about the wine which like the glass had been sent to the Palace from the Archdruid's home.

"I thought things were settling down," Uirb lamented to Urgart as they rubbed round the chased designs on the King's cups. "When I heard that stranger druid man from Eire had taken himself out of the Palace I was very pleased. Not but what I liked what I saw of him, and what I heard him say one night. When I got near him I never felt so afraid as I thought I would feel. Still it's nice to think we're free of him. It's one druid less. I never did see so many druids around this Palace. It's shaven heads and amulets wherever you go."

"Don't talk so much. I don't hear you when you say such things. It isn't lucky to speak disrespectfully of holy men, and

the gods know we need all the luck we get. Give me up a palm-
ful of ashes till I rub this bit. It's our own druids we must respect
from now on and never mind strangers. For that one from Eire,
he's quarrelled and gone away. Over a young slavegirl, if you
please! A girl with yellow hair, a bit out of the common, and
pretty before they had their way with her. Now men like us might
quarrel over such as that, and even royal kings are not above it.
But you'd think that holy men—and yet it's said he quarrelled
with the King and walked off in fierce anger."

"No, uncle, it wasn't with the King. They say Brude would
have liked him to stay. He'd taken to him, loved him like a
brother. And what's good enough for the King is good enough
for me, and I'd have liked it if he'd stayed, for they say he can
cure sicknesses and I might have got him to go to my mother.
No, it was with his Holiness himself he's quarrelled. He said I
don't know what; no one dares repeat it. But they do say it's a
wonder he gets free to live."

"You can't kill holy men, they are immortal. Is this the
King's cup that I'm at now, for I have not seen it before?"

"It must be the Archdruid's. Now that's what's so odd about
this day. Druids we have had before in the Palace, even a host
of them as we have now. But never before have we taken orders
about a feast and the things for the feast from any other but the
Mother or the King. His Holiness has even chosen and sent the
wine they're to have, wine from over the sea! And he's wondering
if the salmon is grand enough for the guests from Fortrin who
have it good their way."

"It's because the feast is given by the Archdruid to celebrate
something. I never know half the time what they celebrate.
Maybe it's a rejoicing because they've got rid of the stranger from
Eire. Take care what you're doing! Handling that glass stuff
again." Young Uirb was holding the glass beaker up so that it
filled with light, he was setting it to his lips. "Put that down,
you rascal, you'll have us both whipped."

For the High King's steward was again upon them, but he
was giving his anxious commands to other servants and had not
seen. "See that there are lights in reserve. The dusk comes early
now. Have the great golden filigree bowl over the Archdruid's
head. He is to wear the Horned Crown—deisuil, deisuil!—Look at
all that bracken on the floor, all over the newly sprinkled rushes!"

"I'll call sweepers," Urgart said hastily.

"Gods! I had almost forgotten," the steward cried, "that slavegirl from Eire, that girl with the bright hair, the one that was given from Tarain to the King and from the King to the Archdruid—"

"The one there's all the trouble over?"

"That's the one I mean. Find the keeper of the slaves. Tell him she is to appear at the feast, sweeping with the others who come to take the bits and bones from under the tables. Tell him to remember she is to appear downcast."

"It'll not be difficult," young Uirb shivering said, "I heard her in the night; I couldn't sleep. That's why my hand isn't just so steady."

"She has to appear where she will be seen by the King."

"Seen! Sir, do you not mean not seen?"

"To be seen, I said."

"The gods, why?"

"Am I here to answer questions?" the steward shouted in rage, "Because His Holiness the Archdruid has said so, that is all." His eyes went to the chamber where the Archdruid would be robing, as if he could be rebuked by even the empty air.

XLIX

THE words were in a tongue he did not understand, and yet their rhythms were familiar, his lesson of a week or two ago. In his own tongue he could accompany the prayer that came in whispers or in a high thin tone such as those use who are in pain. "Our father who art in heaven, hallowed be thy name, thy kingdom come—"

Standing in the shadows of the cellarage below the palace apartments, at the entrance to the noisome prison of the slaves, the King took hold of the doorposts with either hand. His knees were weak under him like a man wounded in battle, he held fast on to the door posts and put his head down on one arm. His bracelets pressed into the flesh of his face.

"And lead us not into temptation, but deliver us from evil." From the abundant evil. From not knowing what to do.

The scent of primrose water and of myrtle came like an offensive thing to his nostrils. He looked balefully up, moving his head on his arm. His sister gazed at him with astonishment in her brown eyes. She stood slim, her youthful lines coming deliciously from the dress of flame colour. He grudged her her round cheeks and her clean sweet smell.

Behind his sister his mother: her dress was of some sort of silk that glimmered in two colours under the pine candle she carried, blue and green like the sea. Its beauty appalled him. He took a fistful of the stuff and caught his mother roughly towards him. "Can't you give her something to cover herself with, at least? You know whom I mean. All the Palace knows, how should you not?"

"Whatever are you talking about, my son? Why are you here? You are missed, and we have been searching for you, afraid of what we should find. Is this a time to be hanging round the slaves' quarters?" He laughed when he heard his mother's deep voice upbraiding him, "Like a lust-crazed boy! Your wife says

o   209

you have not eaten all day—not dressed yet, not washed! sweating still from the hosting exercise—and the hour of the great feast come."

How should she understand? He did not understand himself now. Only his sister was gazing at him with something like compassion; she whispered, "Why don't you break in and take her out, if you desire her so much?"

"Why! Because I am powerless. She is the Archdruid's; a gift I gave him, though she was only given in my name. I cannot take her from him."

But he was unjust to them, who had had no hand in this. He shook himself and stood up straight, and he said camly, "I am not yet dressed, because I do not mean to be dressed tonight. I am not going to the feast. How should I go? It is given as a love feast, to show goodwill between me and the Archdruid Broichan. I have no goodwill for him. I hate him. He makes me false to something in myself that I do not understand."

But his mother had put her hands over her ears. Her coronet went a little askew. She turned in reverence to this side and to that, murmuring prayers of contrition mixed with words of rebuke. "Be silent, be silent, Brude. You tempt the gods. He is willing to be reconciled to you. Do not strain his patience. You will bring us down to ruin with yourself if you do not humble yourself now."

"I am humble enough," the King interrupted her, "I make war on slaves."

His sister whispered to him, "How you are changed, Brude! I hardly know you. I think you are sorry for this slave. It's that that's brought you down here not—not what the Mother said. And yet only last month—Don't frown! I do not blame you, it's a man's affair. But now to be sad because—"

Their mother broke in, "It is unnatural. My son, will you not resist? You are being charmed by our enemies. This priest from Dalriada has used craft to weaken you. You are like a woman. Concerning yourself with slaves! With one captive girl slave!"

"Come away then. But I am not going to the feast. Those who feel like feasting let them feast and welcome. But I will eat with Nechtan and with Drost!"

"And let the rest of your guests sit at the feast? Will you set division in the land over which you are High King?"

Brude stared at her for a moment. Then he shook off her hand, and turned so violently he made the posts of the doorway tremble after him. He strode up the sloping passage that led to the light and air of the ground floor. The women followed him, holding the hems of their dresses from the filth of the passage.

L

THE company of kings and nobles and ladies moved like resplendent birds from over the seas in their many coloured clothing, with its intricate designs, and ornaments of gold and bronze and amber and jet. So large was the company that the Palace servants were bemused by it, and stared unable to lead guests to their places or to pull back seats until the angry voices of the stewards recalled them. The High King and his Mother had their places on either side of the central chair, and at the top of the tables set square to the high table the great kings were placed, North and South together, with their retinues behind their backs. None sat, not even the High King, for the central chair still stood empty waiting for its occupant the giver of the feast.

Most splendid of all was he when he came, not because of the collar of enamelled bronze with its ancient and holy patterning that covered his chest, not because of the bracelets with the serpent head clasps that he wore on his thin arms, but because he carried on his head what was more awful than a crown, the headdress on which stood the Horns of Life and Death. As he entered the hall those near fell back from him, turning their heads to avoid seeing him again; if they were conscious of heinous sin they trembled and indeed many of the Southern Kings trembled whether or no, Talorgan and Drost from Circind, and Nechtan the father of the new Heir. He took his seat in the central chair and with upraised hand gave the signal for all the guests to sit and for the servers to set the food on the tables.

The smell of roast meat vied with the smell of pinewood. But though the mouths of the guests watered they remained mute. Even the King—Broichan leant forward and peered at him from slanted eyes. The King wore a dull coloured robe without any ornament! His face was glum. A penitent, ah, that was it! Still, it was a pity for it seemed to have a sobering effect upon the company. The Archdruid laid himself out therefore to be gracious and cheerful. With fatherly smile he addressed those nearest to him.

"The dusk is coming in early now—may the God of Light send us his favour in dark as in bright hours! You, sir," to Tarain of Orc, "Are more fortunate than we in summer with your long northern light.—Do not spare the food!" he bade another royal guest, a prince from the province of Ce, "The wild duck is to be recommended. Come, gentlemen! Let us honour the High King's presence with high feasting. Let us eat in love and unity of spirit, with our High King united with us again in reverence and obedience to our country's gods."

Brude said nothing, moving the morsels round on his plate. It was the Old Heiress who replied for him. "It is an illustrious gathering indeed, with guests from South and North. We are thankful to your Holiness for the feast."

And as no one spoke after her she went on, "I regret the departure of the stranger from Eire only for this, that he might have beheld our Archdruid seated at the head of our table—"

"You are very devout!" the Archdruid said sharply. "But it is all one whether he sees or does not see. He has gone from our minds as from our Kingdom. No need to speak of him."

He looked from one to another of the kings and princes and chiefs, calling kind remarks to one and another. He spoke in the old tongue to a kinsman of Roith, from a far glen in the West, pressing on him the roast pig fed on apples; and in the new to Urpant of Fortrin, praising their seatrout and salmon from the River Tay as equal to the Nesa's own. He pressed a king from Circind to taste wine, "It was shipped at a harbour in your province. Glad are we to have so prosperous a province in unity with ourselves." He brought up topics to set them talking together.

Yet in the silence one could hear what his own druids, sitting at their own table behind him by way of retinue, were whispering together. "I myself as a young man practised under a notable worker there. But with the spread of the new religion standards have fallen. We are discussing the practice of the magic art in Eire, Holiness."

"The source and spring of all true science is our own land!" Broichan said. "They come from over the Gallican Gulf, from Eastern lands to learn from us. It is a waste of breath to discuss the art of Eire."

"Indeed, Master, indeed! All the same, if we had found out how that Christian druid came through the locked gates, not only barred but hallowed—"

"This is a feast in the royal Palace. Let us leave such topics till we are met in our own assembly."

But those druids further from the Master did not hear the rebuke. "Is it perhaps they have knowledge of how to render physical matter into such a substance that it can penetrate baser matter such as wood or iron?"

"More likely they know how to overcome the will of those opposing them so that they see and acquiesce in that which their reason would otherwise tell them was impossible."

"Illusion of the eyes do you mean then?"

"How can you say illusion, when they were found in the courtyard, palpable to the senses?"

"Royal Lady!" cried the Archdruid to the Old Heiress. "Have I your permission to have the screens over the windows withdrawn? It is close and hot in the hall with so many present. Besides there may be thunder in the air."

Then as she turned away to beckon a servant he spoke over his shoulder sternly, "Those matters you discuss are matters of science. It is unwise, indeed forbidden, to speak of them before the unlearned." And with a glance towards the kings and nobles now happy with their food and drink, "Our guests are in any case without interest in them.

"Sir, you must taste his wine!" he called to one of the princes from Fibh, handing him a beautiful bronze cup, "I venture to recommend it. It was brought to me from Italy by a disciple of my own now gone to reside there but recently back on a visit. It will put you in such a glow you will no longer have any care even regarding the Saxons! Or if you prefer it, this from Gaul which came in the ordinary way of trade. Let the lands south of the Bannag be troubled and lose the finer things of life; we in Alba remain in peace and prosperity. The favour of the gods is on those who do their will. But, if a nation falls away from obedience, forsaking their mothers' gods and setting aside the commands of their priests—Come, do not spare it! It is a change from our mead."

Under his attentions and the wine they began to talk freely.

"They say in Eire the great kings drink wine from Gaul. We asked one of the monks who came with—"

214

"Did you have speech with him? I wanted to, but I dared not."

"I wish he had stayed to be at this feast. They say he had a bard's training in his youth, and a man from Eire would be a change. Not but what we have a fine variety of guests in the High King's hall."

"I wish that priest Colum was here. We should know where he was then. Now, who can say? At any time by his magic art he may appear, right in the midst of us. If he came through locked gates what's to hinder him coming into the hall with doors and windows?"

"I wish you had not said it. It's eerie not knowing when a man will appear, or what he might be taking it into his head to do. They say he was very angry."

Heads were turning uneasily.

"Be silent, sir!" Broichan cried to the king from the province of Ce who had last spoken. "You are fuddled with wine. Why are these windows gaping open?" he shouted furiously to the servants, through the tuning of the bards' harpstrings. "Let them be screened every one. It is autumn and the nights cold and you have the winds blowing in upon our guests."

"Master!" the Old Heiress answered, "They were all covered. Only you yourself, Holiness, desired us to have the screens withdrawn. We will have them covered again instantly!" she added quickly, startled at the fury of his face. He was gasping for breath to speak.

"Is my authority in the Palace grown so small you bandy words with me? Now you see what your bad example has done!" he turned to the King, and was enraged more by the sight of the fixed look on Brude's face. "So, my son, you still flout me! You will not bring more than your body to my feast? Your mind still is dreaming of your new friends." He spoke through closed teeth, trying not to say the words aloud.

"Come along, begin your singing," he commanded the waiting bards. "It will be more profitable to have to listen to your songs than to the chatter of fools."

Through the bards' long singing the guests had leisure to talk softly among themselves. Sometimes the Archdruid heard them in a pause, sometimes he made up from the movement of their lips what they said.

"We are safe, do not trouble your head. He has left the province."

" Hasn't he left it and escaped away?"

"After his bitter words!"

" I did not hear exactly what he said — but they say he cursed—"

" Not the Exalted One, surely? He would not dare!"

" He fears nothing."

" He is still here?"

—" He is still here! He must remain here. For if he goes from the province, so he told me, I would die!"

A harsh cackling laughter came from the head of the high table.

Those next to Broichan turned suddenly to him. His hands trembled on the table. He spoke through the bards' song. " He has not left our province. Not because he does not fear us, but because I have so willed it. What is his power to my power?"

They shrank a little from him, took up their nuts and wine, leant forward to hear the singing; whispered again to each other.

" That slavegirl yonder—it's the one they had the words over. Look the other way. Don't look round yet. With the bright hair. Sweeping with the others."

" I can't see her anywhere. Not—such rags and in the Palace! In the King's presence?"

" The King would not notice such things."

" There's something wrong with the King. He is thinking of something it isn't good to think of."

" They say, they are charming when they are not sad. Next year I'll get Orc to give one to me, I have a sword he fancies."

. . . " Why does she smile?" the Archdruid cried out suddenly in a shrill voice that cut through the harps and voices. " Be silent now, stop singing. Why does she smile? How dare she smile at me? Bring her here, and the Keeper."

" She does not smile, Holiness," said the Keeper hastily, " She has no cause to smile. You may see that on the contrary—"

" Bring me a light. Take one from the wall. I thought I saw her smile. I told you to shackle her."

" Master, she is shackled. See, the chain on her ankles, she can scarcely go. It was with the pain she screwed her face, and your Holiness thought she smiled."

" She is shackled, Master," others averred, "On her hands and feet. Do you not see?"

" It is dark. Bring me a light, why will you not? I think she has slipped her chains. He has undone them and freed her."

"Master, the King is angry. Do not say it aloud. The King is close to you, he can hear." Broichan's chief druid laid a timorous hand on the Archdruid's sleeve.

" — He has undone them as he undid the bolts of the gate."

"Master, do not say what you should not!"

"I will say what I please!" Broichan cried in a voice like a woman's scream. "The King may hear if he please. The King may see. This girl is mine still and I will do what I please with her. I will exact labour or send her to the Grove or give her to the young men. We are here to celebrate my victory over the stranger from Eire and over his God. Fill your glasses with the wine. Bring more wine and mead. Fill your glasses and your cups and drink with me." He took the glass beaker in his trembling hands, when the servant had filled it, and raised it up to drink. "I have beaten him, Brudean!" He looked at the King and set his lips to the rim of the beaker.

And in that moment came the crash of breaking glass and a voice high and thin crying. The wine ran like blood from an open wound over the robe and mantle of the Archdruid. Many thought he was wounded when he fell on the floor.

Five slaves bounded forward with cloths to mop up the spilt wine on the floor. But on their knees upon the rushes they stopped, stayed by the stillness. One of them laid the pieces of glass together very softly so as to make no sound.

Stillness, but for the high thin screeching whose only respite was when a gasping more terrible took its place. Time stood still as the people, kings and nobles, stewards and women, gazed in horror at the most holy druid of the Land fallen on the floor, writhing, crying from twisted face with foam-flecked lips. His hands plucked at the floor. From his mouth always came the unbelievable crying.

The druids closed in together and started the great incantaion for one bewitched. But the High King, active at last now, called some of their number who were known for medical skill to tend their Master, and he got men to run for a litter and bring it to lay him on. So they carried him from the hall, his moans and gasping half covered by the incantation.

LI

The knowledge that there was sickness in the household drew them, the old skilled women. They came shuffling to the House of the Druids, carrying water and fresh bedclothes; and one, the oldest among them, carried the polished mirror with which she could decide between life and death. But when they entered the outer room of the Archdruid, where stood the Old Heiress, they grew timid. Not even the authority of their skill could take away their awe in the presence of science. Within the archway of that inner room lay he who was not only a patient but the holiest and most dreaded of wise masters, very companion of the hidden ones.

And all the time to be heard was a strange unearthly babbling which would at times as it were curdle into words,, words in the old language. They heard *Fire,* and *Burning. I am burning, burning.* A druid grey as a ghost in the dim room glided towards the women and took the cup and the water jug and with these entered again the inner place. There came to their ears the gentle familiar sound of pouring water. But the moment after the horrible babbling increased. The words were clearer to hear if not to understand. *I cannot move, I am chained! Feet and hands. Let me up, let me rise! The chains hold me down. Ah—* The shriek was so agonised that even the women, expert in every kind of disease and pain, trembled at it. Huddled together they moved back to the door, the oldest thrusting the bronze mirror hastily into the hand of the Old Heiress who alone stood her ground.

She went forward slowly and heavily as if she were a moving pillar of stone. *Fire,* and *Chained.* Were the tormented words in her mind or in the air? A murmur of men's voices and a mutter of druid prayer drowned the next shriek, but she heard the words that followed it. *Who was it who screamed? Did you hear, did you hear her? It is the girl with the bright hair and foreign speech. She has entered me, she is in my throat, she is screaming in my throat*— The Old Heiress stood stock still and heard them, and they seared her as if the leech were cauterising a poisoned wound. Not bright, she said to herself, but dark hair. She was clenching the handle of the bronze mirror so tightly it was as if she had taken a naked sword into her hand.

She was just inside the inner room. What lay upon the bed was screened from her by the grey-robed men. Some had their heads bent, rotating their shoulders sunwise, some were saying their incantations, breaking off to get their breath back or to exclaim, "It takes three to hold him on the bed!" The awful cry came, anguished and thin, *It is I myself, I am laid on the altar, chained and bound, I cannot move. And the sun is moving up the sky. O Holy One, stand still! Pity me! The noontime shaft is falling at the entrance stone. They are stabbing it into my side. Keep the knife away,—you are making a mistake! Talorg, Aniel—you have made a mistake. I am not the sacrifice, do you hear me? I am the priest! Ah not the knife again!*

Her groan made the druids in front of her turn from their absorption with their Master. "Royal Lady, you should not be here."

She answered through swirling darkness, "The King sent me. My son sent me to see if I could serve in any way." She was glad to feel a discreet finger set below her elbow, with its small support the darkness thinned and her head steadied. She whispered, "Is this an illness like those of other men? How can he die, being immortal?" At the thought that she was holding a mirror for his lips still in her hand she was seized with fright lest it should be construed as blasphemy and dropped it to the floor, though none heard the noise it made for the shrill babbling which had begun again.

"It is a visitation from the gods?" she said in a low tone to the druid nearest her. She could not hear the reply he made, she only noticed that the lips he moved were dry and grey. *Is this Cernunnos? The end and the beginning— the Dark One. O tell him to forgive me! If I have arrogated power that was His, if I have offended putting on my human flesh the Horns of Power— forgive me, Lord. Spare me, let me escape. I am the priest. Take the knife out of my side.*

The druids pressed back from the bed, pushing her back with them. Some had crossed their arms over their bent heads and were covering each ear with the opposite hand. It is not meet for any to be present when the Dark One comes to take his High Priest.

Then one man only stood by her. It was Brude! She fell forward upon him, clasping his arms, thick with muscle, the embossed gold bracelet above the left elbow. She gave a whistling sob of relief and forgot that he was in disgrace. "Brudean, come away. I came because you asked me and out of reverence. But we must not go in there. The Dark One is coming. Even his men of science have gone away."

He led her into the passage, then he himself turned into the doorway again, and so to the inner room.

The Archdruid struggled up to peer into the King's face. "Is it you? Is it you indeed, my treasure?" He stretched up crooked hands, "I thought I had lost you."

"You have not lost me. I am your fosterson."

"But your soul is lost to me. Once I had you, all. But it is all one now, it does not matter. For I am sick. O I am sick, Brudean! I burn as if I were passing through fire, I am all burning. I do not know whether it is my body or my mind. And a knife twists in my side, here, see the left side. Can you find nothing at all to cure me with? Send to the South. In the Far South, in the Island of Mona, near where your father came from they are skilled in leechcraft. Why have you not sent there? What are you, a conquering king, and yet so helpless to save me? The knife twists in my side, I cannot get breath."

The King stooped over the rumpled bed, and said in a voice so calm the sick man looked up at him with hope and longing, "I have sent for help for you."

"Where, where? Over the Bannag? To Myrdinn? Ah but the time, the time! I cannot wait. I am consumed by the fire and my breath will leave me. When will help come, Brudean? If that priest should leave the province I am sure to die. Have you sent to Myrdinn?"

"No."

"Where then?"

"To the man himself, the priest Colum."

Broichan gave a loud cry. "You have betrayed me to him! And all I ever did I did to make you great."

"I have not betrayed you. I have sent for help to him. You know he is renowned as a healer."

220

"Ah! But he may have left our borders. It is why I am going to die."

" Well, I have sent. Even if he is on his way my messengers will overtake him. He will come back and help you."

' He will never help me. We are enemies. I still have that slavegirl. I did not know she would enter my throat and scream!"

" Be still. He will help. He must."

LII

THE two messengers came so suddenly upon them that they almost rode down the folk who had brought the blind child. The earth spurted up from the horses' hooves as they drew to a halt.

"From the Exalted One," they cried leaping down, "From the High King Brude. It is very urgent. Where is your master?" And when Colum, stilled from his prayer in the inner room, came out to them, "The King is sorely afraid for the life of his Archdruid who, he says, lies at the Palace mortally ill. We do not say it, — deisuil! We would not dare say it. It is the King who bade us ask the Christian druid to come with all speed and save his Archdruid's life. We have brought these spare horses, it is quicker than a chariot, one for him and one for his attendant."

Colum answered, "My two attendants shall go. Lugne and Diarmaid, will you get ready and ride with them to the Palace? I must stay here."

"Master, the King has expressly asked for you. These young men are not druids of such distinction as yourself. They may come with you but you yourself must come too. It is the Archdruid Broichan, sir, the King's adviser and fosterfather. Both his importance and the severity of his—situation—call for your own attention.'

"What has happened to him?"

"It was on the night of the great feast, there at the very table, he fell to the ground. We would not dare to say it of so great a man of science: had he been as one of us we should say he lay between life and death."

"Tell me what ails him."

"He cannot freely breathe but gasps so that it is a terror to hear. But it is worst when he is awake for then he is like a man in torment."

"He suffers pain?"

222

"Every breath he draws, he draws with pain. He cannot always speak, but when he does he terrifies all his attendants, even his druids go little to that room. His mind is possessed, deisuil! May we not be overheard — He is as if lying bound awaiting doom. He cries of fire and of being chained and of the knife. He is possessed. Indeed it is not a doctor but an exorcist he needs, so they are saying. If you can do anything, come. The King beseeches you."

"I will come later. But I will immediately send my two young men."

"The Christian druid hates him? Is that why you slight him, letting only your disciples go? He is in such state it will take the strongest science to relieve him."

"I do not hate him any more. I wish him health and peace. It is perhaps he who hates me, and in his state of weakness, I should not go near him. My men will do all it is necessary to do. It is our God who acts in us, and He can use them as well as he can use me. It is all one whether I am far or near." They still looked crestfallen. He had to persuade them. "I will teach my disciples what to do. I will send by them this white stone— it has the blessing of the High God on it."

"Ah!" they looked much relieved. "Now we understand. But the master will instruct his young men how to use it?"

"Father!" Diarmaid said, shocked. And Lugne put his hands behind his back so as not to receive it. "A druid stone!"

"Take it. It is what he will understand."

"But, father, he is ill. It seems like mocking him."

'I am not mocking him. He will understand. Come near and I will tell you what to say. He is sick as much in his soul as in his body. This stone is only a symbol of faith. He must have faith and make his heart pure. Say to him—"

THE Archdruid lay inert upon the bed; only his hands moved, plucking at the covering. He turned his eyes. "How are you now?" the King asked him, modulating his great voice.

Broichan's eyes rested on the King, his dry lips moved. "Why does he not come?"

"He will be here soon. I heard he had not left the river lodge but stayed as if he knew we needed him. As soon as he gets my message he will come. I sent horses for him."

"Brudean my dear! You are my consolation. You do not forsake me. Ah, he is fortunate to have caught your love, for where you give your love you give it for ever. Should he not be here now?"

The King went to the window and stood looking out, down the royal road to the River. He stood as if he did not wish to turn again. The voice that came from the bed was querulous. "Why did you send for him? I can get well without help from him. I gave you no permission to send to him."

"Master, you were gravely ill," the Old Heiress ventured from her seat beside the door. "Your fever was so great. And your mind was— not here. Who could ask you what your will was? Your druids permitted it, seeing they could do nothing. Let it be now." She rose and came nearer to the bed. It is not that I love him, she said to herself; it is only that I cannot imagine our life without him. "I know you do not wish to see this stranger, I do not either. But neither do we wish to see you pass to the shades. My son is sure the priest has power to cure you. We must humble ourselves and ask him."

"At anyrate," the King came back from the window, "It is not from himself we are asking but from his God, who is now my God too."

The Old Heiress whispered, "Do not excite him." For the sick man was becoming perturbed again, moving his head feebly as if to hide his face among his pillows.

"I am afraid of his God. I am afraid of him. I lie helpless here as if chained. What shall I do if he comes here? He has such power that he has taken your soul from me and filled you with an independent spirit. What will he do to me? I am helpless, I cannot move, I cannot escape him."

Together they straightened the covers, for no others dared minister to him. She mastered her face so that it did not show her repugnance for the duty. And she spoke softly as to any sick man, "Do not be afraid, Master. We will stay in the room." She raised a cup of water but he could not drink it.

"Your hands are shaking!" he said. "Are you too afraid of him? What reason have you? It is I. I witheld that slavegirl from him. I have her chained still. And she shall remain so! In that at anyrate I can thwart him."

The Old Heiress dipped her finger in the cup of water to moisten his dry lips, though she was afraid to touch him. "It is not that I need!" Broichan said pettishly. "What good does it do? It only eases the misery of the moment. It is release from this hideous curse that I need, from the knife and from the screams." And the Old Heiress put the cup down on the table and turned from him and went from the room.

"Be at peace!" the King shouted from the window. "I see grey gowns coming in by the gate. I am going to meet him. Do not be afraid. His God is merciful, it will be strange if he does not show mercy. Trust him, he will know how to cure,"

The sentries stood aside with deep bows for the King. He went with long strides through the courtyards to the gate and met the two young monks dismounting. But Colum he saw was not with them. "So we were too late?" he asked his own men. "Why did you not ride westwards after him?"

"Not too late, Gentle King," Lugne replied, "Our Abbot is still at the River. He was waiting to be sent for."

"He knew my foster-father would fall ill?"

"I think, sir, he knew."

"Does he not know how ill he is? Is he not himself coming?"

"He will not come at this time but later. We are to give his message to the Archdruid if your Exalted Highness will permit us to go to him?"

"I forgot the need for haste," said Brude sighing a little. "Will you follow me?"

"Is he coming?" the sick man tried to raise himself on an elbow as they entered his room.

"He has not come himself, foster-father." In a moment the

look of relief was followed by a look of wild despair. "But here
are his men who bring a message from him. He has taught them
how to cure you."

The druids crowded close round. "It will be a matter of
prayers. They are always praying. I think it should all be done
in the open air."

"No, they will have brought herbs. They are fonder of
herbs than incantations."

"Take care! You will see their master suddenly appear in
our midst."

"I told you it would be safer in the open air."

"Be silent and let our guests speak," commanded Brude.
And he looked expectant at them. In answer Diarmaid drew from
the pocket of his habit— a round white stone. "Our Abbot sends
you this white stone. He says if you get water—"

"Yes, yes, we know."

"— and place the stone in it—"

"The stone will float on top of the water. We know."

"But— we do not believe it any more."

"O but we do!"

"It is all in the mind of the believer."

"The priest from Eire is making a mockery of our practice."

But, "Quick! Bring the water!" Broichan cried from his
bed. "I will try anything."

"This we understand. This the Archdruid can easily do,"
said the King's mother to the monks, "Your master is kind. We
thank him for entrusting us with his powerful stone. It shall be
returned to him when the Archdruid is cured. We believe in the
science of your master and are grateful to have it used on our
behalf."

"It is a stone from your own River," Lugne gently said,
"And our Lord Abbot does not ask it back again. He has blessed
it and prayed for the Archdruid, in that way it has the power of
God in it."

"The water!" Broichan said. They brought him a silver
bowl of water, the King steadying it with his hand over the
Archdruid's hand, and the white stone.

"Stop!" the monks said. "Our Abbot says, let not the
Archdruid drink until he has set free the young slavegirl. If he
commands her release and drinks, he will immediately begin to
grow well. If he refuses to free her and drinks, his illness will
increase until it carries him away."

LIV

It was delicious to be together again in the strange land that itself seemed to have grown familiar.

" Now, what of Dornaig?" Colum asked Cannich and Comgal at the gate. " Did you find the place Finbar used to tell us of in our schooldays? Is there any teacher there now, or any church standing? Do the people remember the settlement at least?"

They looked round cautiously at the men of Alba who were close around them.

"You may speak freely," Colum said.

So they told him. The church of Finbar's day had fallen, they had seen only its foundations on the ground. But there was a secret cell, and people gathered to it still though their teaching was the concern now of travelling clerics alone, those who risked life and slipped past the Valley of Science and the royal seat, either going by sea or going far to westward through lonely straths and glens where the folk were quiet and little disposed to betray anyone who did no wrong.

Now maybe the old road would open up again and Christian teachers come and go freely to build up the people in their faith. Would the shield of Brude's protection cover such travellers, even against the malice of the old religion?

As if in answer there was a stir among the people. A company were riding out of the palace gate, Nechtan of Dunduirn with his armed retinue. Between their lines, surprisingly, rode three women: the Young Heiress rode with two women to accompany her. The party reined horses and Colum went forward to bless them. The women were mantled close for riding, but from one of the attendant ladies the fold of cloth fell revealing a young pale face and bright hair. She leapt from her horse first of any and came to kneel at the Abbot Colum's feet, stroking the stuff of his faded garment. He put his hands over her head and spoke to her in a low voice, before calling his blessing to the others.

Looking over her shoulder at him, between smiling and weeping, she went slowly back and mounted her horse again, and they all rode off down the hillside.

"Why!" Comgal said, "It is only now I realise it, you spoke to that young girl in our own tongue!"

And Cannich, "She looks different from the Alban people. Who is she?"

"She is our little fellow countrywoman," Colum answered, still looking after the riders as they went down over the slope of the hill. "She was a captive here, a slavegirl, put in my way as I now see to tempt me. She will go safe to Dunduirn, and there they will find means of sending her to Dalriada and so to Eire."

As they went into the courtyard of the Palace, before they went to the King, Comgal and Cannich asked, "What about the Archdruid, Colum, and his hold on the King? May we, when we go south by the communities along the east coast, tell the clerics that the road is safe for them? Is the Archdruid no more to be feared?"

"He is still to be watched! I will stay on a little longer here, though I shall thereby forego your company. I must stay longer with the King. Before winter I hope I shall go back to Dalriada through our desolate glen. When I remember Connal and my own men on the Island I can scarcely endure to remain here. But remain I must."

A Guest
That Flew Away

LV

BRUDE held the Archdruid on his arm and walked slowly and patiently, fitting his steps to those of the convalescent. The sun came in, warm for an autumn season, and the King's eyes turned now and again towards the door.

"You are eager to be off somewhere," the old man said. "My dear son! It is no holiday from cares for you to share my sickroom."

"It will not be a sickroom much longer. Soon you will be out and about again."

"I wonder, I wonder, Brudean! We shall see. I hardly long for health when my illness brings me so much of your welcome company. You do love me still then? I have not lost you?"

The King answered gently, "I shall always be your fosterson. You brought me up as a child." But even as he said the words, his eyes went to the door again.

"Not so fast, my dear!" The Archdruid said playfully. "You are a rough nurse!"

There was a sound of voices, a deep roar of laughter. The King's arm tensed in all its muscles so that the druid turned to look at him. Brude's face, eager as a boy's was turned to the doorway. The Archdruid angrily shook himself free from the supporting arm.

"Now I know for what you have been waiting! You have been expecting him to come to the Palace, is that it?"

"He must be in the hall. I have something to give him and and must see him. What harm will it do?"

"O no harm, no harm. No harm but what is already done. Your heart is his. You tend me kindly and speak of fosterage. But he has only to be heard in the courtyards and your thoughts run to him. Go to him then, go now!"

"Why no," the King answered peaceably, "I did not mean that there was any hurry."

The Archdruid said to himself, almost with envy, "What peace it is for a man to be a fool!"

"But he is going away soon."

"Why did he not go when his friends went?"

"The other two abbots have gone by the East to visit the communities in Ce and Circind. Talorgan has gone with them. The Abbot Colum goes back by way of the Glen. He is anxious to see his kinsmen in Dalriada, and the Island I granted him. Yesterday the guides who brought him here were found, seeking him through the Palace. And he longs to go home now."

"I am glad to hear the news!"

"If you will forgive me, fosterfather, I must go now to the hall. What I have to do is best done in the presence of the kings and nobles."

Broichan stretched out his thin arm for the King's support again. "If you will bear with me, Brudean, I will go with you." And Brude had out of courtesy to give it. Not only he but his bodyguard had to slow steps for the old man.

The sentries cried out for the High King as they entered the doorway of the hall. Colum was there with Roith's brother, and Tarain and his cousin a prince from the mainland of Cat. He came to bow to the High King, then greeted the Archdruid, "I am glad to see you, sir, up and walking again."

Broichan muttered whether thanks or abuse, and went to a window seat where he could see what the King was at. He saw Brude take from his attendant a great round brooch and give it into the Abbot's hands. Drifts of his explanation came, "Connal, in the presence of my lords—so that it may be widely known he has his former state—"

Then apart from the rest the High King and the Abbot walked up and down; their voices were too quiet for the old man to hear. Sometimes the stranger spoke and Brude nodded as he listened; sometimes Brude asked a question and the stranger answered with a smile. The stranger was instructing him whom till now only he, Broichan, had instructed. He was teaching him, enjoining him, going over some matter like a schoolmaster over and over, and the King repeated it. Ah holy gods, to see it happen before one's very eyes! He groaned and felt his hatred like poison in his body. He tried not to observe or listen to them, but he must ever follow them with ear and eye, as the tongue will ever touch a bad tooth.

Colum saw the Archdruid coming towards Brude and himself, and stopped speaking. Broichan came and walked between them, and they slowed their pace to his.

"Do I hear that you are now disposed to leave us?" As Colum nodded, "That is sad news for some of us! For the King here, who has grown so much your friend."—

The King smiled but watched the Archdruid warily.—"It is a pity such great friends should have to part. We must think of some means to keep your spiritual adviser longer here, Brudean."

"He says he must go, fosterfather. But he will come again."

"O! But I should like to help him to stay longer with us, to stay so long there would be no need for the effort of another visit. Yes, now, let me see what I could do."

"Sir!" said the King, grown stern.

"You are fond of one another. No? It is his god you love? It is much the same. I must think of some way."

"I have declared our guest to be under my protection, as King and ruler of Alba."

The Archdruid took no notice of him. He turned to Colum. "Tell me, Master, on which day do you propose to go from us?"

The King made a sign to warn him, but Colum immediately replied, "On the third day from now, if the wind is favourable —and I am still alive!"

"I am glad you say, if the wind is favourable. For the elements are not in the High King's power. Your going depends a little on my pleasure."

"Leave him alone," cried the King furiously.

"You do not understand," the Archdruid said, smiling patiently. "You do not see that I am playing a sort of game with him. But he and I are both in our own ways men of science; we understand life can be like a game of chess, Brudean, to put it that way. There are many moves in that game. Do you think that the head of religion, the Archdruid of Alba, has been worsted by this Christian priest? It might appear so. But all that has happened has been of my permitting, my contriving I might have said. It paves the way for his final overthrow. If he goes, as he says he will, on the third day I fear for his safety and for the safety of any men who travel with him."

The King took his fosterfather by the arm, this time not gently. "You made me receive him with hostility. But I will send him away in honour as well as safety. What do you mean to do to him?"

233

"I shall do nothing directly to hurt him. It is very simple. It is no more than a game. He procures by prayer or any means a favourable wind on the third day to blow him down the Long Glen. I by my craft will get a contrary wind which will keep him against his will here. If he cares to sail into the weather I shall call up, it is his own doing."

"He cured you. You crossed him, and he might have gone away. But he waited and he cured you. Have you forgotten so soon?"

"I thought it was his god who cured me? He boasts great things of him! Good then, but you will see if his power is greater than the power of our own gods. You and these lords and the whole of your Land, North and South shall see."

LVI

THE harvesters at the Head of the Loch let the corn shocks fall from their hands to wipe their faces hot from the sun that shone from the clear blue autumn sky. The Loch waters glittered between dark wooded sides, a good sight for those that lived by it in all weathers.

"Look now!" one said, "Is that the High King's men from the Palace again? God of Light, if it isn't the third time they have been here scanning the face of the Loch westward!"

"What's up this time? Can they be expecting more strange holy men coming up through the Glen?"

"They say the High King sends them to look out and see the weather. At the Palace too they're aye looking up at the sky to see will it change. Why folks like that who have plenty changes of clothing should bother their heads about it! It's different for you and me. See and take up your armful, Aniel, and let us get on with the binding while it's dry."

"They say the Archdruid is going to make the weather wild and boisterous to keep the Christian druid from Eire longer here."

"You have it wrong, man! For he's against him. He would not want to keep him. You've got it the wrong way."

They wound ropes of the shining straw and bound round the yellow armfuls. Their piles stood like a little army on the stubble field.

"I'm telling you, His Holiness has said openly he will raise a storm of wind blowing up from the south west to keep the priest Colum here against his will. It isn't for love, it's so that he can disgrace him, him and his new God with him. For he has declared he will go on the third day, and that is tomorrow; and if he can go it's a victory for him. But if he's storm-stayed it is a victory for the Archdruid. I had it all from my nephew who heard it at the hinge of the King's door."

"I wish between them they would leave the weather alone. We have to get the corn in."

"But it'll be worth watching which will win the victory. I have my nephew and his wife and his wife's brother coming here just to see what's going to happen tomorrow. It's a combat between the very gods, as you might say, between the old and the new."

"I don't like it. I wish they would leave the god's alone. I was beginning to like what I heard of the strange druids. Besides, what Brude mac Maelchon and his lords do is what I'm content to follow. Now if this priest and his god are shown to be weaker than the old,—They say he's left his pebble behind, the one that cured the Archdruid's sickness."

"Don't vex yourself, for the weather's set fair. It will stay this way for a day or two more. Look at the small high clouds sailing from the north. There won't be a storm tomorrow, it will be the same as today."

"It can change though, in an hour or less. Sometimes the way it changes isn't natural. My father always said it was because we were near the Grove. The Wise Masters there learn to have influence over the weather and they change it from cloudy to fair and back to cloudy again, just as you would say for practice in the art. It may be clear and hot like this today, and a great storm of wind tomorrow. Deisuil!"

LVII

ASPATTER of rain blown by the south wind into the faces
of the cavalcade as it went along the course of the River
somewhat spoiled the fine clothing of the King and his
retinue. The monks drew up their cowls over their heads,
though the cloth of their grey habits was too worn and threadbare
now to be much use against the wind. The druids of the retinue
of the Archdruid Broichan likewise pulled their hoods up about
their ears, exhanging faint smiles with their leader whose face all
traces of illness had left.

"Who would have said," Diarmaid drew closer to Lugne,
"that the weather would change on the very morning we said
we would go away? It was so fine and clear last night. This
valley is subject to sudden changes of weather?" he asked the
Dalriadan guides who rode with them.

"It is. It's what makes sailing on the Loch dangerous. A
sudden storm will come raving through the Glen, and take a
man unawares. But we have warning of this storm, and since we
are safe on the land we should stay so. Ask the father to put
our journey off till another day."

"Father," Lugne spurred forward and spoke to Colum, "Our
men are asking must we go without fail today? After all, father,
we have been months away from Dalriada, one day will not
make any difference to their anxiety. If we waited even one day
the wind might turn and blow from the north again and we
should have it all our own way."

"We will go on," Colum gently overruled them, "We must
go, for in the minds of the people to turn back would be to
show no trust in the protecting power of God. If the wind gets
up suddenly it will fall suddenly too," he comforted Duncath and
Conn and Fergal. "There's no need to be afraid."

"Colum!" King Brude called through the whistling wind,
"If you turn back now none will think ill of it. If we go on and
find you are unable to make out from shore then it will appear a

defeat and a disgrace." He stopped short, with a glance at his retinue. His men gave way to a few sailors who had come on foot to meet them. "Master!" they said to Colum with a bow in passing to the King, "We have your boat ready and new sails on her. But you are not thinking of putting out today? The wind is contrary and coming hard up the Glen. You will never sail south today, wait till it changes."

"Why are you leaving us?" a woman called from the crowd that was gathering about them. "It's pleasant enough here. We will give you a house to live in and you may teach us your new science, and if you can cure my sister's son's eyes the way you did—"

The King spoke with the rain streaming down his face. "Now we have set out and they know where you are going, I suppose it is too late. We should have altered plans of departure before leaving the Palace. I suppose you must go on, even if you perish I do not fear having to account for you to your kindred seeing they are alien to me. But I shall have my own kings—Nechtan for one, what will he say of me? I shall have let a guest perish with my full foreknowledge. I shall be guilty of your death, you who have given my hidden life to me. Why have you put me in this position?"

"It is only a storm, sir, don't have us dead before our time!"

But the King would not listen. "What a thing to have happened at the very end! I did not think he could so keep up his hatred." And angrily he urged his horse on, riding at the head of his retinue, as doleful as to an execution.

They came to a rise of land from which in a moment the whole Loch came in view. And they felt their breath in their throats. —Where it could be calm and bright, stretching back to the dim mountains of the West it was all dark and grey, crested with white waves like the sea. The wild wind swept against them as they stood gazing, making them hold their clothes down and shield their faces from its bitter lash. Mist and rain filled all the narrow valley. The trees upon the wooded sides swayed helplessly, their leaves rising from them into the churning air.

Brude said with relief, "It cannot be done! You will not make out against such a storm."

The shore was ugly with foam, strewn with the yellowed branches of old trees, spewed from the waters. On it lay their ship with its new sails furled, like a sick bird stranded.

"No, sir," Duncath said, "We could not put out in this. There is no pushing off; or if we got any way out we should be blown back to land. Though better that than to get into midway and then— then—" But he shrugged in despair at sight of Colum's fixed face.

"I will make you this promise again," the King put his hand on the Abbot's, "and with God's aid I will keep it. I will not harry your cousin's land of Dalriada. While I live I will not harry or spoil. And I will let your monks live and work on your Island and they may go among my people. I will not hinder or permit hindrance, so far as I am able, in the work of the clerics in the communities by the east coast plain; I will allow them to pass on their way north. Whether you live or die I make this promise to you. I am very sorry to part this way from you."

"Father—it's the caves and the shelving rocks they told us of, do you remember?" Diarmaid spoke low, in a whisper, so as not to let the Dalriadan guides hear. But they were murmuring their own fears— "unfathomed. Deep as hell. What she wants she takes,— Father, may we not go on foot by the Lochside?"

"Come on, come on!" Colum cried. "Are we going to have it said the men of Dalriada have forgotten the seamanship that brought them once from Eire? Are we to have it said we sail only with favourable winds? We're going to show how we can sail in a contrary wind. It's no worse than a wind, my dear!" he said to Lugne, "So get the sails up as you best can. We will tack into it and make a course this way then that. We shall get on very well, you shall all see.

"God is Lord of all the winds," he called to the people as he blessed them with an arm from which the sleeve was blown like a flag. "He is kind and he has all power."

Then he climbed into the sagging ship and called them by name, "Duncath! Let's see how you can take her out. Fergal! Conn! In with you! Hoist up the sails bit by bit. Lugne, stand by the boom and mind you duck quick when we turn. It's no more than a contrary wind. You have made a way in one before. Let us not keep our hosts standing longer than we need in the rain."

The High King and his people stood bearing forward against the wind, peering through the rainy squalls at the ship as it made out from the shore. It turned this way and then that, a crooked course, but it went fast as if the wind were on its side. Now the waves splashed up and over it,now it swayed as if to keel over. But always it righted itself and went on its way till the distance widened and it grew small to their sight.

And as they went on watching it the sun came through, and the wind died. And in the clearing air they still saw the tiny shape out in the middle of the expanse of water. The narrow valley filled with sunlight.

LVIII

THEY hauled down their sails and brought the boat in, handling it with respect, the way a man after a victorious fight handles sword and shield. Then they spread the sails to dry in a gentle north east wind and themselves sat down beside them on the smooth shore at the southern end of the Long Loch. The water quapped upon the round stones. They sat in weariness and peace and were silent, only the water talking wordlessly.

Colum stood on the shore looking up the long expanse of the Loch to where the land at the northern end of it was bright in a setting sun. Almost he felt he could still discern the form of Brude standing against that wild south west wind with his mantle blown backwards from his sturdy shoulders, watching with perplexed and kindly eyes.

The people by the River and at Airdchartan too—he could almost hear their voices as if they were carried on the breeze, feel the touch of their hands. He could remember them by their illnesses and by confided misfortunes, as if they were his own people. They still seemed very near and real. And yet not only the long expanse of grey water separated him from them but the accomplishment of his task in their country and the purpose that drew him to Dalriada again. In that moment he would have given much to have been able to stay, for he yearned for them, in bondage to fear as they were, hungry for their salvation. How long would it be till they entered into possession of it? How long would the power of the Archdruid and the Valley of Science hold them as if in fetters?

Their help would come, perhaps soon. Now that the High King was a believer the trail up the east coast from the communities of the south would lie open again. They would set up new cells and churches and rebuild the old, rally secret believers and make more, correct into joy the distorted fearful half-faith.

—" Lord Abbot!" his young men, Lugne and Diarmaid, were calling his attention, though chary of breaking in upon his prayer.

He found round them the folk from the village that lay where the river ran into the Loch. They had come up, timidly but in friendly fashion, and offered help in drawing the boat further on to the grass above the shore. Three women came in their gowns of patterned woollen stuff with milk warm from the evening milking. There was room in the houses here, they said, for the little company and a meal was being prepared—indeed smoke from the peat fires and steam from cooking pots rose swaying up into the air.

The Dalriadan guides were quite vexed next morning at the escort which went with them to the next place of habitation, and grudged them the handling of the boat, though by the end of a day it grew heavy enough. "We risked something to come to carry it," they said, "And now there is no need!"

"Need though less risk," Colum humoured them, "And we shall need Fergal to lead us when we come to the forest and there are wild beasts. He knows as much as any man, Alban or Dalriadan, of forest ways."

They were kindly received each day as they went on their journey. Lying safe at night, under rugs in the sharp autumn air, they marvelled at the welcome they found. Had elusive messengers from Brude preceded them, his goodwill going with them to protect them to the debated territory? At anyrate, the people were friendly, and disposed to listen to anything they might say of the new way.

"Almost," Lugne said, "if we were to meet a man who spoke to us in our own tongue we should find it hard to understand him!"

"We shall soon be in the forest," Fergal grunted, "There is little speaking of any kind there."

Their last escort came with them up the hillslope into the forest. The leaves of the oak and beech were yellow and brown, sparse upon the trees, and falling on them as they passed beneath on their laborious way upward.

The second night they made their camp on the pine-needle floor, and lit fires not only for warmth but for security against the wolves and bears. They heard no howling; but a hooting after dusk as if all the owls in Alba were holding conference. Fergal and the Alban men stood up stiff with anxiety, and peered this way and that among the shadowy trees. Colum looked to Conn who had shown such fear on their outward journey, indeed he was murmuring about spirits coming back for Savaintide.

" Spirits they may not be," Fergal said as Colum was reassuring the other, " But I thought that I saw the shapes of men. They were over there— and on that side too; flitting about among the pinetrees. I would rather it were wolves, a man knows where he is with them."

Even while the monks said evening prayer and the sound of the psalm went bravely out into the shadowy forest, Fergal and Conn and the Alban men stood with bows bent, ready, peering in among the trunks of the trees. Suddenly they drew their arrows back: yet with a cry of, " Colum! Father! Father!" a young man leapt in amongst them and fell at Colum's knees. The men of Dalriada cried, " Stop! Hold back!" and thrust the Cruithnian archers aside. And Colum cried out too and put his hands over the young man's head lest any arrow should find it, for he was Gauran's son! After him came others. The camp fires flickered on their thin faces, hollow cheeks, and dark-circled eyes. The young men of Dalriada! He had not remembered that they were so thin.

Then indeed they heard their own language, pouring out. " We did not know if we should ever see you again."

" The guides sent messages, we knew you had got near to the High King's Palace. And then we heard nothing. And the time went on."

" What have they done with you?" the young prince Eogan asked, raising his face shining with tears from the Abbot's knee. " How have you got away? What men are these with you? And the other priests, your friends—?"

" Stand up!" Colum said sternly, but when the young man rose he took him in his arms. " I forbade you to come with me. It is I who must ask: Why have you come now into Cruithnian territory? Don't you know you have come into danger, to no purpose, and you the heir to Dalriada?"

But even while he looked over Eogan's shoulder at the bewildered faces of the Alban men, so far as he could see them between light and shadow, he saw no enmity there, only innocent curiosity. " The Master has met friends? They have come to take him into his own country where we must not go? Good then; we will leave him to their escort tomorrow."

And Colum put his hand over Eogan's as it tightened at the sound of the Cruithnian speech. " I had myself forgotten the news I am bringing home!"

LIX

A FARMER in Dalriada was cutting manfully at the thin
corn stems. Round him the birds were wheeling to snatch
a bite of grain. There must be robins, for the sweet tune-
less song was in the air; but there certainly were greedy
gulls from the sea, and crows. He waved his arms to frighten
them away. Yet he turned back to his cutting with a smile. It
was something anyway that birds thought it worth their while
to thieve in Dalriada again! And as if following the same thought
in his mind he looked down the gentle hillslope to the low
ground where the smoke columns rose from his hearth and the
hearths of his neighbours. Supper would be cooking there, tired
men would sit to a man's meal at the close of day.

True, it was a meagre harvest by other times. But remembering this year's spring sowing and the dearth that went before,
a man must only be amazed to have one at all. He remembered
with a memory that resided in the muscles how the plough had
jibbed and turned askew as he forced it through the soil,
hardened with the feet of fighting men or stiffly rooted with grass
and weeds. For the year before it had never been broken, far less
sown and harvested. Had the birds come wheeling then about
them it was not with a smile they would have been sent away.

So long as this harvest did not draw on them again those
Cruithnians! Sweat rose on his forehead. The curved knife
twisted and failed in his wet palm. He began an invocation to
the God of Light. Then he bethought himself: he tried to recall
instead the prayer the monks from the Island had taught them
only this summer, and before that the Abbot Colum.

A rumour was going round that the Abbot Colum was safe
and coming home. The prince Eogan had sent one of his band
back, a young fellow stuttering with the excitement of his
message. It would be a pleasant thing to show him the harvest.

He heard a shout, and looked sharply up. Higher on the hill
on the grassland and heather his cousins were gathering in the
sheep. They were waving and pointing north where the little

track came out between the hills. He paused, sickle in hand. Fear sprang up like a wolf in his heart again. But it was not the Cruithnians!

A company of people were coming southward on the track, women and men with children on their shoulders, and at the head of them, that was the prince Eogan, and with the prince—Ah, the tall figure and the bright hair into which the brow went deep back because of the tonsure!

"Send to the King!" Niall shouted into the empty air, for his cousins could not hear him. "Send a message to the dun! Tell Connal!" Some drift of what he said must have come to them, for he could see them sway with laughter and point to the south. He turned that way, and saw Connal coming riding, with a couple of men running after him leading horses. On they came across the wide Bog. They would meet the clerics on the road below his field! Niall flung his curved knife away from him and ran, trampling the still standing with the cut corn.

Connal got down from his horse so clumsily he all but caught his foot in the reins. He lumbered to the Abbot's side and put his arms round him, grasping the slack cloth of the habit. "Colum yourself, safe? Safe? You were so long away. Where were you, why have you been away so long?"

"Why, man, don't scold me!" Colum said with a fond look at the convulsed face, wondering secretly of Connal's hair had been so speckled grey before. "We have come safe home to you, my men and I, if that is what you want."

"I should never have let you go! We lost trace of you, your guides brought only perplexing messages. So did our spies, if ever they got anywhere near Brude's place at all. You were at his Palace on the Nesa, you were not there, you could not get in, you could not get out again. We did not know what to believe, and the time went by. Some said you were all of you bewitched, carried off to their druid hell. Where are the two fathers your friends who went with you?"

"Safe, safe too. They've come home by another way."

"Eogan at last could bear it no longer. We should never have let you away. Only what good should we have done you, beaten as we are by him? Eogan went out to look for you, and we thought we had lost him too. How has the High King let you go, Colum? He has asked a ransom for you, is that it? We will make shift to pay it. That is, if you have taken an oath on it. Ailech will help us, for your sake, or else remit our tribute till we raise it. You shake your head! Colum, you've never taken oath to return as his captive for ever?" He licked dry lips. "Ah, that's it! You've given your word you will go back to him."

"In a sense I have. I will indeed go back, but not bound in the way you fear. I have so much to tell you. Look, the people want to speak with us. Only this now about Brude: he is a good and honourable man, a High King indeed, and it would be an honour to be his friend."

"What do you mean? Colum, what is it? You look like a man who's won a victory,—though it's long enough since I knew one! Honourable and a friend? Has he granted you the Island. Ah is that it? So he did respect you as a holy man although of the new way? He has sent you away free and with your request granted? If that is so, I will never say word against him, though he shamed me in his Palace for all his lords to see."

"Forgive it, my dear. Let it go from your mind. It will go from others', you will see. He has promised to live at peace with us. I'll talk of it further, for the people, see—"

"Peace! Did you say peace? It would be a miracle if the Cruithnians gave us peace."

"It was all a miracle. God was before us in the Alban Land and He had conquered the King who conquered you. And Connal, I have a gift for you, but later, later!"

For the people crowded between him and Connal, thinking they had had enough speech. Children ran in with brambles in a leaf and hazel clusters from the woods, "You are hungry after your journey?"

"How is Connad?" suddenly Colum asked. For answer they pointed to a young man on horseback. "A warrior so soon! The cough gone for ever? And the little brothers with their horses of clay?"

LX

THEY rode across the Bog and came to the Long River coiling around the steep rock on which Dunadd stood. They splashed over and came to that one entrance. Even as the thought of her passed through his mind Colum saw Lluan now standing midway on the stairs ready to welcome him again. Her hair was bound in plaits and piled on her fine head and she wore a golden circlet. It was not hard to picture her as she had been in Gauran's day, queen of a little country, but a valiant one. She came down to meet him more eagerly perhaps than she had planned, and in the midst of her formal greeting and her reverent inclining to his blessing she began to ask the questions Connal had asked, How was he? Had he come safe from the toils of the Cruthnians—signing herself—Ah, was it not the mercy of God he should be back in a gentle country? When had he eaten last?

He scarcely heard the questions, he had so many of his own to ask. As he went up he noticed that the walls were rebuilt, the floor smoothed, with steps evened. From the hall they were approaching a warmth came, and the hum of voices; the stench of misery was gone.

"Aedan is coming. He may be here." Lluan looked round. But Colum asked, "Where is the queen? How is she? The child—?"

The child? Yes, he was answered, the child had come, a boy. It was three months cradled and had begun to smile. On Connal's own face a slow smile appeared. Lluan led the Abbot to the door of the women's grianan, and called softly into it. And in a moment out she came, the wife of Connal, Gauran's niece. She had the young child in her arms, and lifted him up for Colum to see, trembling with delight. The baby stretched out his tiny star-shaped hand and took Colum's finger in a warm wet clasp of his own.

Into his memory came the slavegirl in Brude's Palace, and he commended her when she should come to the keeping of the queens. "I shall see to it," Lluan said. "She shall make her home here, or we shall send her to her home in Eire. We have ships now, three have newly been built. Next year they may build a longship for Connal."

He found himself looking down on the kitchens, Lluan not disdaining to point them out to him. Girls sang as they turned the round stone querns, the meal spurting from the sides so that the air was filled with white dust and a sweet homely smell. A mason crouched over a new quern he was completing. Colum leaned down to bless them, and all Dalriada, in field and granary and grinding stone. "He shall carve a cross in the one he is making," Lluan said, "because of your homecoming. — But I must bring Aedan," and as she led him to the hall again she spoke fondly of her younger son. "Though he is so young he is strong. He is like Gauran. That is, in some ways. We tried to rebuild Dunadd after you left us, the grianan at least.

"But in spring we had dark hungry days, and for all our willingness I doubt if we should have done much. It was Aedan. When Aedan came he made the young men quarry stone and he sent others to Loch Awe for wood. And he drove the men though they complained they had too little food to work on, he drove them to repair and rebuild. Eogan was in despair imagining you were lost, and Connal longed for you. But Aedan commanded our men. When is he coming? He was busy looking over the armoury, sending swords and spears down to the smithy. Ah—here, father, is my son Aedan mac Gauran."

Colum saw the young man coming dutifully to greet him and incline to his blessing. Beside his elder brother Eogan Aedan was short, thickset: but he differed most from him in the look of forcefulness he wore. Perhaps the mouth was a trifle wilful, the eyes arrogant with the arrogance of youth? Still, there was a forlorn gallantry about him that touched Colum, and he thought, "This indeed is Gauran's son!" And as he put his hand on the young man's head, bowed briefly to receive it, he said, "You have done well, my son! You have made Dunadd worthy for kings to live in."

"Colum," Connal said, as though to cover up a word that gave him pain, "You say Brude is ready to make peace? How can I credit it?"

"By this!" Colum drew out from the breast of his habit the brooch Brude had sent with him, and himself fixed it on the neck of Connal's mantle, thrusting the pin into the spiralled ring. "He will not trouble you if you do not trouble him. He will not harass you for tribute, since he regards you as an independent king."

Connal seized the brooch on his neck so tightly the pin entered his hand and a drop of red blood spread on the shabby blue mantle cloth. He licked smiling lips, not knowing what to say. But the two young men, with royal breeding in them, dropped on one knee before him in a gesture of homage, and he stood still and straight then, his hands at his sides.

Lluan said through her tears, "You have made peace, God be thanked for it! I was afraid all this rebuilding might draw their attack on us once again. They would take Aedan.—What pity would they show to Gauran's sons?"

Aedan put his arm merrily round her, "Come, Mother, we've had enough crying! It's a feast you must be thinking of now. We must ask all the princes of the kindreds and the chiefs here to Dunadd, to see our cousin the priest home in Dalriada again. And they will see Connal's state."

"I scarcely dared hope you would succeed," Connal was saying. "It seemed as much a dream as Aedan's hope he would get Rederech of Strathclydd to give us men."

"Now he will give them!" the young man cried, "We are a nation again. Or maybe next year when we have our food and our homesteads, and our men under arms. When we show him we are not finished yet he will give us as many as ever he can spare, and we can fight back against the Cruithnians and get back our lost land."

Connal was quick to see the shade on the Abbot's face. "Not this year or the next!" he said sharply to Aedan. "We are at peace with the Cruithnians. Our cousin went to seek it, and though he has not told us all I do not doubt it was dearly sought." Then he said more lightly, shoving the young man aside, "This boy will soon be scheming on the other side! He will make an alliance with Brude mac Maelchon and go to war against Strathclydd and Reged—if not against the Saxons themselves! What's this they're calling you? Aedan Vradog?"

Lluan was indignant at this, "A Deceiver? Who dare use such a word of Gauran's son?"

"Well," Colum said, "That is what Brude's gift means, we may take our place in Alba, pray God it may always be a worthy one. He is to be honoured as a friend, Brude mac Maelchon, not feared as a foe. But he is to be honoured!"

After that they all came round him, women and men, with questions about their late enemies. "Is it true the women rule? Who rules the High King? Is it true that women take a husband for only a year, and that a man does not know who his father is? Did you ever see the terrible Archdruid?"

"You have come through so many perils and have so much still to tell us!" they protested next day, when after mass he said he must go.

"You are forgetting the other half of my petition to King Brude," he reminded them. "I want to see my Island. Have you forgotten I have left a half-score men there waiting for me?"

LXI

HE sent back the longship from the west of Mula, saying
he and his two men would cross to the Island alone.
There were fishers' curraghs everywhere along the shore,
they could find one to take them.
They climbed up a little hill and went down into a bay, and
from there he got sight of it.

Yet it was strange to his eyes. It was as if he had forgotten
it in some measure after all. The outline of it struck him with a
sense almost of foreboding. That odd hump-backed island, that
rising hill on which was the circle of ancient stones, those cold
white beaches fringing the grassland—all spoke to him of the
most searching pain. He remembered, how could he ever forget,
the early desolation of the men who followed him away from
home, cold, storm and sickness, hunger, hostility, fear, confusion
between false and true and keenest woe of all, exile from Eire. He
remembered their first friend the poor young stranger who had
called himself after Oran, and had thought to honour God by
his outlandish sin. His own vigils, his search for the presence of
God.—The wind that blew behind them from over the heathery
moor was so cold on his skin it made him shiver. He passed his
hand over his lonely eyes.

And then suddenly, very small and thin in the wide air, came
a sound. It was so small and thin it seemed to him like the first
cry of a child. Like a woman delivered his heart was flooded by
great joy. The tiny sound had all the meaning of the world in it.

It was the sound, remote, diminished by distance, of the
abbot bell. He crouched on the rough bents of the shore, his face
pressed into his hands. Only his ears were active, hearing,
hearing. As he knew it would be, the tiny sound was over, and
others followed it. He could hear the singing as the voices rose
on a phrase of the psalm, lose the tune to recover it again. He
followed the mass they said, his knowledge of it filling up what

251

was lost to hearing. The deep peace after pain was so like a childbirth that when he moved his body felt spent and strained.

O my Island, my most dreadful and dear, have I indeed come to you again? I am home.

When he lifted his head, he found Diarmaid and Lugne gazing across the Sound with him. He could see distinctly the small figures of his men; he saw the cows spread out driven by, it must be, Grillan; he saw tall Ernan go up to the abbot cell, he saw some come down to the shore searching for dulse for a meal.

And at that he hailed them at full voice, echoes went over the Sound. A company of outraged gulls rose from the rocks close by. He gave them a deprecating grin, and shouted again. He heard an answering shout from the man driving the cows, another from somewhere on the hill. The figures came together from all around, and moved down to the shore. Have they repaired the causeway? Did they manage to cut the stones?

He ran to the sailors who were leaning against their curragh. "Push out, quick. I must go over now."

"Father," they said reproachfully, "We were waiting for you!"

Up and down, up and down, in the little hills and hollows of the waves they went as if they were dancing. When they were up on a crest he could see his people, they got larger every time he saw them from the crest of a wave.

They were gliding in between the two jaws of the rocks, sagging on the pale sand. It was like all homecomings in one to have their tumultuous welcome, to talk in the midst of talking, to ask questions and be too happy to hear the replies. For they were all here, safe and sound as he had left them; he pored over each face in turn, although they jostled each other to and fro. "Baithene, and Grillan, and Scandal, and Ernan, Mochonna . . ."

LXII

THE strong west wind ran over the heather and the yellowed grass, the cows on the machair below him had their tails blown over their backs. Diarmaid settled himself behind a hillock, and thought of the community in the east of the Island lying snug and sheltered. Good for it, when such a winter as this came, to lie in the lee of the hill.

Good for the Abbot now to have some shelter. For it was a rough journey they had gone last spring. That spring and summer—if he had known he never could have gone! And the Abbot had borne the brunt of it. He needed shelter now, shelter and peace.

But he got no peace. And who should know that better than Diarmaid his doorkeeper! For all the winter gales they had constant visitors, men of Dalriada and of the Cruithnian folk, there was no end. They had guests who came from farther too, messengers from priests and abbots in Strathclydd, a nobleman from Rederech's court with a message straight from his king. There had been one whose tongue they could not understand, he was from the far south, from the queen Lluan's country. There had even come, and come if you please to stay! one of the dreadful Saxon people from the east. And how he had found his way through the lands of the nations who hated him, and what it was that made him find it — it was as great a mystery as any other. They could not understand very much of what he said, but he seemed determined to become a lay brother. "We shall be having the wolves come next!" Diarmaid had heard one of the seniors say under his breath. They found the fellow had an aptitude for meal and flour, and were trying him out for their baker. And who would say what his work had been before?

Sometimes he, Diarmaid, could not help resenting it. He secretly wondered if ever the Abbot did too. One could feel homesick not only when one was lonely but when one was sur-

rounded by folk of another sort from one's own. Once or twice
he had said, "Lord Abbot, do you think we shall ever have a
guest from Ailech? Perhaps from Gartan itself?"

It was not wise to think of home, of Gartan where he and
the Abbot had both been born, though with many years and
many ranks of society between. The hills were the same for them
both, and the little river that ran between, with its pools and its
eddies and its waterlilies and its fish and its birds that flew down
to nest among the reeds. To stop such thoughts Diarmaid set his
face towards the shore. The wind was like the thunder of horsemen. The sea was driven crashing in the holes and caves, spouts
of water rose high into the air. White breakers crested the sky-
line. Pity any guest should come riding the seas just now!

He was a strange man, the Lord Abbot, though usually
friendly and near. Who would have said when this wind rose in
the morning he would have sent his doorkeeper away to the west
of the Island to watch for a guest? "A guest from our own home,"
was what he had said. How was it possible? Guests came by the
good little harbour in the east and came up the causeway into
the community. Who would come by the west? Unless indeed
one were storm driven.

As he watched he saw something in the air. It might have
been one of the breakers, but it was too high. He lost it from
view, he found it again, and it came nearer and fell on the shore
below. Diarmaid made his way to the place among the rocks
where it had fallen. Salt spray stung his cheeks, his feet slipped
on the wet stones, but he found the place.

And there was a great bird, white but stained grey and
brown. Diarmaid stared at it, for it was the very thing he had
been thinking of: it was a wild swan, such as he had seen on
the lakes at Gartan or coming in overhead in strong flight from
the sea. He gathered the bird up off the shore; carrying her in
his arms he went to the shelter for the herdsmen nearby. He
laid her down; and exhausted, she lay where he put her. Her
beak was open and her eyes glazing. From her wet broken
plumage seawater dripped blood-stained. Diarmaid felt among
her feather for hurts. She struggled weakly but he stroked her
speaking as though she were human, "Don't be afraid. You are
in sanctuary on Colum's Island." He brought her fresh water
from the burn to drink, and after a while she took some; and
then he washed the salt water from her wounded wing.

The abbot bell sounded in the lulls of the wind. He did not want to leave her, but he had to go. He made a cover for her with his habit, and went in his tunic back to the community.

The Abbot was thronged with men after vespers, and Diarmaid thought he should not be able to get near him, even supposing he had anything to say to him. But the Abbot himself came to him, looking at him closely with a smile, and said, "God bless you, my son! You have found the guest I was expecting and have cared for her? In a little I will come and see her too."

And a day or two afterwards, as Diarmaid was in the west of the Island watching the cows again, and petting his wild swan, the Abbot came and went into the shelter with him. Diarmaid had found her things to eat, and fed her with them, weeds from the pond and small fish. "You might be a swan yourself!" said the Abbot admiringly. "They do not often eat when they are ill." And he stroked her feathers, and spoke to her, "It was too long a journey for you to take to visit us, my beauty. And at this time of year! You might have died in the midst of the stormy seas. You might not ever again have sailed on the calm lakes.

"Dairmaid!" he said raising his head, "I think she has come from the Suilech Lough, and before then she nested at Gartan. She has fed on the lake where these yellow lilies grow. She is from our birthplace, she is our sister."

"Sir," Diarmaid said, delighted, seeing she was beguiling the Abbot from his graver cares, "I think we could keep her. She might stay here. I could make a fence of willow by the pond and cover it on top so that she couldn't get away. After a while she would get used to living here and stay of her own will."

But the Abbot shook his head, smiling, "Why, Diarmaid, would you make a monk of her? I'm afraid, whatever brought her here, she will not want to stay. Now that this wing is mended and the weather clear she will want to go."

And he took her up, and carried her outside the shelter, and laid her down on the machair grass. She lay quiet a moment, and half in earnest half playfully he signed her as if she were a human soul. She gazed round her then, and moved her wings uncertainly. And then she rose dizzily from the ground. And then she straightened out her long neck before her and beat her beautiful strong wings with a flanging sound, and mounting she circled once or twice above them, just as if taking farewell. Then she set her head towards the south west, and flew away over the sea.

The Abbot and Diarmaid stood watching her till she was out of sight. And Diarmaid when he looked away at last found his eyes filled with tears. He said, " She is gone, father. We shall not see her again. We might have kept her for our own."

But Colum shook his head again laughing ruefully; and putting his arm round Diarmaid drew him away from the shore. " She does not belong to this land; but you and I do. We loved her very much. Now let her go."